Firefly Summer

KATHLEEN Y'BARBO

ISBN: 1-942265-04-2
ISBN-13: 978-1-942265-04-7

DEDICATION

To those who made sure my sweet tea and Jesus not-just-on-Sunday Southern heritage was well learned, not by books but by example.

If you're Southern, either by birth or naturalized, then you may recognize the women I write about in this story—although I promise they are (mostly) made up.

If you have not yet visited the South, bless your heart!

And to the real Bonnie Sue, the real Sue Ellen, the real Robin, and the real Shirley.

You are queens among women. Long may you reign!

"I know, Lord, that a person's life is not his own. No one is able to plan his own course. So correct me, Lord, but please be gentle. Do not correct me in anger, for I would die."

Jeremiah 10:23-24 (NLT)

CHAPTER ONE

"Next rider in the College National Finals is our oldest in the competition today. He's almost finished with medical school, but first he's got to finish this ride. Give Trey Brown a hand, ladies and gentlemen!"

Sessa Lee Chambers shifted in her seat to watch her five-year-old son stand in rapt attention as the cowboys in gate seven moved in perfect synchronization. One held the gate, one held the rope, and another sat astride a bronc that looked as if it would easily take the rider's head off if given the opportunity. A fourth man spoke energetically into the rider's ear, his words lost on the cheering crowd inside the Sam Houston Arena.

Her attention shifted back to Ross. Was that...a smile?

"Come on, cowboy," Ross shouted over the din as his lifted his little red cowboy hat to mimic the others now crowding the gate. "You can do it!"

Clutching her throat, Sessa fought back the tears that were already blurring her vision. Ross hadn't smiled or spoken a word since his father died nearly one month ago. Taking him to the rodeo had been Ross's grandfather's idea. Get him outside. Expose him to some good old-fashioned commotion. Let him pet a horse or two.

That last one was the most difficult of all. Just last week, her dwindling finances had caused her to sell the last of Ben's beloved horses to an old friend who lived south of town. Bud Jones would take good care of them, this she knew. What she hadn't known was how heartbroken Ross would be at their loss.

Of course, because she was too far gone in her grief to see anything, it had been Daddy who'd pointed out Ross's sadness.

And not very nicely.

But he was right. And she had to do better.

The gate opened just a few feet away from them, and the horse bucked out, jarring her thoughts. The rider bounced with legs out and hat flying, but he held on until the buzzer sounded.

"Now that was a ride, wasn't it folks? Hard to believe he's thirty one!" The speakers blared with the announcer's excitement. "Good job, cowboy!"

Funny. The man striding victoriously across the arena was two years older than she. Her memories of college were brief and dimmed by time and distance. One semester was all she'd gone, but she'd somehow managed to meet Ben Chambers, marry him, and forget all about any ideas of pursuing higher education. Looking back, it was the worst decision of her life. Then she looked at Ross and realized that decision had been the best.

Ross waved his hat like the others standing at the gate. "Good job, cowboy!" he echoed.

He was still waving the hat when the long-legged cowboy ambled by. "Good job, cowboy," he repeated.

To Sessa's astonishment, the cowboy stopped right there and knelt down to get eye-to-eye with Ross. She couldn't hear what transpired over the noise of the crowd, but a moment later, one of the other men was handing the cowboy a pen.

Ross ran toward her as fast as his little legs could carry him. "Look, Mama!" he shouted. "The cowboy signed his name on my hat! He said someday I could be a cowboy just like him!"

"Hold on there, cowpoke."

Sessa looked up to see the sandy-haired cowboy once again kneel beside Ross. "I said you could be a cowboy like me, but only if you study hard and keep your grades up so you can get into college. Oh, and be sure and listen to your mama."

He looked over Ross's head to offer Sessa a wink.

Through the haze of numbness, she felt a twinge of...something. Attraction, maybe. Unwelcome as it was. She let her gaze drop to her son, avoiding further eye contact with the cowboy.

Oblivious, Ross beamed up at the man, one hand clapped to the hat on his head, steadying it. "I will," he said. "I promise."

The cowboy straightened Ross's hat and then stuck his hand

out to offer the child a firm handshake. "I have a feeling I'm going to see you again someday," he told Ross as he rose.

"Me too!" Ross said with a broad grin.

He wore his grin, and that cowboy hat, all the way home. Even as he fell into a deep slumber in his bed, Ross still bore the traces of that smile.

And of course he wore the hat.

CHAPTER TWO

Fifteen years later

Venting her frustration, Sessa fashioned a block of the finest ash into the shape of a lion's nose then moved to the table where the next task awaited—carving a replacement ribbon for a century-old prancing carousel horse.

Every satisfying jab of the chisel had chipped away at another piece of her resentment until exhaustion, and the completion of the piece, forced her to quit. Still the aggravation teased at her, daring her to believe that the Lord was out to get her.

He had to be.

She set the well-used carving tool in its place and shook her head to remove the sawdust from her hair. Out of the corner of her eye, she noticed the thick file of papers neatly packaged for mailing.

Today of all days, she should be on top of the world. Unlike some of her smaller commissions, the pieces strewn across her workspace could soon be replaced by several dozen intended for use in the Smithsonian's traveling carousel display. After years of careful planning and despite the death of its founder fifteen years ago, Chambers Carousel Restorations had a real shot at hitting the big time.

Her husband, rest his soul, would have been so proud. On the other hand, their son Ross would be unimpressed. What a cruel irony that she and Ben had worked to build something to pass on to the next generation, only to find that their only child entertained no interest in the family business.

If only Ben had lived to help raise him. Maybe Ross would have been the man she hoped he'd become.

But then, Sessa could spend hours thinking about what might have been. Instead she chose to live in the present, only thinking of her prodigal on carefully chosen occasions. She went back to her work only to find her control had slipped.

It happened more often these days. Sometimes a glance at her son's baby pictures would bring a memory to mind, while other times it would be the sound of laughter from a child on a radio commercial or the photograph of a dark-haired boy in the newspaper. Other times her longings might stem from a conversation between herself and her mother, some snippet of a past memory that would turn happy then stab her in the heart. Then there was the red cowboy hat on the shelf in his room, faded by the years and dusty from her own inability to spend much time in a place where memories hung deeper than morning fog, that hat gave rise to the best memory of Ross she had.

The day he spoke. The day some stranger turned a boy from inward to outward. To horses and riding and rodeo. She smiled and batted at the dust motes dancing in the sunshine.

Remembering Ross as the baby, the child, and the young man prevented her from thinking of him as the adult he had become. The adult she barely knew and hardly recognized.

How long had it been since she'd seen him? The months had stretched long and distant until nearly a year had gone by since his last visit. Even then, he'd been someone she loved but did not like. It shamed her to think of how relieved she'd been when he'd left.

And now this. An impossible situation with no good solution.

Her smile faded. This.

A litany of if-only's assaulted her, and she covered her ears to stop them. When they'd finally quieted, Sessa reached for the next piece, a delicate rabbit's ear made of maple.

Wood shavings littered the floor of her studio, and a fine dust danced in the rays of morning sun. Seemed she might never come to terms with the guilt plaguing her.

"Guilt is not of the Lord." She reached for a piece of cheesecloth and gave the prancing horse's nose a thorough cleaning. "You're doing the right thing. There's absolutely no proof."

But the right thing seemed so wrong. And the proof was in

those eyes. In the dimple in that tiny chin. In that bawl that sounded as if it came all the way up from those tiny toes.

Her cell phone mocked her, daring her to do what she knew she should, and even as she made a swipe for it, she felt the pain of doubt. "Lord, I can't," sprung to her lips in a desperate plea. "I'm too old, too busy, too... You're the one who made me, so you know how terrible I am at doing more than one thing at a time. Surely you understand."

The clock over the door read exactly eleven-thirty. One hour from now the decision would be taken away from her; it would be done. All she had to do was wait it out.

Cradling the phone in her hand, she blew a fine film of dust off its black surface only to watch the particles settle on the envelope. All her dreams, the hope for a secure future, lay beneath the dust of shattered plans. Somehow, with the Lord's guidance, she could make new plans, find new dreams.

Slowly she punched in the number she'd been given last night, a number she tried to forget yet couldn't help but remember. An eternity later, the phone rang. Sessa cleared her throat and said a prayer for guidance then found her voice when a young woman answered the phone.

"I'll meet you at the bus station." Sessa hung up before she could take back the words. "I did what I should have, didn't I, Lord?"

Even as she spoke, she knew the answer. "I can do all things through Christ," she said on an exhale of breath, "who gives me strength."

"Well amen to that!"

Coco.

Sessa heard high heels clicking on the concrete and knew the cavalry approached. What was it about her best friend that brought her running at the first sign of trouble, even when she had not yet been told about the trouble?

To the untrained eye, Cozette "Coco" Smith-Sutton hadn't aged a day since she reigned supreme as Sugar Pine High's head cheerleader and then married the quarterback—after he successfully completed his college career at Texas A&M and made it into the pros, of course. The fact that she'd also held the titles of Homecoming Queen, Cotton and Corn Princess, Miss Sugar

Pine (twice!), and fourth runner up to Miss Texas should have disqualified her as friend material for a woman who would rather read or spend time in her father's workshop than just about anything else.

And yet Sessa and Coco, who began life together as babies in the church nursery, had defied the odds to remain closer than sisters all these years. Coco had been her rock when Ben's delivery truck rolled off the highway that icy night so long ago, had tucked Ross into bed at her place alongside her boys on nights when Sessa's work kept her in the workshop because not working would have seen the electricity turned off or the mortgage not paid.

In turn, Sessa had brought casseroles and fended off well-meaning church ladies when Coco's mama died and her daddy suddenly became the most eligible bachelor in the Over-Sixty Seekers Sunday School class. She'd also held Coco up through the long dark days and nights after media darling and NFL quarterback Ryan "The Rocket" Sutton, the man that ESPN called unstoppable, stopped loving perfect Coco and her boys and took up with a twenty-something stripper from Fort Worth.

Oh, they fought. For all her sweetness, Coco could go sour fast if she found out you were doing one of the three things she detested most: hiding something she thought she ought to know, telling a lie, or messing with Texas.

"I'm out in the workshop," Sessa called as she tossed off her gloves and swiped at the sawdust in her hair.

"Well of course you are," she said. "I was just heading to the grocery store and thought I'd see if you needed anything."

Today Coco had poured her long lean legs into white jeans, thrown a turquoise top over them, and finished the ensemble with matching turquoise high heel sandals. While Sessa's hair was moderately tamed in a messy bun, Coco's artfully created blonde ponytail looked as if it had been styled in an exclusive Hollywood salon instead of by Vonnette over at the Hairport.

She dropped her keys into her signature oversized designer purse, this one the same color as her heels, and removed the sunglasses that hid her perfectly made up face. A dozen silver bracelets jangled as she rested her hand on her hip.

"Honey, you look like something the cat drug in. What's

wrong?"

Right to the point. Typical Coco.

"I've been better."

Coco's green eyes opened wide. "What has Ross done now?" She continued walking toward Sessa. "No, do not answer until I can get you inside and pour you a cup of coffee. You look like you need something stronger than that, though. A pity neither of us drinks."

"Coffee won't fix this."

"Don't be silly. Coffee fixes...wait—" Coco shook her head. "This is really bad, isn't it?"

Sessa managed a smile. "Or really good. I can't tell which."

Coco reached behind Sessa to grab a length of cheesecloth, and then used it to dust off just enough space on the workbench for the both of them. She climbed up and motioned to the spot beside her. "Come on, then. Spill it."

With the sun shining in from windows covered with a healthy measure of sawdust, Coco's face was hidden in shadows, though her blonde ponytail shone like spun gold. In that moment Sessa was fourteen again, a girl sharing secrets with her best friend in the privacy of her daddy's workshop.

Only she wasn't ten, and Daddy had long since gone home to Jesus. And she wasn't worried about silly things like popularity or pimples, things that had seemed so life-changing then.

She climbed up to settle next to Coco. "You know you can't go to the grocery store in those pants now."

Coco shrugged. "Didn't really need to anyway. That was just an excuse to come see what was up over here. So come on. Fess up. What's our Ross gotten into this time?"

Our Ross. Sessa reached around Coco's back to hug her and then straightened and studied the splinter that had been plaguing her thumb since yesterday. "Fatherhood, apparently."

Her best friend didn't move a muscle. "You sure, Sessa?"

"She has his eyes and that dimple in her chin is just like his."

"She?"

Sessa nodded. "A baby girl. Tiny thing. Probably not more than a month old. One at the most."

"You don't know for sure?"

She met her friend's gaze. "I was a little surprised to see her and her teenaged mama on my doorstep, so no, I didn't think to ask."

"Anyone we know?" When Sessa shook her head, Coco continued. "I see. Are they here now?"

"No."

When the silence stretched on, Coco gave Sessa a nudge. "There's more, isn't there?"

Sessa let out a long breath and batted at the dust motes swimming in the shaft of sunshine. "She's coming to live with me, Coco. My granddaughter."

Coco held up both hands then scooted off the workbench to turn and face her. "Wait just a minute. You mean to tell me you are taking in a teenager and her baby just because the child's eyes match your son's, and she's got a dimple in the same place as he does?"

"Just the baby." Sessa ignored the question of the baby's parentage. This child belonged to her son, of this she was certain. "And I don't have to take her. Her mother gave me a choice."

"A choice?"

"Yeah, though not much of one," Sessa said. "She's leaving at 12:30. I can either pick my granddaughter up at the Greyhound station or forget she exists."

"She told you that?" Coco held her hand out as if to interrupt any possible response. "And by the way, does this baby's mama have a name, or did you forget to ask that, too?"

"Her name is Skye."

"Just Skye?"

Sessa shrugged. "That's all she offered. At the time, I didn't figure the rest mattered."

She paused. "Anyway, she's a sweet girl, really. Said she admits she's made stupid mistakes and she needs to make some things right before she can be a good mother to Pansie."

"Your granddaughter's name is Pansie?"

She nodded. "With an 'ie' because she was born to be different. Or at least that's what her mama said on the subject."

"Well that's the cutest name I've heard in a long time. I can't wait to get my hands on her and love on that child." Coco cocked her head to one side. "So, are you going to just stand there, or are you going to go get that baby?"

"I'm going," Sessa said with a strength she hadn't felt since the wind was knocked out of her yesterday.

"Well, you can't go get her like that! Look at you. You're covered in dust." She reached over to prove her point by shaking sawdust out of Sessa's hair. "Get inside and make yourself presentable, and then we'll go together."

"Coco, I need to do this by myself."

"I understand," her friend said. "But you're still going to get yourself cleaned up. Now hurry up. What time did you say you had to be there?"

"Twelve-thirty."

Coco grabbed her by the shoulders and marched her out of the workshop and into the sunshine. "Go. I'll close up shop here."

Sessa took one step and then returned to envelope Coco in a hug. "Thank you," she said as tears threatened. "It's just until Ross comes back." Both of them knew the unlikeliness of Ross Chambers returning to Sugar Pine with the maturity and intention to raise a child.

"Of course it is." Coco's reply held all the enthusiasm of a true friend who shared both your hope and your reality.

~*~

"I'm sorry, Mrs. Chambers, but she's going to need a change."

"All right." Numb, Sessa accepted the soggy blanket-wrapped bundle.

The girl, still a kid herself, blinked back tears and tugged at the hem of her neon green tank top. Her skin was pale as Mama's porcelain teacups, and she wore her chestnut hair in a messy bun. Her lower lip trembled slightly as she seemed to have to work up to a smile.

This was one brave girl. Scared, but brave.

"She's three weeks old today. I named her Pansie Skye."

Sessa tried not to tremble, not to allow the emotions to well up, as she held her only grandchild. "Oh," she managed.

"Yeah, it was Ross's idea. He said since my name's Skye, and we made her in the..."

Skye's voice trailed off.

Sessa focused on the baby, and images of Ross began to form.

Dark hair, dark eyes, these were the first Sessa noticed yesterday. In her mind, her son's tiny fingers latched around her own as the baby's did. Eyes of deepest mahogany peered up from beneath the garish oversized pink and yellow lace bonnet she knew would cover inky black hair.

"...and so, thanks to the lady who runs the home where I stayed while I was pregnant, I've got a plan now. I'm gonna get my GED out there, and then I'll get a good job and send her a bus ticket so we can be together."

Sessa opened her mouth to point out the impossibility of sending a bus ticket for an infant and then thought better of it. "Well, it sounds like you've got a quite a plan for things now."

"I do, and I promise I'll come back for her just as soon as I can." She smiled at Sessa and pointed to the Greyhound behind her. "It's too bad things didn't work out between me and Ross." She shrugged. "Oh well, I gotta jet."

"Jet?" Sessa repeated, still numb. The newborn began to whimper, her lip a defiant curl and dark lashes held tight against rounded cheeks.

"Yeah, jet." Skye placed on the floor beside Sessa a blue striped bag stained with fat blotches of brown. "See ya, Pansie-poo." She touched the brim of the baby's bonnet and whirled around to dance up the steps of the bus. "Mama'll be back real soon. You'll see."

The Greyhound roared away in a cloud of smoke and diesel fumes, and it was all Sessa could do not to chase the roaring silver monster down Barton Street and demand that Skye end the cruel joke and take her child back.

When a pair of questionable characters pressed near enough to smell, the baby began to howl in earnest. "Hang on, honey." Sessa gathered up the bag and bounced the baby in her arms.

Inside the less than sanitary ladies' restroom, she set the baby on the changing table and placed the bag beside her. How long had it been since she changed a wiggling child?

A lifetime ago.

Keeping one hand on the now-screaming infant, Sessa popped open the snap and peered inside the bag. A single diaper and a formula-filled bottle of questionable vintage lay atop a stack of four wadded, stained sleepers and a wrapped package of saltine crackers.

There was nothing in the way of hygiene products beyond a sample-sized container of powder and a single wet wipe in a plastic bag. A second plastic bag held an envelope with the name *Pansie Skye Chambers* scribbled in a childish hand. The author had turned the dot over the 'I' into a flower and had colored it in with a bright pink marker, even adding green leaves on either side.

Carefully, Sessa slid the envelope into her purse and regarded the baby with a frown. "All right, Miss Pansie." She picked at the ribbon holding the bonnet on the squirming baby, "let's see what's under this ugly hat."

For a moment, the baby stopped crying to look up at her through wide brown eyes. As the yellow ribbons fell away and the hideous bonnet came off, a head full of dark curls stole Sessa's breath.

"Oh my, you're beautiful. A precious miracle."

For a moment, in the dingy restroom of the downtown bus station, Sessa felt the presence of God in the form of a tiny, smelly child. Her eyes clouded with unshed tears, and her heart thumped wildly.

"Thank You, Jesus," she stammered, "for not allowing me to miss this blessing."

Unimpressed, the blessing opened soft pink lips to resume screaming.

Improvising, Sessa managed to clean the baby and change her into the least dirty outfit of the lot. Somewhere along the way, the baby stopped crying, although Sessa's ears still rang as she tossed the bag into the trash.

Only then did she realize that without a car seat, she had no way to transport this precious bundle. She thought of calling Coco, but she wasn't ready to share this child with anyone just yet, even her best friend.

As she stood in front of the bus station considering her options, Jim Bob Winston drove by in the only cab in Sugar Pine. A product of a different era when cab drivers were a bit more necessary in this town, everyone suspected Jim Bob kept the Sugar Pine Cab Company going because otherwise he'd have no excuse to get out of the house and away from Vonnette's lengthy honey-do list.

"Thank you, Lord," she said as she waved the elderly man down and walked over to the now-open window of the dark green vintage Chevy sedan. "You wouldn't happen to have a car seat, would you?"

Jim Bob eyed Pansie for a second then returned his attention to Sessa. "I keep one in the trunk just in case. Why?"

"I need to make a Walmart run," she said as matter-of-factly as she could manage. "But first I need to borrow a car seat."

"Why don't I just take you?" Jim Bob climbed out of the cab and headed for the trunk. "I don't mind, and it looks like you've got your hands full already. Not having to drive is one less thing, that's what I always say."

In fact he did always say that, so much so that Vonnette had the phrase embroidered on his dark green cap, on the matching vest he wore when he was on duty, and on the business cards he handed out.

Jim Bob set up the car seat like a pro, leaving her to make a mental note to ask him to set up the one she'd be buying for her car. "Climb aboard," he said with a grand sweep of his arm. "My chariot is your chariot."

Sessa climbed in and, with only a little help from Jim Bob, managed to situate Pansie in the car seat. As soon as the cab set off, the little darling fell fast asleep.

"Just leave her be," Jim Bob said as he pulled into a parking space at Walmart. "I'll keep an eye on her while you go get what you need."

Somehow Sessa managed a trip to Walmart for supplies and the ride home without deciding that she'd lost her mind. Ignoring the priority envelope readied for mailing on her kitchen counter, she carried the still-sleeping baby through the kitchen and into the small bedroom next to hers while Jim Bob unloaded a portable crib, a car seat, and a stroller along with a half-dozen bags full of diapers, formula, and baby items. Looking over the receipt, she knew her bank account would be screaming as loud as her new granddaughter.

"Expect Vonnette'll be here soon as she hears what you've got," Jim Bob said as he took it upon himself to pull the portable crib out of the box and fit it together.

"I expect she will," Sessa called from the kitchen. "But do me a favor and let me tell her. I'm going to need a little bit of time with Pansie before I'm ready to talk about how I got her and who she belongs to."

Jim Bob came into the kitchen, breaking down the big box as he walked. "Pansie is it?" At Sessa's nod, he reached down to tickle her chin. "Looks just like Ross."

Their eyes met over the squirming child. "Yes," she said slowly. "She does."

A moment of understanding passed between them, and Sessa knew her father's best friend would have taken the secret of a baby's arrival at the Chamber's home to his grave. "Thank you, Jim Bob," she said. "I'll call Vonnette tomorrow. And I promise to leave out the part where you drove us home."

He folded the remains of the port-a-crib box under his arm and grinned. "I'd be much obliged if you'd do that, Sessa." He paused at the door, and Sessa scooted around to open it. Again their eyes met. "You're a good woman, Sessa. Your daddy would have been proud."

Jim Bob left her with those words hanging in the empty space between them. Proud of taking this child in to her home? Yes.

Proud of how close she came to letting the problem ride away on a Greyhound bus? Likely not.

But that was Daddy. He always did have strong opinions. Always did what was right.

Pansie let out a wail. "All right, you." Sessa hurried to see how much she remembered about making a bottle and feeding a baby. Only when she'd settled in the rocker and started it in motion with the hungry infant in her arms did she allow that she might be able to do this.

Emphasis on *might*.

The bottle soothed the child once again into a peaceful slumber, and despite the bone-deep fatigue settling around her, Sessa couldn't bear to put the baby down. Instead, she lit a lamp, eased into her favorite chair by the window, and stared down into the face of heaven.

Her phone buzzed with a text from Coco. *Well???*

Sessa managed to type one-handed, *She's perfect but I'm already exhausted.*

If you need me, just say the word.

Tomorrow. Sessa set her phone aside. She'd tell Mama tomorrow, too.

"Now what?" she whispered as the quiet settled in around her.

Now you raise your granddaughter, came the soft reply, not from a friend's text but from the Friend she counted on above all.

Raise her, she did. The first week with a newborn in the house was a blur. Nothing beyond baby care and the occasional shower stolen during Pansie's naptime seemed to get accomplished. Had Mama and Coco not arrived every day to each take a shift, she would have died of exhaustion before the end of the first week.

The priority mailer with the signed contracts inside lay on the counter near the door, resting in the same spot she'd put it on the day she went to pick up her granddaughter. Restoring the horses would have to wait for God's timing—and Pansie's.

On a few occasions, Sessa thought about mailing it. More times than that, she'd prayed over the paperwork as she made formula or washed bottles. Once she took Pansie out to the studio while she put the finishing touches on the reproduction lion and prancing horse and called for the delivery truck. When the dust caused Pansie to sneeze, Sessa made short work of calling the delivery truck to cancel and heading for the house.

She spent part of an afternoon crunching numbers with Pansie in her lap and another hour generating sketches while the baby napped. Mostly though, Sessa just played grandmother, or mother, or whatever the combination of the two could be termed. Mama chipped in to change diapers, do endless loads of pink laundry and, of all things, bake pies. What a newborn needed with pies in the house escaped Sessa, but the stolen moments she and her mother spent over custard pie and coffee while the baby napped were priceless.

"Did you mail that envelope?" Mama would always manage to ask.

"Not yet," was always the answer Sessa gave.

Conversations with Coco went in a similar fashion. The difference with Coco Smith-Sutton was that more than once, Sessa had to grab the envelope out of her hand to keep her from taking it to the post office herself. And bless her heart, Coco did everything else that needed doing, often anticipating Sessa's needs before Sessa did.

At the end of the second week, she gave in and mailed the signed contracts. She'd worked too hard to give up this chance.

Until Ross came for his daughter, she and God would handle the operations of Chambers Restoration together, and Mama and Coco would help with Pansie as needed. If God meant for her to fulfill the museum contract and take care of an infant, then she had no business questioning His will.

She knew in her heart this season of mothering the baby girl she'd always wished for would eventually end. Soon Ross would restore his relationship with the Lord and with his family, this she knew with as much certainty as she knew her own name. Until then she would rely on faith and prayer and revel in the soft lacy pink things and the scent of freshly scrubbed baby skin and glossy dark curls.

Later that evening, with the baby bathed, dressed in a newly washed yellow sleeper and safely tucked into her father's hand-me-down crib that had replaced the portable crib, Sessa took a moment to ponder the events of the day. She'd sent her mother home early, eager for a rare evening alone in the house.

"Lord, how will I manage until Ross comes to claim her?" She paused to touch the newly framed photo of Pansie that held a prominent spot on the mantel. "Worse, how will I manage when he does?"

As she headed down the hall for one last check on Pansie, the sentiment was quickly replaced with another familiar verse from the fourth chapter of Philippians, one she'd called upon on many occasions in the almost fifteen years since Ben's death, often in response to Ross's subsequent troubles.

"My God will provide for all my needs through His great riches," she said under her breath as she placed a hand on the infant's back to feel it rise and fall. "Bless this child and the children who gave her life, Father."

Pansie stirred a bit and made a puckering motion with her lips. A soft whimper escaped like a sigh while the baby's tiny fingers curled into a fist. At that moment, Sessa knew this was a temporary arrangement, one meant to be savored but not lingered upon.

Wandering into the kitchen, Sessa drew near to the window.

Her gaze landed on a glass jar she'd brought in, an almost

antique made filmy by a layer of dust. Ross's empty lightning jar. She smiled. How many summer evenings had she and Ben spent on the back porch watching their little son toddle around trying collect lightning in a jar from among the collection of glowing insects buzzing about?

"Someday you'll do the same thing, Pansie Chambers," she whispered as she touched the jar and wiped away a finger's width of dust. "Someday you and your daddy will collect lightning in a jar."

She looked up at that topmost shelf, at the red cowboy hat still sitting there. When the time was right and Pansie was older, maybe she'd take her to a rodeo. Or better yet, teach her to ride.

Peace settled about the nursery like a soft pink blanket, interrupted by the ringing of the phone she'd left in the kitchen. Sessa closed the door and hurried to locate the phone atop a stack of freshly laundered crib sheets.

"Hello," she said as she checked the clock on the oven. Half past ten. Late to have phone calls. She should have checked to see who was calling before she answered.

Her heart jumped. It could be Ross.

"Mrs. Sessa Lee Chambers?"

The voice sounded clipped, official. Her heart sunk.

A call from her prodigal would have made the day perfect. A call from a stranger only served to irritate. "Yes," she said, "this is Sessa Chambers."

"I'm sorry, ma'am. It's about your son, Ross Benjamin Chambers. I am correct in understanding he is your son?"

Sessa huffed in disgust. So much for the perfect day. "So what is it this time? Drunk and disorderly, breaking and entering, possession with intent to sell?"

"No, ma'am." The caller paused. "He's been murdered."

Words and phrases chased her thoughts, failing to capture them. Stabbed. Ranch outside Houston. Drugs. Cash. Man in custody. Did she want to be notified of the trial?

"Trial," she echoed. "No. Please no. Just..." She pressed back a sob. "Just tell me where my son is now and how I can bring him home."

Another flurry of words, of explanations she chose not to grasp and details she hoped to forget. She hung up the phone knowing two things: she would bury her son next to his dad, and she never wanted to set eyes on the face of the man who robbed Pansie of her father.

CHAPTER THREE

Exactly two years later

April meeting of the Pies, Books & Jesus Book Club
Location: Bonnie Sue Tucker's home
Pies: two peach and two pecan, brought by Carly Chance
Book title: AND THE LADIES OF THE CLUB by Helen Hooven
Santmyer

Sessa heard her cell phone buzz from the depths of her purse. Much as she wanted to ignore the call, it could be Pansie's babysitter. Now that her granddaughter was solidly in the middle of the terrible twos, anything was possible.

She glanced at the number. Not one she recognized but local to Houston, which was less than an hour away from Sugar Pine.

Before she could say hello, a deep voice said, "Sessa Lee Chambers?"

Her heart sunk. "It is."

"This is Roger Hart with the *Houston Chronicle*, and what with the new events associated with your son's death and the subsequent trial I hoped to—"

Sessa ended the call and threw the phone back into her purse. Coco gave her an *are-you-okay* look from across the room. She nodded, though she wasn't.

A meeting of the Pies, Books & Jesus Book Club was the last place a girl could expect some privacy. And right now that was exactly what she needed.

"Pass the whipped cream and sprinkles, please, Sue Ellen?"

"That's ice cream and pecans, hon," the owner of the town

diner said as she studied Sessa. "Is something wrong?"

"Oh, of course it is." Sessa felt her phone buzz. With the back of her foot, she shoved her purse further under her chair. "I'm fine. I've just been so busy working on those orders and that Pansie, well, she's a handful, so I don't sleep much."

Coco nodded toward the kitchen and then stood. Sessa rose and snatched up her full-to-the rim glass of sweet tea. "I'm just going to go top this off."

Thankfully Sue Ellen was kind enough not to point out the lameness of her excuse. Instead, she smiled. "You go right ahead. I'll save your spot."

Sessa stepped into Mama's kitchen right behind her. Before the door closed completely, Coco had turned to face her.

"All right. I want to know right now what you plan to do."

Sessa eyed her friend, clad tonight in a lime green sundress and matching earrings, and shook her head as she set her tea glass on the counter. "About what?"

Coco rested one hand on her slender hip and gave her a sweeping look that sent Sessa heading for the mirror Mama kept hanging by the back door.

One last look before you go out is never wasted time. Mama could have embroidered that one on a pillow for all the times she'd said it.

"What are you doing?" Coco demanded.

"I'm checking to see what you're talking about."

Coco's chuckle held very little humor. "Honey, you look just fine. Great, actually. You really should wear that color of blue more often. It does fabulous things for your eyes." Her manicured and bejeweled fingers swept an arc in front of her. "Never mind about that, though. What I meant is what are you going to do about that man?"

Sessa shook her head. "What man?"

Her perfectly drawn brows rose. "The man who...you don't know, do you?" Her expression fell. "He's out. The man who killed our Ross. They let him out."

She let the words hang between them for far longer than they should. Such was the friendship between her and Coco, though. The unexpected call from the man at the *Chronicle* was beginning to make sense.

"Why?" she managed, though it came out as a whisper.

"Seems like Ross didn't go to that doctor's house by himself that night. The fellow who was waiting outside..."

Her best friend seemed to search for the words, so Sessa took a guess. "Told the cops the truth?"

If Coco was surprised at the question, she didn't show it. "Apparently."

"Mama always said the truth would set us free. I guess she was right." She lifted her attention to meet Coco's even gaze. A tear shimmered, and she swiped at it with the back of her hand. "I knew all along he didn't murder Ross."

"Oh, honey." Coco moved forward to hug her. "I know what you're thinking, and I'm so sorry. Neither of us knew that little boy would turn out to be someone who would do what he did."

"If only Ben had lived," she managed. "If I'd been a better mother to him."

She held Sessa at arm's length. "You loved him enough for the both of you. We both did."

Sessa blinked back more tears. "We did, didn't we?"

"Yes we did."

"Still, I can't help but feel like I didn't just fail my son." She rested her hip against the counter and let out a long breath. "I also failed that doctor who lost his medical career. Coco, if I'd just gone to that trial. Maybe if I'd told the judge how Ross turned out." She rubbed her palm over her forearm. Sometimes it still ached where Ross had broken it on his last visit home.

She met her best friend's gaze. "I'm so sorry about all of it. I just wish I could fix it, for Ross and for that doctor."

Tears glittered in Coco's eyes. "I know you do, honey, but you can't go back in time, and there's nothing you can do now." When Sessa shook her head, Coco continued. "Maybe someday you'll get the chance to tell him how sorry you are, but not tonight."

"Maybe I ought to write him a letter," she said. "I bet I could find out where he lives." She paused. "Why are you looking at me like that?"

"Because you're putting a lot of energy into something you cannot do a blasted thing about, Sessa Lee Chambers. Now focus. If you don't want to go back in there, head on out the back door, and I'll tell them you weren't feeling well."

Though the idea of making her escape was tempting, Sessa

knew she'd never get away with it. Besides, her purse was still under the chair in the living room.

"I'm fine." She reached for her tea glass. "Let's go back in there before Mama comes in to see what she's missing."

"Want me to go first?" Coco asked.

"I'll do it." Sessa pasted on a smile and opened the kitchen door

"So nobody's said anything about the big news," Robin Chance, the owner of the Pup Cake Bakery and Doggie Diner was saying as she sipped at her tea. "They've let that doctor out. What do y'all think of that? He only served a year's time, and now just because some kid says he was with Ross and they planned that robbery, he gets to—"

"Hush. You know Sessa doesn't want to talk about that," Mama said. "Although how she managed to stick her head in the sand and ignore anything having to do with the trial is beyond me. That boy was my grandson, and you know I adored him, but that poor doctor. I feel for him, really I do. I heard he was planning on giving that boy money to pay for college. Can you feature it?"

"Bonnie Sue?" Vonnette nodded not so subtly toward the kitchen door, and all eyes turned to Sessa.

"Like I said," Mama repeated. "Sessa does not want to talk about that, so we are most certainly not going to talk about that, are we, honey?"

Most days it was easy enough to ignore her very opinionated Mama, but with those words hanging in the air and every member of the Pies, Books & Jesus Book Club waiting for her reaction, Sessa decided enough was enough. Yes, the man who'd gone to prison for killing her son was being released. The residents of Sugar Pine would no doubt have the full scoop before nightfall.

She set her tea glass down next to her copy of *And the Ladies of the Club*, this month's book club selection.

"That's right, Mama. I do not want to talk about that," she said evenly. "Why don't we get back to the book discussion? That is why we're here, isn't it?"

"Well, that and the pie," Carly Chance said with a nervous giggle. The pregnant waitress from the Blue Plate Lunchateria and wife of a former military man who was gone more than he was home rested her hand on the bump where her trim waist once was. Her expression sobered. "And for what it's worth, I can't blame you for not thinking about what happened. Why, if I thought about where Jared was and what he was doing back when he was in the service, I'd just about lose my mind."

Sessa opened her mouth to form a response and found nothing to say. The difference in a wife waiting for her hero to return and a mother knowing her son was neither a hero nor returning was too great. Too painful.

"Thank you, Carly. For the pie and the understanding."

Carly's worried look brightened. "The peach is good, isn't it? I had hoped to make buttermilk but then I ran out of..." She paused. "I'm running off at the mouth again. Look, we love you, Sessa, and if you don't want to talk about this Brown fellow, then we won't talk about him. Isn't that right, ladies?"

A few nods mixed with soft murmurs of agreement. Only Mama kept her silence. Instead she met Sessa's gaze with a determined look. Determined to do what, Sessa could only imagine.

"So, what did you all think of the book?" Mama asked with a tone that told her they'd revisit the unpleasant topic at another time.

"It was long," Vonnette said. "Goodness knows I enjoyed it, but I like to have turned myself into a raisin trying to get that book read before the club meeting."

That comment set the ladies to talking, easing the tension in the room and successfully changing the subject. By the end of the evening, Sessa had almost forgotten about the phone call and the conversation with Coco.

Almost but not quite. The topic simmered at the edge of her thoughts, daring her to consider it.

She carried the last of the pie plates into the kitchen and dunked them into the sudsy water then reached for the scrubber. As she washed the dishes, she could hear Mama bidding goodbye to her guests.

Snatches of conversation, phrases like "she'll be fine" and "give her some time" drifted across the old floorboards to reach her ears. Of course she would be fine. She would stuff down the grief just like she had when Ben died.

Sessa dried off one hand and turned the knob on Mama's old

kitchen radio, the same radio she'd had in that spot on the kitchen window since Sessa was a child. Set to the oldies station since that music was brand new, a lively sixties tune about going downtown filled the room with a much-needed buffer between her and the conversation on the other side of the wall.

A few minutes later, Mama came through the door carrying a coffee cup and a wadded up paper napkin. "That Vonnette always leaves something in the bathroom. This time it was her coffee."

"At least it wasn't her car keys like last time." Sessa chuckled. "I thought Jim Bob was going to have to come get her in the cab."

Mama grinned, then abruptly her smile disappeared. "Oh, honey, we can't all just pretend it didn't happen like you. People are going to talk. They can't help it. You've got to figure out how you're going to deal with it."

Sessa dried her hands and set the towel aside. "What're you talking about?"

"The trial. That doctor." She gave Sessa a helpless look. "Ross. Oh, you know what I mean. He's out. He didn't do it. That young man, Ross's friend, he said some things that probably weren't true but I think he said some that were."

"Well." Sessa pressed past her mother to head toward the spot where she'd left her purse. "I don't know what was said, and I don't care to know."

Mama followed two steps behind. "It's a shame that a boy who was so loved turned into a man who might have killed someone, but you've got to recognize it happened and learn to live with it, especially now that they're letting that doctor out of jail."

Sessa let the words trail her as she snapped up the keys from the depths of her purse.

Mama hurried to her feet and trailed her across the kitchen to the door. "Ignoring what you don't want to deal with might have worked just fine when your heart got broken in junior high, but it's not working now. You know it's the truth."

It was the truth. She just didn't plan on doing anything about it any time soon.

CHAPTER FOUR

Dr. Dalton "Trey" Brown, III, drove slowly along the downtown streets. One elbow propped in the truck window, the 15-mph speed limit allowed him to drink in the once-familiar digs.

Around the corner was the parking garage, and just outside it stood the newsstand where he used to buy his newspapers, at least until the headlines began to hit too close to home. Then he'd settled for hearing the bad news from his attorney.

Today, his first real day back in his old life as a doctor, he planned to buy a copy of the *Chronicle* and read it in plain sight in front of God and everyone. For the first time in recent memory, he had no fear of whose picture would be on the front page.

Or maybe he would take it to a quiet place and savor it alone, just him and the Lord and the *Houston Chronicle*. He wouldn't have patients today, only paperwork and meetings—*if* the chief agreed to reinstate him.

Trey throttled down to allow a pair of bicycle policemen to cross Fannin Street. By habit borne in prison, he averted his eyes and sat very still until they'd passed. Only the sound of a horn honking behind him let him know the road had been cleared.

Easing into the physician's-only parking entrance, Trey found a spot and shut down the engine. He leaned against the well-worn leather of the driver's seat. He'd bought this truck brand new back in college with rodeo winnings.

A rare shaft of sunlight cut between the garage windows and sliced across his left eye, blinding him. He closed his eyes against it. "Lord," he whispered, "I want to do things right this time."

He slid out of the truck, chest going tight at the familiar rows of trucks—and the occasional low-slung sports car. Slinging his backpack over his right shoulder, he walked north toward Turner Memorial Hospital's main entrance. A warm wind caught his hair and blew it into his face, reminding him he hadn't found a new barber yet. Old Jack had retired, selling out his shop on the first floor of the building to a gal who made purses out of license plates and jewelry out of broken machine parts.

Up ahead lay the corner and Bayou City Newsstand, the first milestone in his return to work. He refused to think of the next, concentrating on the coins jingling in his pocket rather than on the doors to the hospital just some fifty-odd yards away.

The old man who used to run the place was gone, replaced by a woman of middle age with a less than enthusiastic expression. He offered her his best smile and waited while she gave change and a copy of *Reader's Digest* to a Life Flight attendant.

"Today's *Chronicle*, please," Trey said a bit more confidently than he felt.

To avoid looking at the actual headlines on the papers displayed across the back of the stall, he concentrated on fishing the quarters out of his pocket and placing them on the chipped red linoleum counter. He'd waited a long time to read a paper like an ordinary citizen, and saving the privilege until his first day back at work seemed the right thing to do. After he met with the chief, he'd find a quiet place to regroup.

The woman complied without comment, slapping a copy of Houston's largest daily paper into his hand. He checked his watch, then folded the paper in half and jammed it into his backpack.

Walking through the doors of the hospital proved easier than he thought; he didn't see a single soul he knew. Most used the staff entrances to avoid out-of-office contact with patients. He, on the other hand, had always preferred to take the front doors in. Dressed in jeans and boots, without his lab coat, he could've passed for a patient himself.

Would he feel more normal, more back to his old self, when he donned scrubs and his white lab coat?

The elevator doors slammed shut on him and a carload of others, but by the time his floor came around, Trey rode alone. All the better to slip in undetected.

Until the doors opened on the fourth floor and there stood the last person he expected to see.

"V-v-v-vikki."

Funny, he'd never stuttered before; not even at the trial. But then she hadn't been at the trial, except for one pivotal day. An assistant district attorney intent on clawing her way to the top couldn't afford to be linked to a common criminal, especially a common criminal who'd just called off the wedding of the century.

A common criminal who might not have gone to prison if she'd testified to what she knew.

"Trey."

She wrapped her voice around his name and made it her own, just like she'd once done with him. What was she doing here? Her presence was a shock—an unwelcome one.

"What a nice surprise," she added in a tone that told him this meeting was anything but chance. Vikki allowed her gaze to slide slowly over him, and then she touched his shoulder, thick with muscles built up while behind bars. "I hardly recognized you. In fact, you look very different."

"I am."

"It suits you."

Oh, but she wasn't different. Not from what he could see. His former fiancée wore the same color blue as her eyes, a conservative dress that managed to look tame and tempting all at the same time. Or perhaps this, too, was his imagination.

He buried the urge to step right back in the elevator.

Vikki repeated his name, this time phrasing it as a question. He watched her lips move, perfect full lips painted a shade darker than the rosy glow on her cheeks.

For a moment, all Trey could do was stand there, snared like a rabbit in a trap. Words, so long practiced and yet never intended to be said, caught in his throat. He licked his lips and tried to dislodge them, hoping he could manage to swallow the sentiments rather than allow them flight.

A man on the other side of forty should never feel this tongue-tied about a woman fifteen years his junior. But then Victoria Carlotta Elisabeth Rossi of the Palm Beach polo-playing Rossis was hardly an ordinary woman. Two years ago they'd been a formidable team, a pair who met over a conversation about a horse and who remained together because it suited them both.

Not so much a love match as a power match.

He stared at her hair, now caught in a twist at the nape of her neck, and wondered when she'd found the time to grow it so long. When he knew her it had been shorter, a spiky blond style that made her look as if she'd just stepped in from dancing in a fresh breeze.

He'd loved it.

He'd loved her.

Until she'd betrayed him.

She moved an inch closer and took his hand, and the scent of something sweet and exotic caught his attention. It encapsulated all he remembered of her, this perfume, and he fought the urge to inhale more of it.

A phone rang in an office somewhere in the distance, ending the thought. He noticed she'd stopped speaking and merely stared.

"Are you all right?" she asked.

No. No, he wasn't.

"Fine, I'm, um, fine. How are you?" he managed as he finally dragged his hand away from her clasp.

"I'm good," she said slowly, her gaze skittering past him to focus on something in the distance. A slow smiled dawned and brightened the already sunlit space as she recovered to stare directly into his eyes. "I'd like to take you to dinner tonight."

The statement toppled what little balance he felt, and he braced his hand against the wall.

Vikki straightened the thick gold and diamond bracelet on her wrist.

Her slender fingers, nails painted the same shade as her lips, were devoid of rings. Not a single gold band or oversized engagement ring in sight.

"Running into you like this was hardly a coincidence. I knew about this appointment before you did."

Shock and dismay cut through the layers of confusion and snapped him to attention. His gaze lifted to meet her stare.

"Don't be so surprised," she said just a bit too sweetly. "I think a man with your..."—she paused to give him sweeping glance before meeting his gaze once more—"talents deserves to return to a position worthy of his skills." Vikki smiled. "Daddy agreed, and you know he's got a little bit of say in how things are run around here. But I won't give all the surprises away."

He hated surprises. Worse, he hated anything he got that he didn't earn or deserve.

Then there was the question of what she got out of this. *Plenty* was his guess.

"Oh, who am I kidding? I never could keep a secret."

"Unless it would keep me off death row," he snapped.

Her unexpected—unwanted—presence, combined with feeling like he was a bug under a microscope and the nausea he'd been fighting all morning created a pounding pulse in his head. His temper flared.

"The answer is no. *No* to dinner. *No* to whatever you and your father cooked up for me. Anything that might have been between us ended the day you testified at my trial."

"Trey, really." Her gaze swept the horizon. "Must we do this here?"

His eyes narrowed. She had to be worried about him making a scene. In her line of work, rumors were gospel by the time they got to the press, and a fight with the newly released Dr. Brown was just juicy enough to end up in the gossip columns by tomorrow.

Why would she risk the fallout for a supper invitation? He didn't get it.

And he was done here.

"Trey Brown. It sure is good to see you."

Interruption welcome, Trey tore his attention away from Vikki's white-lipped frown to see Charlie Dorne storming toward him with the speed befitting a man who was a college running back less than a decade ago. His coattails flying, his horn-rimmed glasses askew, Charlie's hand was already outstretched in greeting and his smile could be seen across the room.

While much of the surgical staff at Turner Memorial had pretended him out of existence during his trial and subsequent incarceration, Charlie hadn't. Charlie had attended the trial when he could and sent him words of encouragement when he couldn't, always assuring Trey he was praying for him. The guy had even taken the trouble to send him a Bible for the duration of his jail term, refusing to take it back when Trey admitted he had no need for the Lord.

The Bible lay under the *Chronicle* in his backpack, well used and with his own notes scribbled alongside Charlie's in the margins of each page. His life had been changed because of that book, and because of this man.

"Hey, Charlie." He checked his watch. Five minutes to spare before his meeting, and so much still left unsaid. "Good to see you too," he added, and it was. Especially as Charlie's presence meant he wasn't alone with Vikki.

Ignoring Vikki, the orthopedic surgeon closed the distance to slap him soundly between the shoulders. "First day back?" He reached to pump his hand like a dry well. "I knew they'd get you back here once the judge heard all the evidence on appeal and declared you innocent."

Innocent. Not exactly what the paperwork said. Thus far Trey could barely consider the word in relation to himself. No matter what the state of Texas declared, and no matter what evidence had been entered in his behalf, a young man was still dead. And he'd held the weapon that killed him. Even if things had been different and he'd never faced jail time, Trey knew he'd have carried that guilt around for the rest of his life.

"That's not exactly how it happened, but the end result was that the truth came out."

Unused to being ignored, Vikki cleared her throat. Loudly.

Dorne, larger than life, wore a smile so broad it had to be genuine. It faded a bit when he turned to stare at Vikki.

"Charlie, you remember my, um, friend, Victoria Rossi, don't you?"

"Sure do." But the doctor's usual East Texas charm was missing from the greeting.

An awkward silence descended.

"Trey." Vikki's nails clamped on his forearm. Her eyes cut to Dorne in a sign Trey recognized. As if he was going to get rid of the other doctor to be alone with her.

His one saving grace was the fact she wouldn't make a scene in front of Charlie.

He shook her off. "We're done here."

But she wasn't. She leaned in again.

"I made reservations at the Lancaster," she said, voice low.

"I said no." He turned, but could feel her seething beside him. Charlie had the good manners to pretend interest in an awful painting hanging nearby.

"You're a smart man, cowboy." Now her voice had a dangerous tone to it.

Cowboy. If indeed he still were just that, life would be much simpler.

"Too smart to pass this up. If you want to stay on the fast track to chief, you'll be there."

Trey watched her walk away, her words, almost a threat, ringing in his ears. When she disappeared around the corner, he faced Charlie, now leaning against the wall watching.

The clock over Charlie's head told Trey he was almost late for his appointment with the chief. An appointment he suddenly did not want to attend. After his stint in prison, he knew the cost of mistakes. But thinking about stepping into the chief's office made him want to vomit.

Unlike Vikki, Charlie had appeared at just the right moment.

"You got a minute?"

"Sure." Charlie pushed off the wall. "But don't you have someplace to be?"

The elevator dinged, and Trey pressed past his friend to step inside. "Yeah, but I'm having second thoughts about showing up now that I know what it's about. How about I reschedule and buy you breakfast instead?"

CHAPTER FIVE

Trey's phone call to the chief's office was blessedly brief. He left a message with the chief's secretary that he was meeting with a colleague and needed to reschedule. He would have to face the chief soon—he wasn't officially back on the payroll yet.

A few minutes later Trey and Charlie grabbed a small table in the far corner of the hospital coffee shop on the basement level just as a couple of EMTs vacated it. While Charlie unloaded milk, orange juice, one sausage biscuit and a donut from his tray, Trey watched the lunch crowd and stirred a second packet of sugar into his coffee, trying to sort his thoughts into words.

Trey stared past Charlie to the bank of elevators on the opposite wall and the throng of nameless strangers milling about. His phone sounded, and quickly he squelched the noise without looking. He'd told the chief's secretary she could leave the new meeting time on his voice mail.

And if it were anyone else, they could wait. His conversation with Charlie was way overdue.

"I read that Bible you sent me."

Charlie raised his glass of milk in mock salute. "Good for you. Guess you had plenty of reading time."

That's what he loved about Charlie. Anyone else might have danced around the topic of his incarceration, but not this guy.

His gaze settled back on Charlie. "Took me awhile, but I got it, this me and Jesus thing. Thank you."

With a chuckle, the surgeon reached to give Trey a high five. "Well, all right."

"Yeah," he said through the steam coming off his cup.

The doctor leaned back in his chair and gave Trey a sideways look. "You're not considering letting Vikki lead you back to that old life, are you?"

"No!"

He shook his head. "But?"

"But..." Trey paused to consider his words. "I need some advice."

Charlie leaned forward and placed his elbows on the table. "Sure."

Working up his courage, he gave voice to the fear dogging him. "Have you ever felt like you don't deserve it?"

"It? Oh, *it*." Charlie slapped the table and jostled the glass of milk, causing it to spill. Swiping at the mess with a napkin, he smiled. "Every day, Trey. Every day. But then that's grace, man. Undeserved but freely given."

"Yeah, but I feel like I should be doing something to make up for all I've done wrong." He paused to watch a trio of nurses look his way then quickly avert their gazes. "It just seems too easy."

"Easy and hard all at the same time, I'd say." He tossed the soggy napkin toward the center of the table and gave Trey a direct look, his smile gone. "This is personal isn't it? It's about your acquittal."

Trey sipped at his coffee without actually tasting it. "I still don't feel like a free man."

"Give it some time. The ink's barely dry on the paperwork that says you didn't do it."

"But I did do it. I killed that man." A couple turned to stare, and he lowered his voice a notch. "A twenty-year-old kid is dead. By the hands that are supposed to heal, not kill. No amount of time is going to change that."

"No, it won't."

"That's it? It won't?"

Charlie shrugged. "Sorry, pal. That kid would have killed you if you hadn't defended yourself. You know that."

Sometimes he thought he did. Other times, he wasn't so sure. He'd known that boy. Mentored him. Taught him how to stay on the back of a bucking horse. He'd had high hopes he'd do well in rodeo and in school.

Was even willing to put money behind his hopes.

Trey inhaled deeply, then let the breath out slowly as he

nodded to a pair of orderlies vacating a nearby table. "I don't fit in this life anymore. In medicine, I mean."

Speaking the words aloud crystallized all of it—the swirling emotions that had suffocated him since his release, the feeling that it was wrong to come back.

"Sure you do," Charlie said.

His cell phone rang again, but Trey ignored it to lean toward Charlie. "I can't even hold a knife yet, Charlie. I threw up on my kitchen floor just trying to cut a bagel." The phone rang again. He was beginning to think he shouldn't have gotten out of bed at all. With no family to speak of, no one to call him for an emergency, it could only be the chief.

And his expectations.

Charlie seemed to consider the statement a moment. "Why do you think that is?"

Trey ran a hand through his hair and shook his head. "That's the million dollar question."

His friend didn't waste a minute. "I know a guy who might be able to help. He's a specialist at this sort of thing. While I look for his number, you answer the call."

Numb, Trey pressed the button and held the phone to his ear. "Brown here."

The chief of staff's rant began with a question and ended with a statement. In as few words as possible, Trey promised to appear within ten minutes under penalty of continued loss of his license and possible banishment from Turner Memorial altogether. Trey placated the chief with the appropriate apology and promised to be in his office right away.

Doubt slammed him hard as he hung up the phone, making him wonder whether he would ever operate again. Skepticism hit him harder when Charlie reached for the notepad in his coat pocket, wrote down a number, and then pushed the slip of white paper toward him.

"He helped me, and I know he'll help you."

"You mean you..." The words died as he tried to enunciate his shock at the idea of such a level-headed guy as Charlie Dorne having need of a counselor's help.

Nonplussed, Charlie nodded. "Yeah, me." His gaze, while direct, seemed to indicate his thoughts were elsewhere. "When

Dee died, I had a real bad time of it." He pointed to the paper. "I'm still here because of this man."

Faint remembrances of signing a sympathy card for Charlie upon the demise of his wife teased at his mind. Back then it had been just one more document to sign between surgical orders and medicine changes. Fresh shame gnawed at him. Before he could comment further, Charlie stood and grabbed his tray.

"Better get yourself up to the chief's office stat," he said. "You've got less than half of that ten minutes left."

Trey stood and tucked the card into his shirt pocket. "How'd you know?"

Charlie pointed to the phone clipped to Trey's belt. "I've got ears."

He lifted his backpack to his shoulder and joined his friend in a chuckle as they walked toward the elevators. "I guess I've tried his patience enough for one day."

The surgeon pressed the up button. "Make that call." He paused as they stepped into the elevator and then he slid Trey a sideways look. "Or I can call him for you."

"Yeah, sure," Trey said. "If you think of it, that'd be fine."

~*~

They shook hands and parted ways when Charlie left the elevator on the fifth floor. All the way to the top, Trey rode alone and tried to pray. Somehow, his elusive needs didn't quite collect into any coherent thoughts.

An hour later, after all the papers were signed and the lawyers had departed, the moment was properly celebrated among the staff. Trey left the chief of staff's office a full-fledged doctor with a brand new license to practice medicine in the state of Texas and a place on the staff of Turner Memorial Hospital. While there was no direct mention of him being placed on the fast track, the chief's toast over champagne left little doubt that was at least an option.

Unfortunately, that license would do him no good if he couldn't hold a knife, and the fast track would be a slippery slope unless he decided that's what he really wanted. Then there was the issue of Vikki. He certainly wouldn't be meeting her at the

Lancaster for dinner, but he would have to speak to her about any continued involvement in his life. Those days were over.

He balled his hands into fists. Somewhere behind him a door opened.

"Dr. Brown," the chief's secretary called, "you'd best get down to OR seven. Dr. Santini's looking for you."

Santini.

He'd promised to scrub in with his former friend at ten, and his watch read five minutes past. Once more he was late. Another bad impression made on his first day back at work.

Work.

What was his work anymore? Cutting people and sewing them back up? Was that why the Lord allowed him to still hold a scalpel after he'd used one to...?

Trey pushed the bloody image away with a roll of his shoulders and slammed his fist against the wall with a satisfying thud. "Tell him I'm on my way, Peg." He stalked down the hall toward the stairs.

Twenty minutes later, shame chased him back to the parking garage, the contents of his stomach left on the floor of OR 7. There was a virus going around, or at least that's what he overheard one of the nurses saying as he made his exit. He should take a day or two to feel better. This from Santini as he diplomatically stepped over the mess and sent an intern out to arrange for another operating room.

With the car door closed, Trey turned over the ignition and positioned the air conditioner vents so they were blowing directly on him. Closing his eyes, Trey leaned back against the headrest and once again tried to pray. This time all he could manage was a roughly mumbled, "Help me."

The buzzing of his phone jarred Trey. He reached into his pocket and saw that the name on the caller ID matched the one on the card Charlie Dorne had given him.

That was fast, Lord.

"Dr. Brown, this is Tom Glenn. Charlie told me you'd be expecting a call," the counselor said. "Am I interrupting?"

"Your timing is fine, Mr. Glenn."

"Call me Tom. I'm calling because I have an unexpected cancellation for this morning at eleven, and I wondered if perhaps you'd like to take that slot."

~*~

Trey arrived with a few minutes to spare.

He found the chair nearest the door and waited long enough to get nervous. Just as he was about to bolt, the door opened, and a guy who looked as if he'd just stepped out of the Houston Texans locker room called him by name.

"Come on back," Tom said as he led Trey down a hallway decorated with Louisiana State University memorabilia. "Charlie tells me you played for the Aggies."

"Running back," he said. "I mostly warmed the bench but I made a couple of touchdowns senior year."

"Middle linebacker," Tom said. "I stopped a few touchdowns in my brief college career. And a few running backs."

Tom glanced back in time for Trey to see him smile. Trey joined the counselor in laughter, and the ice was broken.

"Come on in and make yourself comfortable."

Unlike the nondescript reception area, Tom's office was decorated in that slick modern style many of Trey's colleagues favored. The furniture was all chrome and black leather, and the modern art was good. Very good, judging by the Kandinsky painting by the door and the Picasso lithograph holding a place of honor between the floor-to-ceiling windows that offered a view of Memorial Park and the polo grounds.

He took a seat across from Tom's vintage Karl Springer desk, ironically an almost exact copy of the one Vikki had in her office. "Thank you for fitting me in. Where should I begin?"

"First we pray." After a brief prayer for God's guidance that settled Trey even more than bonding over football, Tom returned to the topic at hand. "I find the beginning's the best place, although I'm always curious as to whether my clients can sum up their issues in a sentence. Can you do that?"

Could he? Trey thought a minute. "I killed a kid I'd been mentoring. Now I can't hold a scalpel without losing my lunch." He let out a long breath. "Sorry, that was two sentences, wasn't it?"

Tom appraised him, chin propped on steepled fingers. "You

murdered a kid?"

The question—the same one he'd asked himself often during his incarceration—knocked the breath from his lungs.

"You didn't follow the case?" he grated.

"I'd like to hear it from you."

Was that a *yes* or a *no*? Trey didn't want to tell the story again. Didn't know if he could.

Eyes on the floor, he focused on regulating his breathing. When he felt like he could speak without vomiting, he recited, "I was coming home after an evening out. Came through the garage. I walked in on him. He was trying to open the safe in my home office."

He blinked against the memories. He could see it. The hall light shining behind him. The dark office. The adrenaline surge when he noticed movement behind the desk. A head turning toward him, light slanting across a face.

Ross.

"Why was he there?"

Tom's voice broke through the memories.

Shaken, sweating through his shirt, Trey looked up from the floor. "What?"

"Why was he there? What did you have in your safe that he wanted?"

He shook his head. Pried his fingers off the armrest. They *ached.* "Cash."

Tom nodded slowly. "He was robbing you."

He hesitated. Memories swirled. Had Ross really been after the money? "I thought so. He had to be."

Hadn't he?

His eyes closed as he searched through the images of that night. The glint of light off of Ross's weapon. Reaching for something to protect himself. Anything. Coming up with the sterling silver scalpel his late parents had given him when he'd graduated med school.

He shook his head, an attempt to shake out of the fragmented reality—the memories overlaying what he saw even now in the therapist's office. "Everything happened so fast."

Tom stood up, startling Trey, whose gaze followed him to a sideboard and small fridge in one corner of the room. He retrieved a bottle of water and handed it to Trey.

He gulped it. The shock of cold coursed down his gut.

"We can come back to that night." Tom returned to his chair. "How well did you know Ross?"

Not well enough. "I mentored him through a program at Star of Hope."

Trey had suspected Ross was using. Hard to ignore the physical signs. He'd hoped to draw Ross out of the lifestyle. Help him live up to his potential. He'd been a brilliant kid.

Trey'd been blindsided when evidence had been released during the trial that implicated Ross as a dealer.

How could he have misjudged someone so completely?

"Was he a regular visitor to your home?"

Trey blinked, trying to find his footing in the conversation again. "He'd been over a few times." Mostly they'd gone out to Trey's barn, his land outside the city limits. They'd shared a love of horses that transcended the differences in their circumstances.

In all that time, Ross had never mentioned his mama. But the prosecutor had mentioned her often during the trial, along with Ross's baby girl. A mother and a daughter who would go on without Ross in their lives.

"You lost someone you counted as a friend."

Trey wanted to deny it, deny the connection in the face of Ross's final betrayal, but he couldn't. "Not as much as his mama lost. She lost her son."

Tom's eyes saw too much. Trey shifted in the chair as the other man scrutinized him. "You lost a lot."

Trey shook his head.

"You lost your license. Your fiancée."

He and Vikki had been done before that night, but Trey didn't correct the other man.

"You lost your reputation. Your position."

"He lost his life!" Trey's words burst from him, and he shoved up from the chair. Emotion swamped him, making it hard to think, to breathe. He pushed both hands through his hair. "All those things—they don't matter."

When he'd been stripped bare in prison, in those darkest days, he'd found what did matter. Only when he'd had nothing left.

"And performing surgery?"

Trey whirled to face the therapist, heart pounding, hands still gripping his hair. An ugly surge of emotion had words boiling on the back of his tongue, but he swallowed them. One visit, and the man had pinpointed Trey's pain.

Before, he'd lived for surgery. Thought he'd been born to it. That moment when he located the patient's problem, when he'd used the tools of his trade to heal, it had always delivered a flare of triumph. He'd won. He'd saved lives.

Until Ross. Until he'd used his superpower to kill.

Tom watched him patiently.

"You don't pull any punches."

The doctor nodded. "Can't help you if I do."

Trey let his hands drag down his face. How he wished he could wipe away the past three years. Go back in time and drive around the block instead of going home.

"Think about that moment when you picked up the knife this morning."

He didn't want to, but his mind followed Tom's words back to the operating theater. Santini's expectations. The watchful nurses.

"What did you feel? Fear? Or guilt?"

Nausea rose and Trey forced his eyes open. Forced a breath into his lungs. Out.

He shrugged. "It's all mixed up together."

Tom folded his hands. "I can teach you exercises to help alleviate the fear. We can deal with anxiety. But the guilt...it has to be worked through. You've got to be able to forgive yourself."

"How can I, when I stole a little girl's daddy? Do you think Ross's mama can ever forgive what I've done?"

"Maybe you should ask her."

Reeling, Trey fell back into the chair he'd vacated earlier. "You think I should talk to Ross's family?"

If he dared, would they even let him apologize? He could imagine several scenarios, and none of them ended happily. He didn't even know what Ross's mama looked like.

Every day of the trial, he'd scoured the courtroom, looking for the mama that the prosecutor kept bringing up, but no sobbing, heartbroken woman had been present.

She hadn't attended, not one day of the weeks-long ordeal.

Would that have changed things for him, facing down her

recrimination?

Could Tom be right that apologizing might bring him some closure?

Several protests formed in his mind. Each of them died a swift death before he could speak them aloud.

"I see you're thinking about it," Tom said.

"I am."

He leaned forward. "What do you really want, Trey?"

"What do you mean?"

"You've got your license to practice back, correct?" At Trey's nod, he continued. "I think the question you need to answer, whether or not you make your apologies to the boy's family, is what you plan to do with that license. What you plan to do with your life."

CHAPTER SIX

"If I'm going to meet a man, he's either going to have to quilt or sing, because the only two places I ever go are Quilt Guild and church choir. Besides the book club, that is."

At her mother's words, Sessa looked up from her remains of the Blue Plate Lunchateria's East Texas version of California Cobb salad. Where had that come from?

"Well, I guess he could tap dance, but I don't see how that would be attractive at all." Mama peered over the gold rims of her designer glasses, her face a mask of innocence as her fuchsia nails tapped the tabletop next to her best friend Vonnette. "What? I've been alone ten years, you know. Maybe it's time."

Bonnie Sue *alone?* Hardly.

Sessa shook her head and took a healthy sip of iced tea. Between her mother's friends at church and book club and Sew Busy fabric shop, Sessa practically had to schedule a meeting with her a week in advance just to see her alone.

She formed her words carefully. Perhaps it was time for Mama to step out from beneath her share of the duties and pursue the social life she'd lost with Dad's passing. "You know Doctor Easley has had a thing for you for years."

Her mother's eyes narrowed. "That old coot? What in the world would we have in common?"

The fact that the good doctor was nearly five years younger than Mama seemed irrelevant. Compared to her vibrant, blonde, soon-to-be-seventy tap-dancing mother, every man over the age of fifty seemed old.

Most days she made Sessa feel old.

"You know, we should find *you* someone nice, Sessa." Mama

demurely placed her napkin over her unfinished slice of apple pie and slid her a sideways glance. "I was just telling Vonnette that I felt like the Lord was calling me to pray for a man for you."

"I had a man. When God wants me to have another one, He'll tell me Himself."

Mama looked nonplussed, but then she usually did. "Well, maybe He *is* telling you—through me."

"Listen to your mama, Sessa, honey," Vonnette said. "Just because you've had a bad ride or two, that doesn't mean you need to climb off the horse."

Sessa shook her head. "I have no idea what you mean, Vonnette, but I have a good idea that if the Lord wanted to speak to me, He would do it Himself."

Vonette reached across the table to press her hand atop Sessa's. "Bless your heart."

Her eyes narrowed. "What do you mean by that?"

"Well," Mama said, "it is no secret that when you were dating, you had more than your share of unfortunate experiences."

"Unfortunate?" Vonnette cackled so loud that half the diner turned to look. "Bonnie Sue, do you remember the time you and I had to go fetch her from the police station after she went out with that English teacher from the high school?"

"He seemed so nice," Sessa said. "I didn't know he'd set fire to his last girlfriend's car. You should have seen his expression when she showed up at the restaurant and threw a drink in his face. I'd have called the cops for her if she hadn't."

Mama giggled. "And you were brought in for questioning."

Sessa cringed at the memory. "It wasn't funny."

"Well it is now," Vonnette countered. "After all, they let you go once your mama and I went down and vouched for you." She shook her head. "Oh, but what about the time you went out with Coco's cousin? The astronaut from Clear Lake?"

"And he brought his helmet," Mama supplied.

"Into the restaurant," Vonnette managed as she fell into gales of laughter.

"That wasn't as bad as the time you set me up with Ray." She gave her mother a pointed look. "Do you remember Ray, Mama?"

Her mother offered a distressed look. "In my defense, I had no idea he was so much older than you. His mother and I were college roommates, so I just assumed her son would be, well..."

"Younger?" Sessa supplied. "I was willing to ignore the twelve-year age gap, but when he took out his teeth in the restaurant, that was too much."

"You've had some doozies of dates, Sessa Lee," Vonnette said. "No wonder you gave up dating."

"Can you blame me? I cannot recall a single pleasant date," she said. "It may take me awhile to get the message, but even a slow learner like me eventually figures out that if God wanted me to date, He'd make the experience a little more fun."

She'd been slow to learn, this was true. But she'd finally realized that the anticipation of a date with Mr. Right wasn't worth the pain of yet another disappointment when her date turned out to be Mr. All Wrong.

"A few bad dates is no reason to up and quit."

"More than a few, Mama. I'm the queen of bad dates." She shook her head. "Well, no thank you. This queen abdicated a long time ago, and I am perfectly happy."

Mama pursed her lips. "You don't throw out all the apples just because one goes bad." She paused. "You know, I've had the strangest feeling all morning like the Good Lord was going to bring someone real soon for you."

"She sure has," Vonnette said. "She told me first thing this morning that she just knew today was the day."

"Today's the day," Sessa echoed with more than a little sarcasm. "Whatever you say. Name it and claim it."

"I do resent your tone, Sessa," Mama snapped. "You might be grown, but you weren't raised to disrespect, and I am certainly not going to sit here and—"

The bell on the Lunchateria's front door jangled, signaling another diner had joined their midst. "Well, well," Mama said. "Would you look at that?"

"What?"

Sessa swiveled to follow her mother's gaze in time to see a golden-haired cowboy with broad shoulders slide onto a stool at the lunch counter. Their eyes met, and something clicked in her mind. A jolt of recognition shot through her; she knew him from somewhere. As soon as the absurd thought occurred, she dismissed it.

"It's him," her mother whispered. "The man God sent you. I just know it."

The stranger offered a curt nod before removing his Lone Star Feed cap and placing it in his lap. While the man was undeniably easy on the eyes, he hardly looked like he came directly from the Lord.

That didn't stop her hands from trembling.

"I'm telling you, it's *him*," Mama said a bit louder.

"All right, *Mother*." She turned to face her mama once more. "That's enough."

"But, I was just telling Vonnette..." Mama reached for her tube of Pink Passion lipstick. "Well, never mind what I told Vonnette. Let's get back to what we were talking about before your gentleman came in."

"Mama!"

Again she feigned innocence as she flipped open her silver compact mirror. "What I was saying is if you don't want to be embarrassed at the PB & J meeting tomorrow night, you might want to get some advice on your pie crust skills from someone who knows how to make them. I *could* try to teach you to make pie crust again, but that didn't work out so well last time, did it?"

The PB & J.

Sessa groaned. She'd completely forgotten the ladies from the Pies, Books, and Jesus book club would be meeting at her house this month. Not only had it slipped her mind that it was her turn to host the event, she hadn't yet finished the novel the group would be discussing.

And she hadn't even begun to attempt the pies.

With a pair of prancing reproduction carousel horses due to be finished and shipped out to the Detroit Museum on Friday and the house a wreck from her granddaughter's newest obsession of hiding Tupperware in the oddest places, Sessa would likely spend half the night working to catch up and clean up. The other half of the night would be spent reading.

At least that half would be fun.

"Why don't I let Pansie spend the night with me? I'm sure you'll have your hands full tonight getting ready. You've probably still got some reading to do." Her mother returned the lipstick and compact to her purse and reached across the table to place a hand on Sessa's arm. "And speaking of my great-granddaughter, honey, isn't it about time to pick Pansie up from Mother's Day Out?"

Sessa jerked her wrist up to check her watch. Ten minutes lay between her and a late fee. She'd never been late before, but she'd cut it close more than once.

"I'll go get that precious darling," Mama said as she slid out of the booth and straightened her matching fuchsia slacks and top. "You can get the check."

"So much for saving five bucks. Bye, Vonette." She chuckled as she rose to follow her mother.

While Sessa stopped at the cash register, Mama departed the Lunchateria with a regal wave and a promise to come by later for a change of clothes for Pansie. She watched her mother walk toward her car and marveled at the gene pool that had gone dry between Mama's generation and hers. Somewhere between Betty Crocker and Susie Homemaker, Sessa had become Bob the Builder, adept at woodworking and home repair and lousy at baking pies and scrubbing floors.

Out of the corner of her eye she saw the cowboy dousing ketchup over a plate of meatloaf and potatoes, the muscles in his arm rippling beneath the faded denim of his shirt. If he were heaven sent, maybe cholesterol and fat grams really didn't count in eternity. At least this man ate like they didn't.

"Hey, Sessa. I'm looking forward to tomorrow." Sue Ellen Benson brushed past her with a tray balanced on her shoulder. The tall brunette wore red today, a color that complemented her dark skin and made her look more like a fashion model than the owner of a small town Texas diner.

"Me too," she said with a grin.

Of all the ladies in the PB & J club, Sue Ellen was one of her favorites. Only Coco had been her friend longer.

Sessa and Sue Ellen had gone from childhood friends to new brides together. While Sue Ellen stood poised to celebrate twenty-five years of wedded bliss this summer, Sessa would mark seventeen years of widowhood next winter.

She watched her friend match wits with a pair of mechanics from the bus barn before turning to navigate the aisle back in her direction. Funny how their situations had drawn them closer instead of apart. While Sessa envied Sue Ellen's close relationship with her husband, she also gave thanks that God had given her the ability to spend time alone and enjoy it—at least until Pansie had arrived in her life.

Carly Chance, Sue Ellen's second-in-command, hurried to the cash register as quickly as she could, given the fact she was nine months pregnant. "Can't wait for tomorrow night," she said as she touched her expanded belly. "I just loved that book. I got so involved in reading that I almost forgot I'm carrying around two extra people here."

"Now that is the mark of a good book." Sessa handed Carly the check along with a ten-dollar bill then waved away the change. She leaned toward her and lowered her voice. "Don't tell my mother, but I'm looking forward to finishing the book tonight."

Her friend chuckled. "Pansie keeping you busy?"

"Pansie and the Detroit Museum." She shouldered her purse. "And remember that contract for the Smithsonian's traveling exhibit of carousels that fell through?"

Sue Ellen nodded. "Two years ago, right?" Her hand went to her chest. "That just about broke my heart when the project got put on hold."

"Well, I got an email this morning saying the funds have been released, and the project is back on. They'll be announcing their choice before the end of the month." Anticipation and hope rose as she said the words, but on their heels came a wave of worry and the niggling feeling that she would be passed over.

Carly's smile widened. "How can you stand it?"

"I'll be too busy to think about it," she said, though she knew that wasn't true at all. The Smithsonian contract was a huge deal.

Two years ago, she'd come so close to landing it, only to find the project had been placed on hold. At the time she thought it must be God's way of allowing her time to raise her granddaughter without the complications of fulfilling the biggest restoration job of her career. No way could she could have done both.

But now that Pansie was a little older...

While she climbed into her car pondering the possibilities, she also found her mind wandering to the mysterious stranger with the affinity for meatloaf and potatoes with extra ketchup. Maybe it was Mama's comments, or maybe it was something else, but she couldn't shake the feeling she knew him from somewhere.

All the way home, she alternated between searching her mind for the source of muscle man's familiarity and trying to put him out of her thoughts altogether. Back home she traded her sundress for jeans and T-shirt and headed for the back of the property, where her studio stood beneath the shade of a trio of ancient pecan trees. With Pansie spending the night at Mama's, best not to squander the hours she could be working.

As she strolled past the garage where Pansie's baby swing and cradle had been stored, she gave passing thought to the day she'd purchased those things. What a precious blessing that child had turned out to be.

She hurried past the garage and unlatched the door to her studio. Before she could swing the door open, her cell phone rang. The caller ID showed unknown caller. Probably Pansie's pediatrician calling to remind her of her check-up next week.

She kicked the wooden block in front of the old door to keep it open and greeted the caller.

No response.

"Hello?" she repeated as she closed the distance to the switch to flood the space with light.

"Mrs. Chambers?" The voice was deep, halting, and distinctly Southern.

"Yes." Sessa opened the door of the small fridge Mama had given her last Christmas. Bypassing a Baby Bop cup filled with milk, two pears, and a small container of apple juice, Sessa reached for a bottle of water and took a healthy swig.

As the silence lengthened on the phone, irritation began. She really should get something accomplished. "Hello? Who is this?"

Apparently not the doctor's office.

"I'm sorry. I never meant to..." The last word was choked off by what sounded like a sob.

"Excuse me? Who is this?"

The line went dead.

Sessa shook her head and tossed the cordless phone onto her workbench. "I really need to stop answering calls where the identification is blocked."

She turned to study the project at hand. An authentic Allan Herschell Company Half and Half horse lay in pieces on the surgical table turned workbench. Made in 1949, the great beast's cast metal head and legs sported new paint, but its wooden body still needed some work. Its companion, a standing zebra with flowing mane restored and crated for shipping, stood in the corner of the room next to the pieces of a second crate.

Friday morning, Jared Chance, the UPS driver, would arrive at precisely ten-thirty to pick up both horses. Neither Jared nor the curators in Detroit would understand if she didn't meet the deadline. Not only that, but Jared, who hated to come all the way out Firefly Road just to go back empty-handed, would most likely tell his mama.

Robin worked down at the Pup Cake Bakery and Doggie Diner and delivered cupcakes and homemade dog treats to Vonnette and the girls at the Hairport every Monday. Once Vonnette got wind of things, she would be on the phone to Mama, who would then call Sessa wondering why she had to find out from Robin that Sessa was falling behind on work. And goodness knows they'd all think she was slacking off and not working as hard as she ought to be. Which of course wasn't anybody's business, though that's exactly what made it so interesting, she supposed.

Whoever said living in a small town was peaceful and quiet had never lived in a small town.

Sessa turned her attention to the equine "patient" sprawled on the stainless steel worktable. A little paint and some chiseling along the horse's flank, and it would be ready to go. She could probably be finished in a couple of hours.

She went over the horse's body with fine sandpaper then wiped it clean with cheesecloth. The paint went on next, in colors painstakingly chosen to replicate the original.

Hours later, leaving the paint to dry, she returned to the kitchen to take on an even harder project—making pies for the PB&J ladies. Once she'd placed them in the oven, she could turn her attention to straightening up the house then move on to what would obviously be the best part of the evening, finishing the novel.

Tomorrow she could start bright and early on the remainder of the Detroit Museum project, finishing the horse with varnish and checking the zebra for last minute touch-ups. If all went well, she would have everything done before noon when Mama would return with Pansie.

"In a perfect world, anyway," she muttered, reaching for the measuring cups.

While she gathered the flour and other ingredients, her thoughts gravitated back to Ross, who had loved to help her cook just like Pansie did now. Those same eyes that had looked up at her two decades before now watched her again from the eager face of her granddaughter.

"That's the Lord's blessing and a sore subject all at the same time."

She shoved away the memories with a roll of her shoulders and moved her consideration to Pansie's mother, who had all but disappeared from the face of the earth. Just a kid herself, that girl had no idea what she was missing by not being here to appreciate her daughter.

Thankfully, neither did Pansie. "Enough of that." Maybe she thought about the past far too much and the future far too little.

Sessa reached for the flour canister and dusted the counter top, then reached into the fridge for the piecrust dough. It was a true mystery how God determined who ended up raising who, and a bigger mystery at why she was chosen to bring up the feisty toddler. Only He could explain the reasoning behind it all.

Behind anything He did, actually. She'd stopped trying to understand on the day Pansie came to live with her. No, that wasn't true. It was the day she lost Ross.

It wasn't like she had contemplated Ross' death every day for the past two years. Some days she was just too tired, either with childrearing or work. Other days, thoughts of Mama and her dating misadventures or Pansie and her quest to run faster than she could walk held her mind in a welcome—or sometimes unwelcome—distraction.

For good reason she'd avoided attending the trial, shunned the media, and refused to hear any details about the man who'd ended her Ross' life. She never wanted to set eyes on a picture of Dr. Dalton Brown, III, wanted no image in her mind to imagine standing over the dead body of her son. For the same reason, she forbade any discussion of the man—or the subject—in her presence.

Besides, if she knew him, she would have to forgive him. To hate a nameless, faceless stranger seemed much less of a sin than to refuse to grant forgiveness to a flesh and blood man.

Then she accidentally caught a glimpse of him when she turned on the television a week or so ago. He'd been let loose. Not pardoned but released a free man when his conviction was overturned.

Meaning to turn the blasted thing off, Sessa had hit the pause button on the remote and frozen the killer's face on that big flat screen television she'd splurged on last Christmas. Suddenly there he was, the man whose face she'd avoided.

The man who'd ended Ross's life.

The cameras had been trained on him as he left the courtroom at the end of the trial. He wore a suit and tie in a dark color, brown maybe, and his hands were shackled in front of him, a Harris County deputy ushering him out a side door to begin his prison sentence for murder.

The caption beneath the photo said three words: Doctor Declared Innocent. That much she'd already heard from Coco.

She'd found a chair. Sunk into it. Sat very still with the remote in her hand and the image of that doctor providing the only light in a darkened living room.

Her finger had wavered above the off button. Then her eyes found his. And she knew.

The man on that screen, the doctor the jury had sentenced to prison, was no more guilty of Ross's death than she. He may have held the knife, but she was the one who'd allowed her grief at losing her husband to overshadow her responsibility to raise up their only son to be a good man.

She and her selfish grief had failed Ross. That doctor and his knife were just the last stop on a road that started at her door. Ignoring that fact was what had kept her from driving to Houston and testifying. Had kept her from standing up in court and admitting her son was every bit the kind of person who'd do what was claimed he'd done.

It was surely the reason why she'd pushed every detail of this bone-crushing loss into the safe place where she now kept these sorts of memories. Sessa balled her fists and declared once again to the Lord and herself that she had learned from her mistake.

Pansie would never face life with a parent who was absent even though she was standing right in front of her.

But what about that doctor?

Could she have said something that kept him from leaving out that side door? That kept his eyes—innocent eyes—from looking into the lens of that camera as he tasted his last moments of freedom?

"Gwammy?" Pansie's gleeful cry arrived in the kitchen a moment before she did.

"Who's that?" Sessa called, grateful for the respite from her guilt.

"Pansie and Nanny." The dark-haired angel launched herself toward Sessa then giggled when her grandmother pretended to drop her before hefting her securely into her arms.

"I missed you so much." Sessa breathed in the scent of baby shampoo and squeezed the little girl tighter. "I think you grew a foot while you were at school today, Pansie girl." She swiped at the red Kool-Aid ring around her granddaughter's mouth.

A matching stain decorated the front of her pink OshKosh overalls, and a few dots embellished her white Keds. The entire outfit would have to be thrown into the wash before the color became permanent, and Pansie would need a bubble bath and a scrubbing as well.

Such was life with Pansie Chambers. How dull Sessa's world would be today if the little girl hadn't come to stay.

A rhyme. Sessa smiled.

Mama strolled in with Pansie's diaper bag slung over one shoulder and a stack of mail and Pansie's sippy cup cradled in her arms. "You know how that girl loves seeing what's in the mailbox," Mama said as two bills and a Priority Mail envelope tumbled from her arms and slid to the floor along with the cup. "You've got mail."

Sessa knelt to retrieve them, allowing Pansie to wiggle out of her arms. While the toddler made haste for the Tupperware drawer, Sessa set the cup and bills aside to rip open the red, white and blue wrapper and snatched out the letter.

A familiar logo danced across the page, and her heart lurched. She read the first sentence and then the second. The words swam in front of her eyes.

"Nanny, look," Pansie called as she tossed a yellow plastic cup lid into the air. "I cook."

"Yes, darling, you cook very well. Maybe you can help Grammy with her pies tonight." Mama settled beside her on the floor and blew Pansie a kiss. "What is it, Sessa?"

Her eyes scanned the page, drinking in the words one more time. "I got the job," she breathed.

"What job, Sessa?" Mama leaned in to read over her shoulder. "Oh! You got the *job*! The Smithsonian wants you to do the restoration work for the carousel exhibit!"

Numb, Sessa nodded. "They do, don't they?"

"But that wasn't supposed to happen until the end of the month." Mama shook her head. "And yet here it is!"

"Yes." Sessa lifted her gaze to a place well above the ceiling of her kitchen and gave thanks. "Here it is."

Of all the candidates, the Smithsonian had selected her to facilitate the restoration project that had been in limbo for almost two years. The job was huge, the honor of being chosen even bigger.

Their gazes locked, and Mama began to giggle. Sessa joined her, and Pansie chimed in, though the child had no idea what had them tickled.

"Gwammy funny," the little girl said as she attempted to walk in circles with her feet stuck into a pair of green plastic tumblers and a blue salad bowl on her head.

"My Pansie girl's pretty funny too." Sessa sagged against the cabinet. "Mama, how am I going to accept this offer? There's just one of me, and there's so much to do in such a short time."

Her mother shrugged. "I don't know, honey. What were you going to do before the project got put on hold?"

"I thought I might put an ad in the paper, maybe hire someone to help with the carpentry end of things. I'd even thought I could delegate some of the basic painting and prep work."

Mama patted her arm and smiled. "Then I suggest you get busy placing the ad. It's nearly four, and you know how Ella likes to set her watch ahead so she can get home from the paper in time to see Wheel of Fortune."

"You know, if I take on this project, I won't have time to hunt for a husband."

She couldn't say what prompted her to speak the outlandish words. Maybe it was that ounce of fear that *she couldn't really do this project, could she*? Or maybe it was the memory of that split-second connection with the handsome cowboy in the diner.

And Mama knew she wasn't on the market for a husband, but she only narrowed her eyes slightly and waved away the comment with a regal sweep of her hand. "The Lord's already taken care of that, Sessa. I told you that back at the diner."

Before Sessa could respond, her granddaughter waddled over to place a salad bowl on Sessa's head. "You Queen, Nanny," she said. "Gwammy too."

Mama climbed to her feet and clasped Pansie's hands in her own. In a regal tone, she replied, "My precious Princess Pansie, I will have to pass on your generous offer." She cast a glance past Sessa's head at the pitiful excuse for piecrust hardening on the counter. "It appears the Queen Mother will be making pies tonight."

Sessa set the envelope and its contents on the counter. "I beg your pardon. I am perfectly capable of making pies for tomorrow night."

"Of course you are, dear. Because you've learned so much since your last attempt. You weren't considering peanut butter, were you? Although I'm sure none of the ladies remember those peanut butter pies." She shook her head. "I still don't understand why you agreed to trade with Vonnette anyway. Not only are you responsible for hosting the club meeting, but you're also providing the pie. What were you thinking, Sessa?"

"Mama," Sessa said when her mother finally took a breath, though her warning tone was laced with humor. Despite all attempts to the contrary, she was an abysmal pie chef. "I can just call down to the Blue Plate and have Sue Ellen or Carly set aside a four pies for me to pick up tomorrow."

"There's no need for that," Mama said. "You celebrate this new job of yours and let me do it just this once. Next month when it's my turn to provide the pies, I'll let you bring them, even if it means they come from the Blue Plate. How's that?"

Sessa knew her mother would never let that happen, but she had thirty days to figure out a way around it. "It's a deal." She scooped Pansie into her arms and headed down the hall. "Let me get her cleaned up a bit and throw a couple of outfits into a bag, and the princess will be ready for her royal coach."

"Don't forget her leotard," Mama called. "Tomorrow's tap day, and the ladies would never forgive me if I didn't bring Princess Pansie."

Mama had been teaching tap dance at the senior center twice weekly for nearly a decade. Before that she'd educated most of Sugar Pine's female population and a couple of the males on the art of tap and ballet at Bonnie Sue's Academy of Dance. While she failed miserably at teaching Sessa the finer points of the art form, she seemed bound and determined not to make the same mistake with Pansie.

Now mostly retired, Mama still managed to teach those two classes each week. When she wasn't busy with any of the other activities that kept time and age from catching up to her.

Half an hour later, a freshly washed and dried Pansie left with Mama. Another quarter-hour went by before the classified ad was written and posted with Ella down at the Journal just before the five o'clock deadline.

The plea for help would arrive on Sugar Pine's front porches with the sunrise. Maybe she'd have a few qualified candidates to choose from and possibly a full-time employee soon after.

With the envelope tucked under her arm, Sessa practically floated back to the studio. The scent of sawdust and varnish settled around her as she stepped inside and closed the door, a comforting blend that felt more like home than any smell she could conjure up in her kitchen or any candle she could buy.

She stood very still in the center of the overhead light's bright circle of illumination, the Priority Mail envelope now hugged tightly to her chest. A giggle started somewhere deep and solid, from a place where joy began and faith simmered. Slowly that giggle floated up on the wings of something bigger, lighter.

Hope.

Delicious hope.

CHAPTER SEVEN

Two days later, Trey tossed the phone onto the seat beside him and turned off the ignition while the garage door closed behind him. Silence enveloped him as he relived the pitiful attempt at discharging his duty to apologize to the Chambers woman.

Calling her hadn't worked. He had known it wouldn't, and yet the thought of a telephone conversation had been much more palatable than actually standing in front of her and saying the words.

He hadn't been able to do that either, although he had sat in that diner for over an hour with Sessa Chambers so close he could almost touch her. Had eaten everything on his plate and pretended to be just any other paying customer. The coward's choice, and yet looking into the woman's eyes and admitting he killed her child was something he hadn't yet decided how to manage.

Maybe he'd been blindsided by her youth and beauty. The mother of a kid like Ross Chambers shouldn't have had that smile or those bright blue eyes. Shouldn't have been surrounded by people who appeared to love her and enjoy her company.

And she surely shouldn't have had a laugh like that. A laugh he could still hear if he thought about it.

What he'd expected, Trey couldn't exactly say, but Sessa Lee Chambers certainly wasn't what he thought she'd be, so maybe Ross hadn't been either. Maybe he hadn't been the abused and forgotten, down-on-his-luck hard case he professed to be.

Trey slammed his palm against the steering wheel. What an idiot he'd been.

The belief that he could have somehow made a difference in

Ross Chambers' life had culminated in what? Prison for him and the graveyard for Ross. And all this time the kid apparently had a decent set of family and friends here in Sugar Pine.

Vikki was right. He was too gullible. But then he'd trusted her even after their argument over Ross had culminated in the end of their engagement.

Fresh anger shot through him at the thought of how easily she'd turned her back on him during the trial. But then Vikki Rossi had calculated the odds long before she was called to testify about the money in his safe. That's what made her so good at what she did.

If she had professed knowledge of the cash there, she might have found herself answering other questions about her association with the victim. Questions that might put a lingering dent in the stellar reputation the up-and-coming district attorney needed to achieve the next step in her lofty goals.

The phone rang on the seat beside him, and he glanced down to see who was calling. Vikki. *Of course.* As if his thoughts had somehow summoned her.

He climbed out of the car and slammed the door behind him, the phone's ring barely discernable as he closed the distance to the garage exit and let himself inside the house. He'd get the phone later.

Or maybe he'd just leave it there until tomorrow.

Tossing his keys onto the table by the door, Trey headed down the hall to his office, where he eased into the Eames chair behind the desk. A stack of medical journals awaited him, and he'd promised himself on the way home from the counselor's office that he'd get to that task today.

His gaze landed on the corner of the desk where the scalpel turned murder weapon had once held a place of honor. He'd left instructions with his attorney to destroy the thing once it was returned after the trial, but he hadn't yet filled the empty spot. Shifting the stack of journals to the empty place helped, but so did turning his back on the desk.

The view through the floor-to-ceiling windows was still the same: a lush planting of palms and oleander ringing the pool where he used to swim laps before morning rounds at the hospital. Beyond the pool he could see the stable where he'd once kept his horses. They were gone now, sold along with all of the tack in the tack room when he believed he'd spend the rest of his life in prison.

Trey shook off the regret and focused on the pool. The thought of seeing just how many laps he could manage sent him after his swim trunks. He'd read through the medical journals later.

Despite the warmth of the evening, the water felt like ice as he dove in. With each lap, however, his body temperature warmed and his muscles strained. No thoughts existed except the next stroke, the turn at the end of the lap, and then the next stroke again.

Then came the prayers. No words exactly, but rather the unspoken rumbling thoughts of a man who knew he ought to trust God with this impossible situation and yet had no idea how to do that. Charlie Dorne would say that the Lord didn't mind a little unbelief as long as it was balanced by the hope that the Man Upstairs would rid him of it.

Trey added that request and pushed harder to finish another lap. And another.

Sufficiently numbed by the combination of the cold pool water and exercise, Trey finally declared his swim over. He'd forgotten how many laps he'd taken but his arms and legs told him it had been a few more than he should have.

He took a hot shower and threw on jeans and a T-shirt to pad to the kitchen and make a sandwich out of the bacon, avocado and leftover rotisserie chicken he found there. Thoughts of his horses returned along with the idea that he just might want to fill those empty stalls in the barn again.

For grins, he went out to the car to grab his phone—thankfully no more calls from Vikki—and then called Leon Doyle, the guy who now owned his horses.

"You're calling awful late, Doc."

Trey checked the time on his phone. A quarter to eight. Late for country folk. Almost lights out for his former cellmates in Huntsville. The reminder jarred him, and he rose to pace the thought away.

"Sorry about that." He moved out of the office and padded down the hall toward the kitchen. "Look, I was calling about the horses I sold you. I was wondering if you'd consider selling them back to me."

Leon chuckled. "Can't blame you for asking, but I'm sorry, son. I just can't part with them. That granddaughter of mine would be heartbroken. She's really taken a liking to them. Wants to barrel race with the palomino. A city girl who wouldn't give her old grandpa the time of day two years ago now spends all her free time here working with those horses. Her mama says her schoolwork has gone from poor to nearly perfect because she knows she isn't allowed to ride unless she's doing well in school. Isn't that something?"

"Yeah, that's something." He let out a long breath. At least some good had come from all of this.

The silence stretched between them. "Well, thanks for taking the call, Leon. Tell that granddaughter of yours I'm happy for her."

"You know," Leon said, "a friend of mine's got a pair of fine geldings he's looking to sell. I'd buy 'em if I thought I could get away with it, but my wife says no more horses until I buy her new living room furniture. I wouldn't mind, but she wants to get rid of my favorite chair. Can you fathom it? A perfectly good chair put out to pasture because it doesn't match the pillows and drapes. I just won't have it."

As much as he hated having to listen to the old man ramble on about his wife's preferences in décor, it sure was nice being treated like a normal human being and not some guy whose story had been on the news off and on for the past two-and-a-half years.

Gradually he became aware of silence on the other end of the line. "Don't blame you, Leon. Now about those geldings?"

"Oh, yeah. Good blood lines and a feisty disposition. Owned by a man named Jones. Bud Jones. Are you interested?"

A few more details, and he knew he was. Five minutes later, Trey was on the phone with Bud Jones, the owner of the geldings. "I apologize for calling so late, Mr. Jones," he began, "but I understand you've got some geldings for sale. Leon Doyle gave me your number."

"He did, did he?"

"Yes sir. He and I did some business together a few years ago.

When I decided to buy another horse, I asked him first. He told me about your geldings."

There was a cough on the other end of the line that Trey knew couldn't be simple upper respiratory congestion. He briefly wondered if the reason for selling the horse had anything to do with the man's health.

"Well I guess you're all right, then," Mr. Jones said. "Come on out and see them tomorrow. It'll have to be early. Five'd be better than six, because I've got things to do, but I'll allow for six so you can see 'em with the sun mostly up."

Of course the sun wouldn't be up until nearly seven in this part of Texas, but Trey wasn't about to argue with the man who might be selling him a horse on such a small point of fact. "I'll take you up on that six o'clock time."

The older man's *harrumph* was unmistakable. "All right, then. I'm on county road 43 about ten miles south of Sugar Pine. Know where that is?"

Sugar Pine. The breath went out of him. "I do," he managed as he wrote down the address.

"Good, then I'll see you tomorrow morning."

"See you then." Trey hung up and tossed the phone onto the chair beside him.

Ten miles south of Sugar Pine.

Ten miles south of any excuse to stand in front of Ross Chambers' family and ask for forgiveness. Again.

~*~

The next morning, Sessa sat cross-legged on the bench beneath the pecan tree and watched a pair of jaybirds fight over the remains of her cinnamon raisin bagel. A cool breeze blew from the south, and with it the pungent scent of moisture, a sure sign rain would darken the otherwise bright morning.

No matter, Sessa decided as she dug her toes into the thick grass and closed her eyes. Like Daddy used to say, "God is in His heaven and all is right with the world. What more could a body want?"

"Well, Daddy," she whispered as she rose and collected her pink *I love Grandma* coffee cup, "this body could use a little more sleep and a *lot* more help."

Rather than taking advantage of a night alone, Sessa had spent the better part of the evening finishing her book before falling exhausted onto her bed a few hours prior to the alarm going off. Anyone else would have hit the snooze button and stolen a few minutes—or hours—of sleep, but not Sessa.

She had work to do.

Rounding the corner of the house at a fast clip, she ran straight into a man-sized wall covered in a white T-shirt and faded denim. The coffee cup landed at her feet splashing lukewarm coffee and cracking the pink mug in half.

"I'm sorry," the wall said as they both reached for the remains of the mug.

Sessa's fingers latched on first, but his hand quickly covered hers.

"I should have been watching where I was going." She looked up and stared into the eyes of yesterday's topic of conversation— the stranger from the Lunchateria.

Oh. *Oh.*

She'd thought him easy on the eyes yesterday, but today with him standing so near?

Well, easy on the eyes still fit, but she hadn't realized his shoulders were so broad. And he was tall, nicely tall, and oh, those eyes. They were the color of amber with flecks of gold.

Sessa shook away her thoughts as she realized they were both still holding the broken mug. The cowboy let go and jammed his fingers into the front pockets of his jeans. Splashes of coffee dotted the front of his shirt just above his belt buckle. "It was my fault entirely. I doubt you expected company this early."

She looked down at her mismatched outfit of gray sweatpants, purple Sugar Pine High T-shirt she'd bought at the cheer squad fundraiser last summer, and rainbow-striped fuzzy slippers. Then she took in the fully dressed man. Before she could respond, the stranger thrust a hand in her direction and offered a shy smile. By now, what else could she do? She took it.

His grip was firm, his hands neither overly large nor small. They looked to be the hands of a working man. He released her fingers, and Sessa once again met his stare.

Mama strikes again.

She must have wasted no time tracking down the poor man through Sue Ellen's lunch receipts. Or maybe she had called in a favor down at the police station. The sheriff had nursed a crush on Mama for the better part of six decades and would do just about anything except break the law for her.

And that was probably negotiable.

"Mrs. Chambers, I'm Trey Brown." He looked off in the direction of the garage and the workshop beyond. Like he couldn't bear to hold her gaze for too long. "Does that name mean anything to you?"

She felt the slightest tickle of recognition as if she ought to know that name. As if somewhere in the past that snaked in and out of recollection, that name held some significance.

"It should, I think," she said slowly, "though I'm not sure why."

At his conflicted expression, Sessa paused and contemplated whether she should ask him directly if Mama had given him the address or just let him admit it on his own. She took a step back and shook the remains of her coffee off the newspaper to give the man a moment to speak.

The stranger's gaze locked with hers, and she tilted her chin up a notch. He seemed inordinately nervous, even for a man who had fallen under the spell of Mama. Surely he would crack under the pressure of her stare and admit Bonnie Sue sent him any minute. She could then dismiss him with a polite *thanks but no thanks*.

"I'm Trey Brown," he repeated.

Did Mama tell him she was hard of hearing? Maybe he just assumed it. A guy with his looks probably didn't socialize with women of her age. Poor Mama. She must have paid him handsomely in order to get him out here.

"So you said."

He looked wary and yet the slightest bit relieved all at the same time. "So you're probably wondering why I'm here."

Oh yes, Trey Brown, I know why you're here. Whatever my mother's paying you, I hope it's worth it.

Sessa squared her shoulders and offered her brightest smile. If he wanted to play this game, she could play right along—for now.

"Of course, I know why you're here," she said evenly "You're applying for the job."

CHAPTER EIGHT

Sessa's prospective employee ducked his head and then took a step backward. "Ma'am?"

"Call me Sessa."

Understanding rose on his face, or maybe she imagined it. "Sessa." He reached to clasp her hand in his strong grip. "Call me Trey."

"All right, Trey." She snatched her hand back just quick enough to feel foolish and then nodded toward the workshop. "How about I go show you what's involved in the work, and you see if you're still interested." A glance down at her feet and she amended her statement. "After I put on proper shoes, that is."

Once she returned with her running shoes on, Sessa didn't figure they would make it inside the door before the truth would come out about why he was here. To her surprise, not only did they get inside, but she somehow managed to show him around the front of the workshop before his expression went from polite to serious.

Mama must have paid him well. She'd see just how well.

"Something wrong?" She watched him carefully.

He was staring at the table where she did her larger repairs and most of her carving. It was an old surgical table bought for almost nothing when Doc Easley closed his practice, just the right height for the detail work her horses required.

The table gleamed a dull silver in the morning sunlight, a dusting of fine sawdust attesting to the work she'd done last night. On one end of the table was her toolbox, open as usual to reveal hammers, larger chisels, and the other tools of her trade. At the opposite end were the tools she used for finer work. There, sitting upright in a wooden block made specifically for the purpose were her smaller chisels, gouges, and carving blades.

Trey's attention seemed to be drawn to the blades, though when he caught her watching, he immediately jerked his gaze away. "You've got a nice set-up here." He moved toward her workbench, where a series of Sol Stein and Harry Goldstein horse photos chased one another across the rough wood surface.

He picked up one from the middle and studied it. "These look..."

"Spirited?" she supplied. "That's a hallmark of a Stein and Goldstein design."

"I had a horse that used to wear this same expression." He carefully returned the photograph to its place in line. "Seems like he was always looking to bolt."

Ironically the man Mama had sent to court her currently wore the same expression. He must have heard about her record of awful first dates.

"If I had to pick a favorite breed of horses, it'd be Arabians," he continued.

"My husband had Arabians." The rare mention of Ben was made all the more uncomfortable by the realization that she'd said it in front of this man.

"Takes an expert horseman to handle an Arabian," he said with a deferential nod.

"Or horsewoman," she quickly replied. "Ben never could ride either of them for longer than a few minutes."

"He was your husband?"

Mama must've told him.

"Yes." She smiled at the memory and then allowed her smile to fade. Thankfully he had turned his attention back to the workbench.

Mr. Brown nodded toward two black and white original photographs she'd situated next to their colorized mates on the wall above the workbench. "What's going on with those colors?" He turned toward her again. "That horse is purple."

"Those are Parker horses. You'd be surprised how hard it is to get the color to match Charlie's originals. I've had several suppliers make the attempt, but so far no one's managed to replicate the correct shade in this one or the other."

When he looked away, she studied his profile. And then it hit her. This was not a man sent to her by Mama, nor was he a man who was looking for the job she'd advertised in the classifieds.

Oh.

The profile, the same one as his mug shot, stilled her hands and jolted her heart.

She should have recognized him the minute the sun slanted across those eyes. The eyes of an innocent man.

Sessa stuffed her hands into her pocket to hide their shaking. No wonder he'd seemed unsure when she hadn't recognized him immediately.

And now she just wanted him gone. He'd say something in a minute, reveal the true reason he'd shown up uninvited.

Instead, he straightened his posture and gave her a curt nod. "So tell me about this job." The warmth and depth of his Texas drawl surprised her.

She allowed her gaze to travel the length of him. She'd already noticed his height. A longer perusal meant she also noticed he was lean at the waist and broad across the shoulders with ropes of muscles in his arms and chiseled cheekbones that could have landed him on the page of a fashion magazine.

His golden-brown hair was cut short, but not so short that his curls were hidden, and he was clean-shaven. He looked nothing like the slender man with the fashionably long hair, expensive suit, and trimmed beard she'd seen on television.

Was that why she hadn't recognized him immediately?

Or had she ignored a beat of familiarity because of the spark of connection she'd felt at the diner?

She could hardly believe the man who had every reason to expect an apology from her was here, in her barn. Calling her bluff about the job.

She struggled to collect her thoughts as she watched him pick up a nag's head painted vivid green. *The horses.* They'd been talking about the horses. "You know President Eisenhower was once employed as a sander in Charlie Parker's Kansas factory. Of course that was before he got into politics."

She was rambling. Sessa wrapped her arms around her waist and determined to shut her mouth, at least until it was time to make that apology she owed him.

"There's probably a joke in that somewhere." He turned his back on the photographs and leaned against the edge of the workbench.

His stance emulated hers. Arms crossed in front, eyes not exactly knowing where to land, and an expression that strayed toward nervousness.

Sessa willed the man to speak first, to tell her what he came to say. Or to make the demand of her that she knew he deserved—an apology for raising a boy who'd almost ruined his life.

He gazed out the window, toward the barn and the paddocks. "Is that where you keep the Arabians?"

Sessa shook her head. "Not for a long time." She tried not to allow a wistful tone to slip into her voice. "Something happened and..." She drew in a breath and let it out slowly. "...and we had to sell them."

"Same here. Well." He turned away from the window. "Not that long, I guess. Two years."

Since he was arrested. This fact filled the space between them.

"Actually, I looked at a pair of part-Arabian horses this morning. I'm thinking of buying them."

"Is that right?" She couldn't keep up the charade any longer. Talking about horses with this man. She snapped. "Look, I know who you are."

"Yes," he said slowly as he lifted his gaze to meet hers. "I told you."

"You did," she admitted, "but I didn't realize...that is, I avoided anything to do with the whole mess. I tend to do that."

His eyes narrowed. "I don't understand."

"You said you were Trey Brown, but I didn't realize you were...*him*," she finally managed. *Doctor* Trey Brown. "So now that I know, well...there's an apology to be made."

Rather than surprise, the doctor's expression turned to relief. "About that. I tried several times but I just—"

"I'm sorry." She dropped her hands and offered those two words with no qualifications. "I'm just so very sorry. If I could go back and do things over..."

Words failed. A charged silence fell.

"*You're* sorry?" He shook his head. "Why would you say that? I'm the one who—"

"Yoo hoo! I just saw Bonnie Sue and that granddaughter of yours at the Hairport. Sessa, where are you?"

Sessa groaned. "Out here." Leave it to Coco to keep Dr. Brown from finishing his sentence. Sessa just wanted him gone.

Before she could explain just who Coco was, her best friend practically raced through the door. "Okay, the truth is, I was just driving by and I saw this strange truck in your driveway, and I thought with you all alone out here there just might be..."

She drew up short as she spied Dr. Brown. Slowly, understanding dawned. How much understanding, Sessa couldn't tell, but it came with a tentative smile.

"Just might be trouble," she continued as she openly studied him. "And I was right. Well, hello. I'm Cozette. Coco to my friends." She extended a bejeweled hand. "What do your friends call you, hon?"

"Coco," Sessa interjected. "This is Trey. He's applying for the job."

"Job?" Her friend didn't believe her, but she did understand a diversionary tactic when she heard one. "Well, all right then. Hey, Sessa, would you mind getting that belt you borrowed from me the other day? I was thinking I'd wear it to the book club meeting tonight."

"The belt?"

Her eyes widened just enough to let Sessa know she wasn't leaving yet. "Yes, you know. The black leather one with the chains and sequins. Remember? You wore it with your leather pants and that sassy black halter top."

She gave Sessa a pointed look and then turned her charm on Dr. Brown. "She looks much better in it than I do, but a girl's got to try and use what she's got, don't you think?"

If Trey had any idea how to respond, he chose not to say it. Instead, he ducked his head and shrugged. Meanwhile, Sessa willed her cheeks not to turn bright red. Much as she loved her friend, she sure could be a pain.

"Come on, Coco. I'll get the belt." She grabbed her friend by the arm and dragged her out of the workshop. "We'll be right back, Trey."

They were halfway to the house before Coco hissed, "What is he doing here?"

"Hush," she said. "He can hear you."

Coco kept up with her, despite the former beauty queen's four-inch heels, as they rounded the edge of the house and headed down the driveway. When she felt they were out of earshot, Sessa stopped short.

"Black leather pants and a halter top? Really Coco?"

She had the audacity to laugh. "Oh, honey, it'll either scare the dickens out of him or make him even more interested. And either way, it's a sight better than your current outfit. Sugar Pine High T-shirt and sweat pants? Really?"

"I wasn't expecting company."

"Obviously." Coco's expression sobered. "What did I interrupt? It looked like you two were having a serious discussion. And not about any job."

"I'd say none of your business, but that's never mattered before." Sessa wrapped her arms around her middle and held on tight. "Do you know who that is?"

"Sure, I do. That's the fellow from the diner that your mama decided was going to be your next husband."

"How did you know about that?" Sessa shook her head. "Never mind. Small town, big mouths. Anyway, yes, you're right. That's him. But do you recognize him?"

"Should I?"

"That's Trey Brown." She let the words sink in, as much for Coco as for herself. "The doctor from Houston who...?" She couldn't say it. Wouldn't.

Coco reached over to grasp Sessa's hand. "Oh."

"Yes."

Her friend shook her head. "Oh," she repeated. "Oh."

"Stop saying that."

"I'm sorry. I just don't know what else to say."

Sessa was surprised Coco hadn't recognized him immediately, with the way she'd been glued to every little detail of the trial, whether on the television or in the papers. But then, the Dr. Brown Sessa had seen in her one and only glimpse of the trial coverage bore no resemblance to *this* man.

Coco's grip on Sessa tightened. "Why is he here? That's a good question, isn't it? And I don't believe it's because your mama somehow prayed him here so you could marry him."

Sessa let out a long breath. "Much as I wish that were the reason, I think he's here to get the apology I owe him."

"Apology *you* owe him?" She rested her fists on her hips, and her bracelets jangled into place. "Honey, you do not owe him any such thing, and if he's going to show up here at the home of the mother of the boy he killed, well, I'm going to have a few choice words with him about just who needs to apologize to whom."

Coco headed back in the direction of the workshop, and Sessa bolted after her. "Oh no you don't!" She snagged Coco's wrist and turned her around. "Do not say a word to him. I only told you this because you're my best friend, and I wasn't going to lie to you."

Coco snatched her hand back and studied the riot of silver bracelets on her arm before turning her attention back to Sessa. "Did you ask him to come here?"

"No."

"So he just showed up demanding an apology?"

"Not exactly." Sessa shrugged. "Look, it's complicated. I came outside to drink my coffee, and there he was, walking around the side of the house. I ran flat into him, which is why I've got this coffee stain on my shirt and there are broken pieces of a mug back by the irises."

"I see." Her gaze flitted to the stain. "That shirt never was the right color for you. I say toss it rather than try to wash it. The sooner the better."

Ignoring the ill-timed fashion advice, Sessa continued. "I'd like to finish what we started, so can you just go on home and let me do this? You're not going to understand, but it's kind of an answer to prayer that he's here."

She twirled the enormous emerald ring on her right hand. "Are you afraid of him?"

"Not in the least."

Coco met her gaze and opened her mouth, probably to protest, because she quickly closed it again. Slowly, she nodded. "You don't owe that man anything, Sessa Lee Chambers. Please do not think you do. He took your son from you."

"My son took two years of that man's life from him," she snapped. "And he did that because I wasn't the mother I ought to have been."

"You tried," Coco said on a rush of breath. "We both tried. Ross was just..."

"Troubled."

"He just chose wrong, Sessa. That's all there is to it. He had everything he could have wanted back here except for a daddy. Well, we're all missing something from our lives. If we go around blaming others and acting like we ought not act, whose fault is it?"

When Sessa said nothing, Coco continued. "It is our own fault. Nobody else but us. Surely it's not our mama's."

"I appreciate you saying so," Sessa said. "I'll call you later. I promise."

Coco paused just long enough to make Sessa think she might not leave. Then she dug her car keys out of her pocket. "All right, but I'm leaving under protest."

"Please don't tell anyone."

She nodded toward the back of the house. "About him? Girl, have you forgotten how small this town is? The mailman was just ahead of me. I doubt he missed the fact there was a strange truck in your driveway." She glanced down at her gold and diamond Rolex and then back at Sessa. "That was less than ten minutes ago, and he was heading toward town. I'd bet you that leather belt and your sassy black halter top—"

"Neither of which exist."

"You'll be getting a call from your mama before noon."

"Not if you were to go back into town and let those ladies know the truck was in the driveway because I'm interviewing help for Chambers Restoration. Any of them who read the paper saw the want ad." She gave her friend a pointed look. "Because that's what a friend would do."

"I was just at the Hairport. Don't you think they're going to be suspicious if I show back up there with that sort of information?"

"Not if you tell Vonnette you wanted her to have the scoop on the fact that I just might be hiring the cowboy from the diner that my mama swears I'm going to marry."

"But that's the man who killed Ross. People are going to figure that out pretty quick, don't you think?"

"Did you?"

She paused and appeared to be considering the question. "No,

I didn't."

"Who did you see when you saw him, Coco?"

"I saw the man your mama's been talking about since yesterday." Her eyes widened. "You're right. But eventually people are going to figure it out." Probably so. The whole town had watched the trial with bated breath.

"He won't be here long enough for them to figure it out. Soon as I say what I need to say, he'll be gone. In the meantime, they see what they're told to see. Just like you did."

Coco's eyes narrowed. "Oh, that's devious." She paused. "I like it."

"Then go." She gave her friend a playful nudge. "Seriously. Go. I want to get this over with."

"All right." She grabbed another quick hug before hurrying back to her car. "But call me soon as you can," she called as she started the car. "And put on something cute, girl. I don't care who he is, he ought not have to look at you in clothes that should be burned."

"Very funny. You're going to see me tonight at the book club meeting," she said playfully. "Surely you can wait until then to find out what happened."

Coco shook her head as she drove away. Of course she couldn't wait. Had the situations been reversed, Sessa wouldn't have waited, either.

She watched the rooster tail of dust chase Coco down Firefly Lane before turning back to the workshop. She did want to get this over, didn't she?

To her surprise, when she peered into the workshop, the doctor was nowhere to be found. Then she spied him on the other side of the fence in the paddock. He saw her watching and waved, then picked his way back toward the fence.

"Sorry," he said. "You've got a nice barn here. Needs some work to make it livable for horses again, but the building's in good shape." He shook his head. "Anyway, where were we?"

"I was about to apologize to you for my son's behavior and the fact you lost two years of your life because of him." She allowed the words to fall out before she could stop them. "I didn't raise him to be what he became, but I take full responsibility for how he turned out. I prayed over that boy day and night, but sometimes I guess even a mama's prayers don't change things. So, given what you've lost, do you have it in you to forgive me, Dr. Brown?"

The doctor stood stock-still for a good minute letting nothing but those words and the warm breeze slide between them. Finally he shifted position and shook his head. "I can't do that."

CHAPTER NINE

"You can't?"

Sessa Chambers ran a hand through her pretty blonde ponytail and looked more than a little confused. Hurt, too, unless he missed his guess.

"I cannot accept what I'm not owed." Trey ducked under the barbed wire fence that separated them. "Look, I came here to say exactly what you've just said. To ask for forgiveness. I took your son's life."

"He intended to take yours."

Trey found her blue eyes and held her gaze. Somehow, it was easier than it had been before. "Do you believe that?"

She looked away. "I think he was capable of it, yes."

He could see the statement pained her more than she wanted to let on. Trey kept his silence and left her to her thoughts.

"Ross liked you," she finally said.

"What makes you think that?"

"He told me." She set off toward the house, and Trey followed. "You saw something of value in him. And he told me that, too."

"Yes, I did," He digested the news that Ross Chambers had spoken of him to his mother. He hadn't expected that. "Ross was smart as a whip and as good a horseman as I've seen in a long time. I thought maybe someday he could make something of those talents."

"He always did like horses. I don't think he ever forgave me for selling the Arabians after his daddy died. He was only five, and I figured someday there'd be horses in the barn again," she said softly. "Someday just never happened."

"So you built horses in the workshop instead."

Surprise again etched her pretty features. "I suppose you could say that. But it wasn't the same. At least not to Ross."

"About that apology. Mine," he hastened to add. "Saying I'm sorry won't bring him back. I know that. But I am. Sorry."

He was making a mess of this. Trey gave up on saying the right words and just reached over to grasp her wrist.

Her eyes widened, but her expression settled to neutral in a heartbeat. "Looks like we're both sorry."

"I suppose we are."

"Then there's nothing left to talk about, is there? We both saw something good in my boy. I guess that's reason enough to agree to disagree on which of us is to blame."

"But, I—"

"Doctor Brown," she interrupted. "Trey. You can beat yourself up all day long about what happened between you and Ross, but like you said, it won't change anything. Did you mean to kill him?"

"I did not," he forced out.

"Nor did I intend to raise him up to be a man who would put himself in a position where someone had to protect himself from him." She looked down at his hand on her wrist, and Trey let go. "Do you want to keep talking about this? Because I don't."

"Not really," Trey admitted.

"Thank you for coming. For telling me what you told me, and for listening while I said my piece."

She wanted to get rid of him. That much was obvious.

But he didn't feel the peace that his therapist had been so confident would follow his apology.

"I can say the same."

"All right, then I guess we're done."

He struggled for words to fill the awkward silence that descended.

"One more thing," she said. "There is no black belt studded with rhinestones, no leather pants, and certainly no black halter top. My friend can be creative with the truth when she wants to be."

"Is that so?" Relieved at the subject change, he shifted his feet. "I'll confess I'm more than a little disappointed. It's not often a man like me gets to meet a woman with such classy taste in evening attire. Not that I'm judging, mind you. I enjoy a pair of leather pants as much as the next guy, but you have to sit carefully when you're wearing the rhinestones. They'll poke you something awful if you're not careful."

She smiled then, a slow upturn of her lips that held Trey mesmerized as he picked his way across a yard that needed a decent mowing. When Sessa slid him a sideways glance, he nearly tripped.

"Watch your step. I haven't paid much attention to the grass out here. I generally trim up by the house with the push mower and leave the rest alone. Guess it's about time to see if the riding mower still works."

He looked across the pasture and then back at the widow. Much as he knew he'd have to go back to his life as a doctor eventually, he wasn't in a hurry. The chief of staff had told him to take his time, within reason, of course. To the chief, that likely meant a day or two. To Trey, that might be a little longer, especially since this woman needed things done around here much more than the hospital needed another doctor. Especially a doctor who had not yet managed to prove he could operate.

"Where is it?" Trey said.

Sessa Chambers stopped short. "Where is what?"

"The riding mower." He spied a tool shed that looked to be as good a place to search as any. Sure enough, when he'd hiked over there with Sessa trailing him, he found an ancient push mower and a riding lawnmower that had seen better days. There was little more than fumes in the gas tank, but he spied a bright red can marked gasoline in the shadows. With any luck, it would be full.

"What in the world are you doing?"

Ignoring the question, he stepped around her to snatch up the gas can. Empty. Of course.

Setting the can aside, he pushed the riding mower out into the sunshine. To his surprise, it started on the first try. Trey turned the key, and the engine sputtered to a stall. The spark plugs were passable but probably ought to be changed. Other than that, it looked in decent shape.

The blonde beauty stepped in front of the mower, hands on her hips. "I repeat," she said with some measure of insistence, "what in the world are you doing?"

Trey nodded toward the field where they'd just walked. "You need grass cut, and I need something to do this morning." Because if he left now, he'd face the empty house and empty life back in Houston.

He climbed off the mower. "I don't suppose you've got a tractor hidden in that barn that I somehow missed?"

"Not anymore. Daddy sold the John Deere about five years ago when he wasn't able to drive it anymore."

"All right, then." He grabbed the gas can and fixed her with a look that he hoped would convey the idea he didn't intend to argue. "You just go on about your day, and I'll be back soon as I can."

Before she could protest, he set off across the yard toward his truck. Trey got all the way to the driveway before she caught him.

"You can't do this."

Trey ignored her as he secured the gas can in the bed of the truck and then walked around her to climb into the pickup and stab his keys into the ignition. As he turned the key, the truck's engine roared to life, and a George Strait tune blared through the radio's speakers. He switched off the music and rolled down the window.

"You simply cannot do this," she repeated.

"Sessa," he said in his best bedside manner tone, "I'm not doing this for you."

She shook her head. "Who are you doing it for? Ross?"

"No." He shifted the truck into reverse. "I'm doing it for me. Do you need anything else while I'm in town getting gas and spark plugs?"

"Town?" Now she looked truly worried. "You don't need to go into town."

"I do if I'm going to get this mower running like it ought to." He paused. "But don't worry, Sessa. I'll keep this between the two of us."

Her laugh held little humor. "Apparently you've never lived in a small town. Nothing is just between anyone in Sugar Pine, especially if my mother or any of her friends have anything to do with it."

Trey eased his foot off the brake. "Then I'll tell them I turned out to be the right man for the job."

"Mowing grass is not the job I posted in the paper." The truck rolled down the driveway. "Everyone in Sugar Pine knows by now that I needed someone to help me with the Smithsonian order, not the field."

"Then I guess you'll have to show me how to help you with the Smithsonian order." He hit the road and shifted into drive. "After I mow the field."

"Not today. I have book club tonight." Sessa's voice faded as he sped away.

"Book club," he said under his breath. "I'll be long gone before then."

In the meantime, however, he could do something about that field. If there was a child in the house—which he figured there must be given the stroller and various plastic riding toys he'd spied through the open garage door—then allowing that grass to grow up like that was dangerous. No telling the critters that had made a home out there.

He couldn't put words to the rock that still sat low in his gut, but that rock was what refused to let him tuck tail and go home. He'd apologized, all right, but didn't feel lighter. And Sessa Chambers had some support system—if her mention of her mama and her nosy friend were any indication—but this was something *he* could do for her.

Trey switched the radio back on and drummed his fingers on the steering wheel as George Strait sang. There was plenty to do at the Chambers place.

But he'd be gone before that book club meeting started. The last thing he needed was to explain himself to a gaggle of gals who probably spent as much time talking about their shoes and their men as they did talking about books.

At least that had been his experience the last time he'd had the misfortune to visit his mama on book club night. Mama. He hadn't thought of how much he missed her in awhile. Something about being around a strong Southern woman like Sessa Chambers sent his mind to places he'd rather not go.

Like home. And family. And what it had been like to just be Trey and not that doctor who went to prison.

The song finished and the next one began, another George.

Another song about life and what was important. A song about the heartland. About home. About hard working men who toiled until the daylight was gone.

Trey pressed the button to silence the music. And wished one more time that that could be him again.

~*~

Sessa half-expected the doctor would come to his senses and keep driving past Sugar Pine and back to Houston where he belonged. Instead, he returned and headed straight to the back of the property to tinker with Daddy's old riding mower.

She tried not to let him catch her watching, but if she stood in just the right spot in the kitchen, she could see Trey bent over the mower with his hands busy working on the engine. Every once in awhile, he would stand and straighten the kinks out of his spine or swipe at his forehead with the back of his hand. Then he'd resume his task.

Never had she been so glad that Mama was making the pies for tonight's meeting. Just knowing Trey Brown was out there tinkering with the mower had her jumpy as a long-tailed cat in a room full of rocking chairs.

Deciding she could use her restless energy in a productive way, Sessa snatched up the broom and tackled the kitchen floor. When Trey fired up the engine on the mower, she nearly jammed the broom handle into the oven door.

"Sessa, girl, you have got to calm down," she muttered as she put the broom away and opted for the dust rag before she caused any serious damage.

By the time the living and dining rooms had been vacuumed and dusted and the sofa cushions fluffed, Sessa had almost forgotten about the disaster waiting to happen in the back field. Almost but not quite.

Because as soon as Mama or one of her cronies figured out just who was toiling away on Daddy's lawnmower...

She shook off the thought with a roll of her shoulders. No sense borrowing trouble. Another one of Daddy's pearls. And worrying about what a bunch of old women might say tonight while the sun was still shining didn't make much sense at all.

She looked at the clock over the stove and found it was blinking again. So was the one on the microwave. One of these days she was going to have to learn how to set those clocks.

Sessa retrieved her phone from her pocket and found she'd somehow missed a call from an out-of-state number she didn't recognize, probably while she was vacuuming. She looked to see if there was a message and, finding none, went back to the home screen to check the time.

It was a quarter past noon. No wonder her stomach was growling.

When had the noise from the mower died?

She returned to the back window thinking she'd spy the doctor out in the field. Instead, she found the field had been mowed, and Trey Brown was nowhere to be seen. She hurried down the hall to the front bedroom to peer out of the blinds. His truck was still right where he'd parked it, so he was around somewhere.

Though the last thing she wanted to do was spend any time with him, the least she could do was make him a sandwich and bring him some sweet tea. After all, he'd been working on that field—and who knew what else—for hours.

It didn't take her long to slice up some ham for sandwiches and put together a tray to take to him. What did take awhile was building up her courage to actually open the screen door and walk outside.

That this man would not only tell her she had no reason to apologize but also would ask for forgiveness of his own humbled her deeply. The fact that she'd been praying for the opportunity to make things right with this innocent man only to have the Lord hear her and arrange for it just flat undid her. She was grateful that he'd come, grateful for the kinship she felt. He'd loved Ross, too. He hadn't said as much, but she'd sensed it.

She spied the doctor by the paddock. Before cowardice could send her skittering back inside, Sessa squared her shoulders and carried the tray all the way across the yard, past the workshop, and over the freshly cut field to where he stood with his back to her. Only when she got within a few feet of him did Sessa realize he was talking on his cell phone.

"No, our relationship was over long before that," she heard him say as she stuttered to a halt. "I don't care what you can do for me."

She'd obviously stumbled onto a very private conversation, but there was nowhere to hide and certainly no way to retreat without the risk of Trey turning around to see her.

She should say something. Should let him know she was behind him.

"Find someone who cares. You won't blackmail me."

Oh no. Sessa's heart sunk.

Whatever was being said on the other end of the line must have appeased him, because he hung up and dialed another number. "Charlie, yeah, this is Trey." A pause. "Good. Great, actually. Yeah, I went to see your guy. Took his advice, actually, and you'll never guess where I am."

The tray was getting heavy, and Sessa could see that the pitcher of sweet tea was now situated dangerously close to the edge. With nowhere to put it down and no desire to intrude on yet another private conversation, Sessa willed her shaking hands to be still.

Perspiration dotted her forehead. She let out a silent breath and prayed he would hang up soon. Men didn't make long phone calls, did they? Maybe she should back away, but she'd lugged this tray all the way out here...

"Am I that predictable? Yeah, that's where I am. Did what he said, yeah. Wasn't as hard as I thought it would be."

Sessa's nose began to itch. She distracted herself by looking at the wisps of clouds just beyond the barn.

At the pair of cardinals—one male and the other female—that flitted around the branches of the old magnolia that shaded the north end of the paddock.

At the way the sun glinted and shimmered off the ice floating in the tea pitcher.

And finally at the breadth of the doctor's shoulders and the muscled and tanned arm that held the phone. The wisps of damp curls just behind his ear, and the way the midday sunshine turned his sandy hair a shade of cinnamon.

He was taller than he'd looked in that video of him leaving the courtroom. Wider at the shoulders and narrower at the waist and hip.

Pleasant distractions, all of them, but her nose still itched with a vengeance. Sessa decided to try and appease the itch by moving her arm just enough to allow her shoulder to reach the spot on her nose that needed attention.

Her first attempt caused the tea pitcher to move closer to the edge of the tray. Her second attempt ended when the pitcher slid to the middle of the tray and the sandwiches nearly pitched over the other side.

A trickle of sweat traced a path down her spine, and she could feel the dampness on her neck. She should say something. Should announce her presence.

Something.

Anything.

"Did a lot of praying on the way. Both times. Yeah, drove here twice before I had the courage to—yeah, twice. I know..." He left the statement hanging and began to chuckle. "Yeah, well, she's prettier than I expected and a whole lot nicer to me than she ought to be."

Much as she was enjoying this part of the conversation, Sessa's itch was turning into the beginning of a sneeze.

Worse, she was hot. And sweating. Neither made for a good grip on the tray.

"Blue eyed blonde, pretty....yeah, I said pretty. C'mon, Charlie, I'm human. I notice things. Doesn't mean that I'm interested in...Okay, yeah...I'll admit I don't know what God's doing most of the time, but I seriously doubt He is leading me to the middle of nowhere to...Okay, yes, it's possible, but Charlie, seriously. I'm a doctor. Yeah, I'm helping her out a little today, but I don't need to think about anything as complicated as..."

He paused. She tried not to sneeze. Her eyes began to water. Heat shimmered on the horizon. She swayed and then caught herself.

"Just cutting a field that needed some attention. Yeah, the mower needed some work. And I'm looking at a paddock and barn that could...No. Just helping. Nothing else. Yes, I'm sure."

Achoo!

The pitcher of tea toppled forward and landed on a clump of freshly mowed grass, but its contents splashed up the back of Trey Brown's Wranglers. Too late, the striped cotton napkin fluttered to the ground at her feet.

The plate of ham sandwiches was safe from falling but not from the sneeze. She dared not think of the fact she had neither handkerchief, nor tissue.

Mortified, Sessa knelt to retrieve the pitcher and napkin and returned them to the tray. With the remaining shreds of her dignity, she dabbed at her nose with the tea-soaked napkin and tried not to think of the man whose work-scarred boots were so close she could touch them.

"I've got to go, Charlie." There was a soft beep as he ended the call.

Embarrassment heated her worse than the sun beating down on her head. Pretty. He'd called her pretty.

She swiped at her sweaty forehead. Her damp neck.

Oh, but she was a mess.

"Hi," he said when she finally dared a look up in his direction. Where she might've expected him to be angry at her eavesdropping—they both knew she'd overheard him—his eyes danced instead. "You brought lunch."

She continued to hide behind the napkin though its use was long over. "I made the attempt anyway."

Trey reached down to offer her his hand, and she allowed him to help her up. His hand was warm. Strong. Work-roughened. She looked down at his fingers, still curled around hers, and tried to think of something witty to say. Failing that, she just tried to think of a way to get out of the situation without looking any more like a fool than she already had.

"Thank you."

The statement took her by surprise. She jolted her attention to his face. To those eyes.

"Thank you," he repeated. "For the attempt at lunch." He held her gaze in a way that conveyed more. Things she couldn't really fathom. Like, thank you for treating me like a human being.

The reminder of where he'd been the past two years—and why—unnerved her.

"Oh." She slid her hand from his grasp and buried her fingers in the front pockets of her jeans. Started babbling again. "I've got more ham. And sweet tea. Inside. In the kitchen, I mean. I could..."

"That would be nice," he said. "Ham. And sweet tea."

His smile eased her nerves.

"Or we could drive into town. I saw on the sign that it's meatloaf and potatoes day at the diner."

"No!" she said a bit too quickly. "I'll go make another round of sandwiches. This time I probably ought to serve them indoors. At the kitchen table. Or out on the patio."

Yes, outdoors was preferable to the close quarters inside. She scrambled to retrieve the tray.

Trey glanced down at the ruins of her first attempt. "Probably a good idea if I just grab a sandwich and a glass of tea and get back to work."

"You've done enough, Trey."

His reluctance to sit down to a meal was a relief and a disappointment all wrapped up together. That smile of his nearly felled her where she stood.

"There's plenty more to do," he said in a tone that told her it would be pointless to argue. "Give me a couple of minutes to wash up, and I'll gladly take whatever you leave me on the patio."

He moved toward the pump at the edge of the paddock with a long stride as Sessa set off in the opposite direction. A glance over her shoulder, and she spied him peel off his T-shirt to stick his head under the water now flowing from the pump.

Her heart fluttered and she stumbled and pitched forward. This time the pitcher didn't fall but she almost did.

Righting herself, Sessa gave up all pretense of dignity and studied her guest openly, albeit from a distance. She'd seen Ben wash up after a day working the fields or the horses and never felt like she did at this moment.

What was wrong with her?

This was Trey Brown. The man she'd tried to hate. Until she saw those eyes on her television. Until she met him.

And she was a grown woman on the far side of forty and well beyond the time when she should be feeling—and acting—like a ridiculous teenager. And yet there he was. And here she was.

And oh, but now he had his shoulders under the water and he was scrubbing at the back of his neck. His tanned shoulders. His tanned neck. And those muscles, now wet from the pump water and...

Oh my. This absolutely would not do.

Resolutely she turned her back on the glorious and appealing sight and marched toward the back door. She would not look. She would not turn and see what he was doing now. These sentences created a cadence that somehow moved her forward and kept her from stumbling.

Much.

Or looking back.

Much.

A new worry, very real and yet slightly intriguing, chased her back to the house. What if this man, this doctor who was present when her child left this life, was more than just a passing acquaintance? What if her prayers for making things right with the doctor that had been so very wronged involved him spending more than just one afternoon in Sugar Pine, Texas?

"Oh, Lord, please don't let it be so," she muttered as she picked up her pace.

And yet at the same time, a tiny voice buried almost too deep to be heard whispered the opposite.

~*~

It wasn't the best ham sandwich Trey had ever eaten, but he'd never forget it as long as he lived. Sessa Lee Chambers was a dangerous woman. Dangerous because she made him forget who he was and why he was there.

Dangerous because he barely knew her, and yet he couldn't get enough of her company. Couldn't even find it in him to be embarrassed about what she'd overheard him telling Charlie.

And dangerous because even after he'd run out of things to do and the daylight was waning, he still found he didn't want to get into his truck and drive home. He did, of course, but only after he stopped by her back door and promised he'd be back in a few days to finish what he started in the barn.

He hadn't elaborated, and thankfully, she hadn't asked. Because he hadn't really started anything in the barn other than imagining what it might be like if it were cleaned up a little, had some fresh straw in the stalls and a decent roof to keep the water out.

And a couple of Arabians like the ones he'd just bought from

Bud Jones this morning.

Trey reached for the phone and then thought better of it and tucked it into his pocket. What was he thinking? He'd only just met this woman this morning, and he was already putting his horses in her barn.

He couldn't explain the draw he felt. It wasn't simply the loss they'd shared. It was something *more*.

Yes, she was a dangerous woman. And he'd sworn off of dangerous women when he broke off his engagement with Vikki. The last thing he needed was to find himself tangled up with another gal who distracted him like nobody's business and got him thinking about...

"What am I doing pondering tangling up with Sessa Chambers, of all people?" He pressed the button to lower the window and then inhaled a deep gulp of pine-scented East Texas air. Charlie's ridiculous question about whether he thought God might have led him to Sugar Pine for a reason other than a simple apology still bothered him.

Maybe He had.

Or maybe He hadn't.

Only time would tell.

It all led back to that second question the counselor had asked. The one where he was supposed to decide what he intended to do with the medical license that had been returned to him.

The one he hadn't been able to fully answer.

Logic and good sense told him the return of that license and the support of Turner Memorial Hospital's biggest benefactor was an opportunity he dare not waste. All those years of climbing the ladder had landed him just a step or two away from the top rung. That same logic and good sense, however, told him in order to complete the climb to the top, he had to get over whatever it was that shook his insides and rendered him useless when he picked up a scalpel.

As he turned off the gravel road and onto the main highway that led to Houston, he felt the peace he'd enjoyed all afternoon fade away with each mile he put between himself and Sugar Pine, Texas. Somewhere in what he was feeling right now lay an answer.

All he had to do was figure out what that answer was.

CHAPTER TEN

May meeting of the Pies, Books & Jesus Book Club
Location: Sessa Lee Chambers' home
Pies: two peanut butter and two chocolate chip, brought by Bonnie Sue
Tucker
Book title: VELMA STILL COOKS IN LEEWAY by Vinita
Hampton Wright

"So I heard our Sessa's got herself a new employee," Vonnette said from her perch on the sofa. Coca sat on the opposite end looking like the cat that ate the canary. "Word is you interviewed him this afternoon."

"*All* afternoon," Carly Chance said.

"And into the evening," Carly's mother-in-law added.

"Yes, I do believe I passed an unfamiliar truck when I was bringing Pansie home around five," Mama said. "Was that your new man, dear?"

"I do not have a new man." She met Coco's gaze across the room. "But I did interview a potential employee for Chambers Restoration."

"What's this?" Bud Jones' wife Annette asked.

Mama grinned at Annette. "Oh honey, you must get out more often. My daughter has been selected by the Smithsonian for a special job. Can you feature it? My Sessa Lee working for the Smithsonian!" She beamed at Sessa. "And what did I tell you about that man in the diner? Mama was right, now wasn't she?"

She ignored her mother to turn her attention to Annette. "I've been given a restoration contract for carousel horses that will eventually be part of a traveling exhibit. I'm still stunned that

Chambers Restoration was chosen. For that matter, I'm stunned that the project happened at all."

"I'm not. Those boys up in Washington just took awhile to figure out who needed to do the work. Of course, I credit the Lord for showing them it was you," Mama said, and several other ladies echoed the sentiment.

"Thank you all," Sessa said. "I give Him all the credit as well."

Mama gave her a sideways look. "Now about that man you've hired to help you. Does he have a name?"

"I haven't hired anyone yet."

"If that's the case, then who mowed the pasture?" Vonnette said. "Jim Bob told me he drove by middle of the afternoon and saw a fellow on your daddy's riding mower. Said it was the same fellow he saw at the gas station filling gas cans and buying spark plugs."

Mama swung her gaze toward Sessa. "Is that so?"

"That pasture was getting high and he...well, he took the initiative to do something about it." Despite the fact Mama and Vonnette had begun to giggle, Sessa squared her shoulders and forged on. "Initiative is what you want in an employee, now isn't it? Not that I'm saying I hired him because I absolutely did not, but you'd agree with me, wouldn't you, Vonnette?"

The owner of the Hairport tamed her snickers long enough to shrug. "I'd agree, but honestly, what I'd look for was a fellow who filled out a pair of Wranglers and had nice strong arms. The better to carve those horses, I do believe."

She and Mama once again giggled like teenagers. This time several others joined in.

"Much as I would love to talk about the hired help, how about Coco and I get the pies that my mama did such a good job of baking? Then we can talk about this month's book. Didn't you all just love it?"

"Oh, I did," Coco said. Bless her. "That Velma, well, she reminded me so much of Sue Ellen's mama, didn't she?"

"She did," Sue Ellen agreed. "I cried in a couple of places because I thought that was exactly what Mama would say or do."

"And that diner," Carly said to Sue Ellen. "Didn't it make you think of the Blue Plate? Sometimes when I was reading the book I wondered if the author hadn't modeled that place after it."

Sue Ellen turned to Sessa. "You did a good job of choosing the book. I don't know how I'm going to pick one when it's my turn. I think this is going to be my favorite for a long time."

"Much as I loved this book," Mama said, "I really don't think we've exhausted the topic of Sessa's man. Or her hired help."

Sessa shook her head. "I did not hire that man."

"Oh, yes, Bonnie Sue," Vonnette said. "I think you're right."

Mama nodded at Vonnette. "Or whoever that handsome cowboy was that I predicted would end up being the answer to all our prayers that she would find a husband."

"*All* your prayers?" Sessa's eyes narrowed as she surveyed the dozen or so women gathered in her living room. "Just who all was praying for me to find a husband?"

Every hand in the room went up. Even Coco's. The traitor.

"His name?" Mama demanded.

"It doesn't matter what his name is, because he's not going to be sticking around to make social calls, Mama. And yes, he did get Daddy's mower working." Several of the women exchanged knowing looks. "As I told you, I didn't ask him to mow the field. He just decided to do it on his own. He was worried about how high it had gotten, what with a little one around." Probably.

"What a nice young man," Robin Chance said. "I think I like him already. I wish I hadn't been busy at the Pup Cake the day you prayed him into the diner, Bonnie Sue."

"My mother did not pray that man into the diner." Sessa's words were sharper than she'd intended. "In any event, yes, he was a nice man. He volunteered to help, and I allowed it. But I did not hire him to work for Chambers Restoration. So I'm afraid all of those prayers were for nothing. Better luck next time, Mama."

Her mother grinned. "Oh Sessa girl, you always were stubborn. It's not up to you to decide any of this."

"Chambers Restoration is my company. It is most certainly up to me to decide who I hire. And I did not hire Trey."

"So, his name is Trey," Mama said.

Sessa's phone rang and she snatched it out of her pocket, grateful for the distraction but surprised she'd been carrying it around for most of the evening. Once again the number was from out of state.

"Excuse me a minute. I need to get this." She slipped into the kitchen, fanning herself. She loved her mama and her friends, but she hated being under the small-town microscope. By the time she'd walked over to the opposite side of the room, she felt steady enough to answer. "Hello?"

Beyond what sounded like the low hum of indistinguishable voices mingled with street noises, there was no response.

She tried again. Nothing.

"Look, I don't know who you are, but this is the second time today you've called. If you're looking for Sessa Lee Chambers, you've found me. If you're looking for someone else, please just stop calling, all right?"

"Mrs. Chambers? Is that really you?" The voice was young and vaguely familiar. "I wasn't sure if I remembered the number right."

"Yes, this is Sessa Chambers. Who is this?"

Coco stepped into the kitchen with her eyebrows raised. "Who is it?" she whispered.

Sessa shrugged, concentrating on the phone conversation she could barely hear.

"How is...?" The line crackled and the rest of the question came out garbled.

"I'm sorry. I didn't hear all of that. This connection isn't good."

"Pansie," the voice said. "I'm calling about Pansie. How is my daughter?"

A cold wave of fear washed over her. It couldn't be Skye. Couldn't be Pansie's mother. It just couldn't. After two years of silence, Sessa and Pansie had settled into life together. She'd begun to hope things would stay the same. Maybe forever.

"Would you please say that again?" She motioned for Coco to move close enough to listen in on the call.

"This is Skye. I miss my Pansie-girl."

Coco made a face. Sessa let out a long breath and closed her eyes. Two years of silence had all but erased the fact that Pansie did indeed have one parent still living.

A parent who had more right to the child than Sessa did.

"Skye," Sessa said slowly, "where are you?"

"I'm at work. Hey, sorry but I've got to get back inside and finish my shift. Tell Pansie her mama loves her and hopes to see her soon." Then the line went dead.

Numb, Sessa let go of the phone. Coco caught it before it landed on the tile floor and then started pushing buttons.

"What are you doing?" Sessa said wearily.

"I'm making sure neither of us can lose that number." When she finished with Sessa's phone, Coco handed it back to her and then pulled her own out of her pocket. "You and I are the only two who have this girl's phone number, at least as far as we know, right?"

"I suppose so." Sessa stared at the name on the screen.

Skye.

Not Skye Chambers because Ross hadn't married the woman who bore his child. Just Skye. For the first time, it occurred to Sessa that she didn't even know the last name of the woman who gave her precious grandchild life.

Skye had a last name. And parents. And maybe even an extended family.

All of these people were related to Pansie, and at least in the case of the grandparents, had as much right to the child as Sessa did. The breath went out of her at the thought, and it took a supreme act of will to inhale and exhale again.

"Sessa? Sessa, honey, say something. Are you all right?"

Pressing the button on the top of the phone, Sessa watched the screen go blank as the device shut down. Only then could she respond.

"No." She forced herself to breathe, keeping the knowledge close to her heart that Skye had chosen *her*, had left Pansie in *her* care. "But I will be." She managed a smile. "We're keeping this between the two of us." At Coco's sober nod, she continued. "Then I'm fine."

Coco hauled her into her arms and squeezed her hard. "Yes, you are fine, Sessa Lee Chambers, but before we go back in there, I want you to just stop and realize that nothing is going to get past God. Do you understand? Much as you love that baby girl, He loves her more."

"Of course."

"You need to remember that the next time she calls, because it's likely she will. Now tell me what she said."

Stepping back, Sessa told her. Still shaken by the surprise phone call, she wrapped her arms around her waist. "How long do you think *soon* is?"

Coco shook her head. "Honey, I wish I knew, but you cannot spend your time worrying about it. You do know that, right?" At Sessa's nod, she continued. "And you also know that whatever happens, you and that precious child will not have to face it alone."

"I know that," Sessa said. "And I love you for it."

"I love you, too, but I have a bone to pick with you."

"And what is that?"

She sent Sessa a narrow-eyed glance. "You never did call me this afternoon after that man left."

Sessa went with the subject change, not wanting to think about Skye any longer.

"Either you forgot, which you *never* do. Or you broke your promise, which you *never* do. Or..."

"Or?"

"Or that man stayed all day, and you didn't have time to call before I got here." She paused just long enough to give her a sweeping glance. "Sessa Lee Chambers, you had a man here all day. Girl, I am going to need the details. Spill it!"

"Hush," she managed. "Yes, he was here until just before Mama brought Pansie home."

"I knew it! So did you apologize to him?"

"I tried but he wouldn't let me." Coco opened her mouth to speak, but Sessa kept talking. "And you'll be happy to know he said it was *he* who should be apologizing to *me*."

"Well now," she said on a rush of breath. "I surely didn't expect that. So he came all this way to make amends with you?"

She shrugged. "He did."

"Interesting. And you really didn't hire him?"

"He said he was going to help with the restoration work once he cleared the acreage, but I don't plan to let him."

Coco gave her a *we'll-see-about-that* look. "So what happened next?"

"He was outside working the whole time. First he fixed Daddy's mower—"

"So I understand."

Sessa affected a teasingly irritated expression. "Do you want to tell this story, or shall I continue?"

Coco shook her head. "Go ahead. Tell it."

"All right, as I was saying, he got the mower running, but it took awhile. Then he mowed the field behind the shop. I told him it wasn't necessary, but he insisted."

Coco was grinning like crazy.

"What?" Sessa demanded.

"I'm just trying to imagine what you were doing while that handsome man was going back and forth in the field. I'd say from the kitchen you'd have a decent view of him, but with the book club meeting here tonight, you couldn't have stood there all day. However did you manage to tear yourself away from the window?"

Sessa shook her head. "You're impossible."

"I've heard the claim made, but I don't agree." A ruckus rose on the other side of the door, and the likely cause was Mama or Vonnette or both. "You'd better give me the short version, because those two old ladies are going to barge in here demanding pie pretty soon, claiming their blood sugar's getting low. Or something to that effect."

"I fixed him sweet tea and ham sandwiches but otherwise pretty much left him alone all day."

"Seriously?"

"Yes. Seriously."

Coco seemed to be having trouble digesting the news. "Okay, well I've got two questions."

"Go ahead." Sessa pulled the pies closer and started slicing them. "Either help or I just might be too busy to respond."

"First question," Coco said as she grabbed the dessert plates. "Is he coming back?"

"He said he was." Sessa counted out the correct number of napkins, added two to the stack, and then tossed them onto the tray with the pies and plates.

"I knew it." She scooted out of the way as Sessa picked up the tray and moved toward the door. "Okay, so second question."

"Come open the door," Sessa said.

"Second question." Coco moved around her to grasp the doorknob. "When he was out there cutting grass, he had to have gotten warm on your daddy's mower. Did he...?" She made to turn the knob but didn't open the door. "That is...?" She made a show of looking around as if someone might be listening. "Did he take his shirt off? Because he sure looks like he might be as pretty under that shirt as he is with it on."

"Coco! You are impossible. Open that door right now."

She shook her head. "Answer the question, Sessa. We had a deal."

Sessa smiled. "All right. No. He did not take off his shirt while he was on my daddy's mower."

Her face fell. "Well darn. I was hoping for a nice description." She still didn't move. "So what is this about having a bone to pick with me?"

The tray was getting heavy. Just like the one she held this afternoon in the field. Sessa balanced it against the counter and met Coco's confused stare.

"Praying for a husband for me, Coco? Really? You of all people?"

She shrugged. "Just because I married a guy who didn't keep his promise doesn't mean I don't want you to find one who does."

A shared beat of understanding passed between them. Coco knew that beneath her independence, Sessa still harbored a secret hope that she'd find someone who interested her past a first date. "I guess that makes sense."

"Of course it does." Coco opened the door. "Now let's go feed these females before they get too cranky."

The sound of Mama and Vonnette's verbal sparring cut through their conversation. "Too late for that," she whispered. "Here comes the pie," she called, and immediately the sparring ceased and the clapping began.

When the slices of pie had been handed out and the coffee cups filled, Sessa set the tray on the sideboard and joined Coco on the window seat. "I always do love book club night. It gets me out of the house and reminds me that not everyone lives in a house of men."

Sessa sipped at her decaf.

A few minutes later, as Mama and Vonnette once again debated a response to one of the book's discussion questions, Sessa leaned toward her best friend and said three words, "Black halter top?"

Coco giggled. "I'll bet that got his attention."

"Actually it was the leather pants that he commented on, but it was more of a joke than any belief that a woman of my age would wear something like that."

"Don't joke about leather pants," Coco said. "With the right top and accessories, they can look cute."

Of course her fashionable friend would think so.

"So," Sessa continued just as the time to answer the discussion question was about to reach Coco. "As to question number two?"

Coco cut her eyes toward Sessa as the person next to her finished answering the question. "What about it?" she whispered.

"He didn't take off his shirt on the mower, but he did take it off at the pump. When he rinsed off. Under the water."

Sessa offered an innocent look that would have made her high school drama teacher applaud. A moment later, Coco jabbed her arm. She refused to look lest her carefully constructed expression slip.

"Get. Out. Of. Town," she hissed just loud enough for those around her to hear.

"Coco?" Mama said. "That doesn't make any sense at all. The question was why Velma was still cooking in Leeway. If she was wanting to get out of town, she surely wouldn't be cooking, now would she? If you don't have a good answer, please just keep quiet next time."

"Yes ma'am," was all she could manage as she gave Sessa another sideways look. "I'm sure Sessa's got a good answer. She's been full of good answers tonight."

"Actually, Sessa needs to go check on her granddaughter." She rose before anyone could complain. "Just pass me by this round, and I promise I'll be back in time to answer the next question."

Moving quietly down the hall, she paused at Pansie's door. All was quiet, so she opened the door and slipped inside. Ella Barnes' granddaughter Kate sat in the rocker reading her e-reader while Pansie slept like an angel in her toddler bed.

"Did she give you any trouble?" Sessa whispered.

"Nope," Kate said. "I read her three stories and then tucked her in with her doll. She went right to sleep."

"Why don't you get a piece of pie?"

"Thanks," Kate whispered as she set the e-reader aside and left the room, closing the door behind her.

Sessa checked the lock on the window and then knelt down by the little bed and adjusted the patchwork blanket that had covered three generations of Chambers children. Finally, she wrapped her finger around one of Pansie's curls. Somewhere between those first months of her life and now, the little girl's hair had gone from the blackest black to a lovely shade of spun gold that seemed to grow lighter every year.

Her mama wouldn't even recognize her.

Sessa froze.

What a sad thought. And who was to blame? Flames of anger rose and then quickly died out. No. Skye had made a wise decision in leaving her child here. To blame her now for having no relationship with that child was unfair.

Then again, it also felt unfair that Skye had intruded on their world tonight in what could be the first attempt at restoring that relationship.

Pansie stirred, and Sessa released that precious curl to press her hand on the little girl's back. The remedy for colic in the early months had become the remedy for undisturbed sleep two years later.

Eyelids fluttered but did not open as Pansie gathered her doll close and let out a long sigh. The slow rise and fall of her little back indicated deep sleep had returned. Still Sessa kept her hand there.

What a precious child. What a precious moment.

Don't let that girl take my baby away, Lord. Please.

CHAPTER ELEVEN

Four days later, Sessa was sanding the hind leg of a pink flying pig while Pansie played nearby when she heard a racket coming from somewhere behind the workshop. Tossing the sandpaper aside, she snatched up her cell phone and patted her pocket for the pepper spray she carried for times like this.

Dialing 911 this far out in the country was pointless, but it was a well-known fact—and a well-used technique—that calling down to the hardware store would dispatch any number of able-bodied volunteers willing to handle whatever trouble awaited them.

It also might bring one of the two members of the Sugar Pine police force, although that depended on whether their radios worked. Funding being as it was, they generally kept a close watch on the goings on at the hardware store and awaited dispatch from there.

Considering it was halfway between breakfast and lunch, any number of fellows might be available to head her direction. Thus, Sessa punched up the contact screen for the hardware store, separated Pansie and her doll from the blocks she was playing with to situate her on her hip, and then went to investigate.

Pansie tugged on the end of her ponytail. "Where we going, Gwammy? I'm not finished building my castle."

"We're going to play a new game. Be real quiet, honey."

She offered a lower lip that warned that a more fully formed protest was imminent. "I need my dolly."

Seizing the opportunity to make a deal, Sessa paused and turned around. "I'll get your dolly but only if you make sure she's really quiet. Promise?"

For once, the fiercely independent child didn't protest. Rather, she rested her head on Sessa's shoulder and clutched her doll against her chest. "Dolly's going to be quiet. She promises."

There. She heard the sound again. This time it was more of a loud clanging followed by a dull roar.

Securing the shop door, she kept to the side of the workshop and eased her way around the corner. There she spied the source of the noise balancing himself on the topmost rail of the paddock. Someone driving a forklift was easing a load of what appeared to be shingles over the barbed wire fence and into a space next to the barn. Apparently Trey's guidance was needed to help the driver avoid plowing down the fence as he delivered the goods, and it was needed from atop the paddock.

"Trey?" she called as she set Pansie on her feet and grasped her hand. "What in the world are you doing?"

"Hey, Sessa."

She swung her attention to the forklift and found Jared Chance at the controls. When he saw her, he quickly silenced the engine.

"Jared?" she said. "Why aren't you working?"

"I took the week off. But since Carly hasn't had the baby yet, and she was getting a little antsy with me underfoot, I decided I'd help my dad over at the building supply. He needed a forklift driver, and I've got the training, so here I am."

"Yes, there you are." She returned her focus to the doctor who had jumped off the paddock fence and was ambling her direction. "Again, I have to ask," she said when he was a few feet away. "What are you doing here?"

"I told you I'd be back in a few days. Well, best I can count, it's been a few days." Trey yanked off his work gloves and stuck them in his back pocket then dropped to one knee in front of Pansie. "Who is this pretty lady?"

"That's my Gwammy," Pansie said.

He chuckled as he glanced up at Sessa. "Well, I reckon your Grammy is awful pretty, but I was actually talking about her." He pointed to the doll. "What's her name?"

"That's Dolly. She's not a lady. She's a dolly."

"No?" He shrugged. "Well how about that? I guess I thought she was, but now that you've pointed it out, I can see she is a doll after all."

"Trey," Sessa said again. "Focus. What's all this?"

He winked at Pansie and then stood. "By all this, I guess you mean the delivery?" At her nod, he continued. "I saw a couple of spots in the roof of the barn that needed repairing."

"A couple of spots?" She surveyed the growing stack of building materials and shook her head. "That's more than enough shingles to cover the roof of the barn."

"And the shed. The garage looks fine, and so does the house, but I had some concerns about your workshop." His expression made her think of a little boy's pleading puppy-dog eyes. Behind the teasing glint, she read earnest hope. "You might not have noticed, but there are a few shingles missing in the back that are going to cause a leak if they're not replaced."

She'd noticed. Several months ago. When the leak first showed up to ruin a perfectly good piece of ash she'd been saving to repair the mane on a hard-to-match standing mare.

Moving Doc Easely's table out of the way of the drip allowed her to carry on as if there were nothing wrong with the roof. Thus, that repair was on her to-do list.

Her very long to-do list.

Sessa tucked her cell phone into the back pocket of her jeans. "Why are you here? Don't you have a job to get to?"

He swiped at his forehead with his sleeve. "Eventually, but not today."

"I guess it's all right, but I can't pay for all of this."

"Wouldn't let you anyway."

Jared called his name, and Trey turned around to wave in his direction. "Got to go handle this. Nice to meet you Dolly," he said to Pansie.

"I'm Pansie," she protested as she thrust her doll in his direction. "This is Dolly."

"Well, so you are. Very nice meeting both of you." Trey reached down to shake one of the doll's cloth hands and then Pansie's.

"No really," Sessa said. "You cannot keep doing these things if I can't pay for them."

He fixed her with an even look, but behind it, she read the hint of vulnerability. "I can," he said. "And I'd appreciate it if you'd let me."

How could she tell him no? Not when the barn really did need fixing.

And not when she recognized the vulnerability in him.

He loped away without a backward glance.

"Who's the man, Gwammy?"

She patted Pansie's head. "Never you mind. Now I think it's time for you and I to go back to work building things. What do you think?"

The toddler shook her head. "I want to watch the tractor."

Of course she did. Sessa sighed. "Just for a minute, then we have to go back to the workshop. You've got a castle to build, remember?"

And I've got to figure out what I'm going to do about Trey Brown.

~*~

Trey's attention was divided between the arriving pallets of shingles and the departing woodcarver. While he needed to be helping Jared Chance situate the building materials in the correct spots, he wanted to see what he'd be missing once he ran out of reasons to return to Sugar Pine. He should've been back at the hospital by now. Yesterday he'd even gotten so far as sitting in his truck in the garage, white lab coat folded neatly on the passenger seat.

He hadn't been able to turn the key.

He hadn't been back to see Tom again, but maybe he could find the closure he needed here in Sugar Pine.

His eyes strayed toward where Sessa had disappeared.

Or maybe it was something else entirely that had drawn him back.

"C'mon, man," the forklift driver called. "Focus."

Trey turned his back on the cause of his distraction and finished guiding the pallets into place. When the last one had been set where it needed to go, Trey helped the driver load up the forklift and then pulled out his wallet.

"Put that away," Jared said. "You've already paid for the materials."

"Yes, but you've done a great job. I wanted to reward you for it."

He shook his head and once again waved away the bills. "Put your money up. If you want to reward me, then do it by taking good care of that lady there." He nodded toward the workshop where Sessa was likely back working hard at carving her horses. Or painting them. "She's a good woman and too proud to ask for help."

"I can see that." He nodded toward the barn. "I'll do what I can to set things right around here."

Jared studied him with the wary eye of a man who'd seen more than his share of trouble and then returned to the process of securing the fork lift. Trey had pegged him for a military guy. The bearing, the stance, the demeanor. He knew it well, and he respected it.

"So you're going to be a father soon?"

Jared's hands paused over the tailgate and then he slammed it shut. "Yeah." He turned to face Trey.

"Your first?"

"Yeah."

"Boy or girl?"

His expression softened. "Don't know yet. The wife and I decided to go old school and wait until the baby comes to find out."

Trey grinned. "Nothing wrong with that."

Jared swiped at his forehead with the back of his hand and then wiped it on his jeans. "Tell that to my mother. She's about to drive us crazy wanting to find out. I keep telling her she'll know when we know. She's not much liking the fact that Carly wants to have the baby at home, either. For that matter, neither am I, but my wife's a stubborn woman. At least she's hired a midwife." His smile faded. "Anyway, tell me man, how do you know Sessa?" He paused. "And why are you doing this for her?"

What to say? Trey decided nothing would do but the truth.

"I was a friend of Ross's back in Houston." He watched Jared's expression change. "I volunteered at Star of Hope Mission and he—"

"He stayed there. Yeah, he told me that was where he crashed when he was in Houston. Did you crash there too?"

"Not exactly. I got to know him through the GED program. I thought I was going to tutor him through the process of getting his diploma." Trey fought not to get lost in the memories. "That kid was so much smarter than I was, it wasn't funny. He could have taken that exam any day of the week and passed it with flying colors. He just didn't want to."

"Sounds like Ross." Jared shrugged. "So why wait all this time to come help Sessa? What's it been since Ross died? Two years?"

"Two years, six weeks and eleven days." Trey straightened his spine and met the soldier's gaze head-on. "And about seven hours." He paused. "I know, because I was there."

Trey braced himself for the younger man's reaction. Tried to think of how he might have responded to hearing this kind of admission.

Truly he didn't have clue what he'd say or do.

"I see." Jared reached up to straighten his John Deere cap, his expression unreadable. "So how'd it all go down, Trey? Did you kill him like the first judge said, or were you just protecting yourself like the second one said?"

Straight to the point. He could only respond in the same way.

"He pulled a gun on me. I reacted with the first thing I could reach, a scalpel my dad gave me when I finished med school. I wish I hadn't."

Jared leaned against the fender and looked away. "I knew that kid from the time he was little. If he pulled a gun on you, he would have used it. Trust me on that."

Trey shook his head. "You don't mean that."

He returned his attention to Trey. "When I say trust me, I mean it. In fact, when I say anything, I mean it."

The edge in his voice told Trey he'd gone too far. He quickly made to remedy the issue. "Didn't mean to ruffle feathers, Jared. I'm just saying that Ross might have had a good life ahead of him. He could have changed. Made something of himself. I used to do a little rodeoing, and I mean, that kid could ride. I'd hoped he might end up in college, maybe riding on a college rodeo team."

"Where he'd have to show up for class and listen to people tell him what to do? Not a chance." Jared shrugged. "Look, it's me who needs to apologize now. I tried fixing him, too. Thought he'd do well by a stint in the military. Even sent a recruiter buddy of mine after him. Big mistake."

"Oh?"

"Suffice it to say that as much as his mama tried to raise him right—and she did—that guy was just plain bad news. Maybe if his dad hadn't died, things would've been different, but I seriously doubt it. I wouldn't be lying to say that he's not missed much around here."

Trey nodded toward the workshop. "I'll bet she misses him."

"I'll bet she doesn't. No," he amended. "I'll agree she misses the idea of Ross Chambers, but the person? No. Trust me. Especially now that she's raising his little girl, the last thing either of them needed was to have that kind of disruption in their lives. You know he hit her? His mama, that is. Left her banged up more than once, though she never would press charges."

The words filtered in slowly... and as understanding set in, Trey's blood pressure spiked. "I didn't know."

Jared seemed to be studying him. "It'd be a harsh thing to say, but it'd be true to state that you just might have done the world a favor."

"Can't see as I'll ever come around to that way of thinking. It runs counter to everything I learned in med school."

Jared tugged open the door on the old truck and then leaned against the frame. "You're a doctor. Why are you here in Sugar Pine roofing that old barn?"

"Because even though I got my license to practice back when the judge set me loose, I owe her a debt I'm still trying to pay."

"Yeah. I can see that." Jared climbed into the truck and closed the door, then rolled down the window to lean out. "I appreciate an honest man, Dr. Brown."

"Around here, I'm just Trey."

A curt nod and he continued. "All right, Trey. Like I said, I appreciate you telling me the truth. You have my word that what you've told me will stay between us."

That Jared—practically a stranger—so easily accepted him, humbled Trey. It had been a long time since he'd felt like he belonged anywhere, like his life had meaning among others. He felt good. Very good.

No doubt people would figure out his identity sooner or later, but Trey wanted it to be on their own and not through idle gossip.

Jared's phone buzzed, and he lifted it to his ear. "Carly? Is it time?" His eyes cut toward Trey, and then he nodded. "Be right there, honey."

"Baby coming?" Trey asked.

"Could be." He stretched out his hand to give Trey a firm handshake. "Look, you stay on the right side of Sessa Chambers, and you'll stay on the right side of me and the rest of Sugar Pine."

"I'll try." He released his grip and took a step back as Jared turned the key and the truck's engine roared to life. "And if it makes you feel any better, babies have been delivered at home since the beginning of time. I'm sure your midwife will alert the hospital if she feels like your wife needs any kind of specialized care."

"I guess." Jared paused, his expression no longer confident. "Say, I wonder if you might be willing to give me a number where I can reach you?" He paused. "Just in case."

Trey caught his meaning, but hesitated, remembering his failed attempt in the OR. "Sure," he finally said. He rattled off his cell number.

Again, he reached out to clasp Trey's hand. "Thanks, man."

Trey shrugged off the thanks. "Go on home. Sounds like you've got a son or daughter waiting to see you real soon. Just one, right?"

The younger man's eyes widened. "Definitely just one. That much we insisted on knowing."

Long after the father-to-be had left, Trey was still thinking about their conversation. Thinking of the admission that Sugar Pine was better without Ross Chambers. Thinking of the news that Ross had harmed Sessa. That the little girl Sessa was raising might have had that kind of man as a father—the kind that might have hurt her.

He set another shingle in place and drove a nail deep into it with a single slam of the hammer. Men who hit women were beyond scum. He finished off that nail and put another in place. Still, God put Trey on earth to be a healer, not a killer.

He'd never get used to the idea he'd been both. Not as long as he lived.

How long he worked at shingling the roof, Trey couldn't say. He'd gotten lost in the rhythmic effort of placing a shingle and nailing it down, then moving on to the next. Unlike surgery, this work was almost soothing. Mechanical. Easy on the brain.

When his phone buzzed in his pocket, Trey nearly dropped the hammer. He glanced at the caller ID. Dr. Santini.

It rang twice more before he decided to answer it.

"How're you feeling, pal?" the surgeon asked him. "Haven't seen you around, and I figured maybe the flu still had you down."

"I don't have the flu."

"Well, that's good news." Santini paused. "Look, I've got a couple of questions for you. Got a minute?"

"Sure." Trey set the hammer down and situated himself in a spot where the roof had been reinforced. "What's up?"

"Yeah," he said, "it's about what happened in the OR a couple weeks ago. Were you really sick or...?"

"Or was I having trouble operating?"

"Yeah."

The truth had been his friend all day. Might as well continue with that line of response on this go-around, though he knew all too well there could be negative consequences. "I can't hold a knife without spilling my guts."

"I see." He paused. "So when you say you can't, do you mean you couldn't that day in the OR, or you still can't?"

Trey thought a minute. "I couldn't, that's certain. But now? I haven't tried."

"Want to try?"

"What?" Trey shifted positions. "Are you asking if I want to come back and operate with you?"

"Not asking if you wanted to. Asking if you will. And before you answer, you ought to know that there's been talk. I just figured I'd give you a chance to shut them all up before it gets to the chief, and he starts believing it."

"The chief told me to take a couple of weeks before I came back full time." Trey knew the excuse, though true, was a poor one. "When?" The word slipped from his mouth before he could stop it.

"Needs to be soon, pal. Real soon."

Trey let out a long breath as he considered his options. Santini was obviously wrapping a warning and a chance to redeem himself into one package. To pass on the opportunity was foolish.

"Week after next?" he offered.

"Friday," Santini countered.

"I'm in the middle of something." He swiped at the perspiration on his forehead. "Can't guarantee I'll finish it by then. A week from Friday's doable, though."

Or at least he prayed it would be.

"Deal," he said. "I'll schedule the OR. You just show up and keep the contents of your breakfast where they belong, got it?"

He grimaced at the reminder. "Got it."

"And there's one other thing."

Trey braced himself for whatever else his friend might ask. After this favor, he knew he'd owe Santini big time.

"It's about Victoria Rossi."

Great. Had there been talk about her, too? "What about her?"

It took Santini a minute to respond. "She and I, well...we've been seeing each other. Not that we're letting anyone at the hospital know yet. But...well, it is getting serious fast."

Exactly how Victoria Rossi worked. Pick her man and stop at nothing until he was hers. He'd been in too deep with her before he realized what happened. Not that he had complained at the time.

"Go on," Trey said.

"Since you and she were, well, you had a thing once upon a time, I wanted to tell you myself before you heard it somewhere else."

"I see."

Let Santini hitch a ride on Vikki's fast track to chief. Trey certainly wasn't interested in either the job or the woman who could deliver it. Helping people was his true calling, and part of him had known it all along.

His phone buzzed letting him know someone was trying to call him. A peek at the phone told him that someone was Jared Chance.

"I really need to grab this other call."

"All right, Trey. See you a week from Friday. I'll email you the records and the scans so you'll be familiar with the patient."

"Yeah, great." He switched to the incoming call. "Brown here. What's up, Jared?"

"It's Carly." The cold-as-ice soldier sounded scared to death. "Something's wrong, and the midwife isn't here. Said she'd be here soon, but she just called, and she's having car trouble.

There's blood and Carly's hurting and...look, Doc. Could you just come over? I'm not that far from Sessa's place. If I try to take her to the hospital myself, I'm afraid I'll kill us both trying to drive and take care of her."

He wanted to say no. Wanted to tell Jared to call 911 instead.

But remembering the young man's kindness—and the oath Trey'd taken as a physician—he couldn't do it.

"Text me your address." He scrambled down from the roof and fumbled for his keys with his free hand. His heart pounded as his gut did a flip-flop. Could he even do this? "I'm on my way."

CHAPTER TWELVE

"Did you hear that Sessa's cowboy delivered Jared's son last night? It's the truth. Can you feature it? He was a doctor all along and didn't say a word about it."

News of the cowboy's heroic efforts had circulated around Sugar Pine faster than a hot knife through butter. The topic certainly hadn't veered from this subject since she arrived at the Blue Plate to meet Mama and Vonnette for lunch.

As Vonnette offered her opinion, Sessa gave passing thought to the idea that since the doctor's secret had been revealed, he might be less inclined to stick around. She wasn't sure how she felt about that.

Mama was still chattering, but Sessa had already tuned her out. Her phone buzzed with a text. From Skye.

Can you pick me up at the bus station when I get there?

The breath went out of her. No. Not yet.

Not ever.

A moment of panicked breathing, and then she thought of Coco's reminder that nothing would happen that God did not allow. And they wouldn't go through it alone.

It still hurt to type an answer.

When? She pressed send and then waited. And waited. *When?* she texted again.

"I swear, I knew there was something special about that man when he walked in here and sat down on that stool over there." Her mother gestured to the stool where Trey had made his debut in Sugar Pine. "And I said then what I'll say now: the Lord meant him for my daughter."

"Mama." Sessa tossed her phone into her purse and slid out of the booth. "I've got to go."

"We're not done talking."

"We are for now." She left a ten dollar bill on the table to cover her meal and hurried to the car, where she once again checked for a response to her text. Nothing.

With hands shaking, she drove to the bus station and parked across the street. Memories of the last time she'd met Skye at this place arose. Good memories, though at the time she hadn't been so certain.

"May it once again be so, Lord," she whispered as she turned off the engine, tossed her keys in her purse, and crossed the street.

A few minutes later, she returned to climb into the car and slam the door. No busses were expected this afternoon or evening. None had arrived this morning. The next bus was not expected until two o'clock tomorrow afternoon.

Irritation chased away her relief. The fact that Skye wasn't here today didn't mean she wasn't coming tomorrow. Or the next day. Or next week.

Sessa drove straight from the bus terminal to the church where Pansie attended Mother's Day Out and let herself into the children's building to tiptoe down the hall to Pansie's classroom. She found the children napping and their teacher, Miss Erin, watching over them from her rocker near the door.

Spying Sessa, she pressed her finger to her lips and slipped out of the room and into the hall. "Are you picking Pansie up early?"

"Well, I had thought to but..." She glanced at the sleeping angel through the door's long window. "I guess I'll let her sleep. You'll be sure no one but me or Mama ever picks her up unless I call and say so, won't you? I mean, that's the rule, isn't it?"

"Well, of course," Erin said. "It's our policy to release our children only to people on the list."

"Okay, good." She returned to her car and drove home, peace slowly descending. Worrying about what would happen never solved anything.

It did give her something to think about, though. Even if that something wasn't what she ought to be thinking about.

Fix your hearts on what is true and honorable, what is right...

Sessa pondered Philippians four, ironically the subject of last Sunday's sermon, all the way home. She'd half-expected to find

Trey's truck parked there, though he was likely catching up on the sleep he'd missed while delivering the Chance baby last night.

Pausing to toss her purse on the kitchen table, Sessa stepped back outside and headed for the workshop to pick up where she'd left off that morning. She needed an outlet for her nervous energy. Her first set of horses for the Smithsonian project would be delivered next week, and she still had a few items to complete before those arrived.

If she allowed it, she would worry about how to keep up the pace that would be required once the horses arrived. Better to keep busy. Surely someone would answer the ad soon, though she'd had no inquiries.

She plugged her phone into the speakers she kept in the workshop and programmed it to play her current favorite version of Vivaldi's *The Four Seasons*. When the music filled the space, she reached for the planer to smooth out a piece of wood that would become an ear for the prancing horse waiting for her on the table.

"I'm fixing my heart, Lord, and I'm depending on you to fix the rest."

"I need to remember that."

Sessa jumped, and the planer clattered to the floor. Trey reached it before she did. "Sorry about that."

She accepted the planer with a shaking hand and returned it to its place on the table. She silenced the concerto. "It's fine. I guess the music was louder than I thought." She crossed her arms over her midsection. What in the world he was doing here? Apparently he wasn't going to offer up the information, and she wasn't comfortable enough with him to just ask.

Instead, she said, "So the whole town is talking about how you delivered Jared and Carly's baby."

How do you feel about that? hung in the space between them.

"I just filled in for the midwife. Apparently she had car trouble."

"And the birth was breech. You saved their lives, Trey."

He ducked his head as if uncomfortable. "It's what any doctor would have done." Trey lifted his gaze. "Do you have a minute?"

"Sure."

Trey leaned against the workbench and seemed to be studying the toes of his boots. "So I've got a business proposition for you.

Hear me out and then think about it before you answer, okay?"

She rested her hip against the other end of the workbench facing him. "Okay."

"As you know, I've been doing a little work on your barn."

"A little?" She shook her head. Even with being interrupted, he'd cleared most of the old shingles from the barn roof.

"I believe you agreed to hear me out," he said in a teasing tone.

Sessa grinned. "Sorry. Go on."

"Okay, so there's more work to be done, but basically you've got a sound structure, and with some repairs to the fencing and some clearing work, you'll have a good pasture. Whoever built it did a good job."

That would have been Daddy's father. She kept that close to her heart and allowed another smile.

"I'd like to board my horses in your barn and rent out your pasture. I'd pay a good monthly rate, of course."

His words were so out of left field that she had to play them over in her head again. Sessa straightened her spine. "You'll do nothing of the sort."

He nodded, but couldn't quite hide the flare of disappointment in his eyes. "I understand."

"No." She walked around to stand in front of him, hands on her hips. "You don't understand. I've waited a long time for horses to return to that barn. I'd love nothing better than for my granddaughter to someday look out her bedroom window and see horses grazing in that pasture."

"So you'll rent out the space to me?"

"Absolutely not. I will not have you paying for what I am freely offering."

"I'm going to insist on paying you, Sessa." He glanced around the workshop. "I know you're probably doing just fine with your work here, but maybe you could set the money aside to put Pansie through college."

"I'd like to see that girl go to college, but I'll not send her on money that wasn't properly earned. However..."

She gave it a thought.

"However?" he prompted.

"However, I do have a counter proposal."

"I'm listening."

"You've been maintaining the barn. I have no doubt that with your horses in it, maintenance will continue. That's payment enough for me."

"Agreed. Now, for my counter to your counter."

"But we agreed."

"We agreed on the barn." He moved around her to stand at the window that looked out over the pasture. "But there's the matter of where the horses will graze. I estimate a day or two's work will bring that pasture to what it needs to be. That's not enough payment."

He turned to face her. "So here's my counter-counter-proposal. It hasn't escaped my notice that you used that advertisement for an employee for Chambers Restoration as my reason for being in Sugar Pine." He shrugged. "I used it, too. However, we both know I didn't respond to that ad." He paused. "So I'm responding to it now. I'll graze my horses in exchange for whatever job you advertised for."

"So you'll give up medicine for a full time job stripping paint, sanding, and carving carousel animals? Because that's what this job entails. I don't think so."

He opened his mouth to respond, but she held up her hand to silence him.

"The Lord will provide. In the meantime, I'll be fine. And I'm not going to change my mind about this, so don't try. Take it or leave it."

Trey once again looked as if he meant to argue. Then, apparently, he thought better of it. Instead, he reached his hand across the distance as if offering to shake on the deal. "I'll take it." He didn't shake her hand. Instead, he retrieved the planer. "But seeing as you don't have anyone working for you yet, I figure I'll act as stand in until you hire someone—as long as you'll give me time to finish the barn, too." He set the planer down on the steel surface between them then looked up, his expression challenging her to argue.

She mustered a smile. "All right, then." She pushed the planer aside and handed him a detail knife. Slipping the ash handle into his open palm, Sessa wrapped Trey's fingers around the knife and then reached for the piece she'd been working on yesterday. "I've seen your work on my barn. Let's see how you do making this piece look like that one."

~*~

Trey stared at the knife in his palm and tried to listen as Sessa explained what he was to do with it. Something about making one piece of wood look like the other. Make a flat piece of poplar look like the ears on a prancer. Or was it a stander?

She'd somehow rattled off the definition of both types of carousel horses without the explanation of either sticking in his brain. What she showed him seemed simple enough. Just a few shaves of the knife against the wood, and then he would use the planer and finish the work. Simple enough even for a novice like him.

But he couldn't make his hand move to pick up the wood.

He stared at the knife, offset as it was with the steel of the operating room table beneath it. For that's what it was, an OR table. She'd said that, too. And something more, perhaps about a doctor friend of her mother's. None of it stuck as he stared at the knife in his hand.

The knife that looked very much like a scalpel stuck into a wooden handle.

The room tilted, and a wave of nausea hit him hard. As carefully as he could manage, Trey placed the knife on the table and turned to walk out into the sunshine with Sessa still talking. He got as far as the driveway before she caught up to him.

"Trey?" Her tone was balanced somewhere between a question and a demand. "What's wrong? Are you ill?"

He was. Again. But pride wouldn't allow him to admit it. Not to her.

So he straightened and turned to face her. Even in his worst moment, one look at Sessa Lee Chambers could turn him around. He made a note of this but couldn't decide if it was a good thing or not. Power of that kind could be dangerous. Or it could be the best thing that happened to him.

"Must be something I ate last night." He couldn't quite meet her eyes as the words tumbled out.

She touched his sleeve, a light touch that lingered just above the crook of his elbow. "Something I can do?" she said in that sweet voice of hers.

He let out a long breath. "Yeah, there is. Why don't you show me one more time what you need done and then maybe grab us both a glass of sweet tea? It's gotten warm out here."

It was. He was. But at least with her busy fetching tea, he might manage to collect himself.

She nodded, her expression still searching. To his surprise, she linked her arm with his. "All right then. But I'll understand if you're not feeling well. After all, it was your idea to do this. I can certainly wait until another day."

But it couldn't. For so many reasons, it couldn't wait.

Shrugging off the effects of holding the knife, of seeing that table, Trey gathered up the tattered remainder of his pride and followed the woman who was quickly climbing into his heart back into the workshop.

This time he listened, mostly, as she showed him what to do. "Now you try." She returned the knife to his palm and then pressed the piece of poplar toward him. "See how the edge there just needs a little work to make it look like the other leg?"

Trey studied the matching piece and then nodded at Sessa. Under her watchful eye, he touched the edge of the knife against the place where the cut must be made. Steadied one hand on the cold metal of the operating table. Gripped the handle of the carving knife. Stared at a blade that looked so like the scalpel he'd once used so expertly.

Just one cut. Just. One.

He let out another breath. Sucked in sawdust-scented air. Let out another breath.

And then Trey slid the edge into place. Made the cut.

"Great job." Sessa headed toward the door, unaware of his fear. "I knew you could do it."

But I didn't, he silently called as she disappeared into the Texas summer sunshine. *Until you showed me I could.* The words danced through the sparkles of dust motes that swirled between him and the door.

Between him and Sessa Lee Chambers. The woman who made him feel as if he could do anything.

Sessa returned to find her new hired hand had done an expert job of matching the carving on the prancer's front legs. So engrossed was he in completing the final details of the project that Trey barely noticed when she slid the glass of iced tea in front of him.

"Just a minute." He turned the two legs over to compare them. "I need to make sure it's exactly right."

Sessa nudged him with her shoulder and gave him a sideways look. "It's perfect. Just as I expected."

She had, though she was still skeptical that he'd actually complete the project given the way he'd reacted to her placing a knife in his hand. Maybe he was ill, though he certainly looked fine now.

She watched him return the knife to its place and then reach for the glass of tea. Sawdust decorated muscled forearms and dusted the rolled up cuffs of his shirt. He'd even managed to gather a light sprinkle of sawdust on his forehead and across one tanned cheek.

Her fingers itched to swipe away the fine coat of poplar. Instead, she searched for a something to say. Something to get her thoughts back to a more appropriate topic.

"So..." She watched him drain half the glass of tea before finally sitting it back on the work table, "tell me about these horses of yours."

"I'd rather show you. If you've got time, that is."

She retrieved her phone to check the time and noticed to her relief that there'd been no more texts from Skye. "How far away are they?"

"About ten minutes to Mr. Jones' place."

"Bud Jones?"

He nodded. "Do you know him?"

"He and my daddy go way back, and his wife and I attend a book club together." She paused. "But as much as I'd like to go see the horses you've bought, I just don't feel comfortable getting that far out of town without Pansie."

"Then let's bring her."

"She's at Mother's Day Out up at the church, so we can pick her up there."

He glanced at his shirt and then back at Sessa. "I'll need to clean up some. Just let me go grab my other shirt from the truck."

"Sure." A recollection of him cooling off at the barn rose. "I'll just take our tea glasses inside and grab my purse."

This accomplished, Sessa went outside to find Trey leaning against the passenger door of his truck. A pale blue button-down with pearl snaps had replaced his dusty shirt, and he'd combed the sawdust from his hair and must've washed his face from the outside tap. With his long legs still encased in faded denim and his boots scuffed from work, only someone who truly knew Trey Brown would suspect an accomplished surgeon lurked beneath this cowboy's exterior.

Enough of that, she determined as she fumbled with her keys. She'd also had enough of the worries about people in Sugar Pine seeing them together. In just their short acquaintance, Trey had proven the kind of man he was. Far as she cared, they could drive right down Main Street waving at everyone.

After somehow managing to lock up and move Pansie's car seat into Trey's truck, she climbed into the passenger seat and allowed him to close the door for her.

Inhaling deeply of the scent of leather and something akin to pine, Sessa settled back in her seat to give him directions to the church. She watched him lope around the front of the truck, tucking any possible feelings other than friendship back where they belonged, deep inside her heart. Trey Brown was a nice man. A good man. And no matter what happened in the past, she'd be glad to count him as her friend someday.

Or as a nice memory who happened along at a time when she needed to find some closure with her son's death. Getting the apology out had been a blessing. Having him not only receive it but offer one of his own had been more than she'd expected.

At times like this, she was hard pressed to forget that the Lord operated on His own time and in His own way. She'd certainly not have chosen for any of this to happen. Not like this. Not with her son.

"You okay?" he said as he buckled his seatbelt and then slid her a sideways glance.

"I'm fine." And she was. Truly.

A few minutes later, she retrieved a sleepy Pansie and settled her into her car seat. Though Pansie managed a smile in Trey's direction, she quickly snuggled into her blanket and fell back asleep.

"Looks like she's a little underwhelmed," Trey said.

"That girl loves her naps. Thank goodness. Old as I am, I don't think I could keep up with her if she didn't."

Trey signaled to turn onto the main road. "I can't imagine trying to raise a child at my age. How do you manage it?"

And that right there was the reason there couldn't be more than friendship between them, no matter that her stomach was full of swirling butterflies. Pansie was a fixture in her life.

"You just manage it," she said. "When she came to live with me she was only a few weeks old. I had no idea what I'd do with her. I mean, of course there was no question I would take her in, but there were plenty of questions about how I would survive the first week."

"I guess it was hard losing your son and gaining your grandchild all at the same time."

"No, it didn't happen like that. Pansie came first. Her mama showed up on my porch out of the blue and gave me until the next day to decide if I would keep her."

Trey gave her a sideways look. "And if you hadn't?"

"Skye couldn't raise her. She was just a kid herself. If I hadn't taken the baby, she would've been adopted out, I guess. Or ended up in foster care. Skye didn't plan to keep her. She made that clear."

"That's a rough choice."

"Not really," Sessa said. "I applaud Skye for realizing she wasn't capable of being a good mother to Pansie and having the good sense to do something about it. She told me she needed to get her act together and that Pansie didn't deserve to wait until that happened."

Trey nodded. "Still...that had to be difficult. For both of you."

"You mean me and Skye?"

"No. You and Ross."

Sessa gripped the door handle as Trey slowed to turn on the farm road that led toward the Jones ranch. "Far as I know, Ross never met his daughter. He might not have known he had one."

"I see."

"Which means Pansie can only have good thoughts about her

daddy someday," Sessa said. "Or at least that's my hope."

"You'll raise her that way. She'll know him through you."

"I hope so."

He slowed to allow the car ahead of him to make a turn. "You don't sound so sure."

"I'm not. Her mother has been texting me. She wants to see Pansie."

"And you don't want that."

A statement, not a question. He understood.

Sessa let that sink in deep, allowed herself to really feel the sense of connection she hadn't known since her first husband died.

"Does it sound terribly selfish to admit I don't? Skye left that baby with me and never looked back. Or at least never kept in touch. Then two years later, she decides she's got to see her daughter again?" Sessa realized her voice had risen and paused to glance back at the still-sleeping girl. "Pansie is hers, but she doesn't know the child. I do. And I am afraid—"

"That she's going to take Pansie away from you?"

All Sessa could manage was a nod as she blinked back embarrassing tears.

"That's a rough one, Sessa. I mean, she's the mother. What if she's done what she said she would do and gotten her act together?"

"Why are you defending her?" Sessa snapped. "She is biologically that child's mother, and nothing more. For her to come back now and disrupt the life we have together, how can that be the best thing for that child?"

"Maybe it's not. But maybe it is." He pulled over and shifted into park, then swiveled to face her. "Look, I know I am risking making you mad here, but your granddaughter is loved, Sessa. That much is obvious when I see you and her together. That's a blessing you've given her. She won't even know her dad. That's what I've given her."

The words struck Sessa in the heart. "And that's a blessing, too."

Trey looked away. "Don't say that."

"Surely you've heard what my son was like. You can't imagine he would be a fit parent for her. So why would I think her mother would be fit, either?"

"Because she might be. Look." He exhaled a long breath. "I'm no expert. I've never had kids, though I always wanted them. But you asked if you sounded selfish so I'm going to answer that. Until you know for sure whether that little girl's mama is fit or not, you can't decide she isn't because you don't want the disruption. To make that decision without knowing what kind of woman Skye is—that would definitely be selfish."

Sessa's temper flared. How dare this man say such a thing?

Because it's true.

She sucked in a deep breath. It was. But how could he know her better than she knew herself?

Glancing up, she found him watching her closely. "I guess I asked for that."

"You did. But then I probably should have warned you that, contrary to what the Harris County District Attorney's office claimed about me, I can be brutally honest."

"Yeah," she managed. "So I noticed."

"You're really worried about this, aren't you?" His fingers drummed on the steering wheel. "You don't want to lose her because you've already lost her father."

"And her grandfather," Sessa said. "But yes, that's it. And it's selfish. I can admit that."

He showed the beginning of a smile. "But what if you don't lose that little girl when her mama comes back? What if you gain a daughter?"

She turned his words over in her mind. "What if?" she repeated as Trey pulled the truck back onto the road. "That might be nice."

"Gwammy," a sleepy voice called from the back seat. "Where are we?"

Sessa leaned around to look at her granddaughter. "Hello sleepy head. We're going to see Dr. Brown's horses."

"I like horseys. Can we ride horseys today?"

"No, sweetheart," Sessa said. "We're just here to look at them."

"I see horseys!" she exclaimed as Trey drove under the arch announcing the Jones Ranch.

Bud Jones came out to meet them as the truck came to a stop

in front of the barn. "I see you brought company today, Dr. Brown. I didn't know you were acquainted with our Sessa. And look here, I see Pansie."

"Papa Bud!"

"Hey there, Miss Pansie." He gathered the little girl in his arms. "What're you doing here?"

"We came to see horseys."

Trey reached over to shake Bud's free hand. "I thought I'd show the ladies the two I bought."

"Right this way then," Bud said to Sessa. "Your friend there's got good taste in horses. He talked me into selling my two best."

"Oh, don't be silly, you old goose." Annette Jones waved from the back porch. "You know he paid you twice what you should have sold them for."

Her teasing tone had them all laughing, which was a relief after the intensity of the conversation in the truck. For a few moments, Sessa was able to forget her worries about Skye. Annette joined them to take the short walk to the paddock.

"Which ones are they?" Sessa asked as Pansie scrambled out of Bud's arms and into hers.

Trey pointed to a pair of Arabians grazing alone a few yards away. "What do you think?"

Sessa stared in wonder. "I think they're beautiful." So similar to the two horses she'd sold after Ben's death. The memory hit her hard. "Just beautiful."

"Beauty-ful," Pansie echoed, causing everyone to laugh.

"Have you decided what you're going to do with them?" Bud asked.

"I have, actually," Trey said. "I'm going to board them at Sessa's place."

"Is that so?" Bud's gaze swung from the horses to her. "Your daddy sure would be happy about that. You know these two were sired by Battalion, don't you?"

"No." She steadied herself by latching onto the fence with her free hand. "I had no idea."

Trey was standing beside her now. "Who?"

She found him watching. "Battalion was one of the pair I had to sell when Ross was little."

He smiled. "Then it's appropriate that these two spend a little time in their father's barn, don't you think?"

Pansie wriggled out of Sessa's arms and made a beeline for Annette. "Do you have cookies?"

Annette laughed. "I swear that little girl must think I carry them in my purse."

"That's because you do," Bud said.

"Well, that's the truth. Come on, Pansie," she said. "I've got cookies in the kitchen, and milk too. Then we'll see if we can catch one of those kitties you like to chase. Your Grammy can come fetch you when she's ready to go. How about that?"

Sessa watched Pansie and Annette disappear inside the house and then turned back toward the paddock. Trey and Bud had walked to the barn, so she wandered back to the fence.

Now that she looked closely, she could see the resemblance the horses bore to Battalion. One of the pair looked over in her direction, and Sessa couldn't resist. She stood up on the bottom rail just as she used to when she was a girl. Then she whistled once and clapped her hands three times.

To her surprise, both horses headed her way with a gallop. The lighter of the pair held back and stomped the ground just beyond her reach, but the other loped almost all the way to the fence before stopping just shy of knocking her down.

Sessa reached over the fence to scratch the Arabian behind his left ear. He nickered and presented the other ear to receive the same treatment. His companion inched toward her and nudged her with his muzzle until she paid him similar attention. Joy spiked. *This.* She'd missed this.

The darker of the pair rested his muzzle against her ear and whinnied softly, its sound almost like a sigh. *Fix your hearts on what is true and honorable, what is right...*

"Thank you, Lord," she whispered. "For reminding me what right feels like."

She continued to divide her affection between the two horses until Bud and Trey returned from the barn. "Want to ride, Sessa?" Bud asked.

"I wouldn't turn down a chance. But I don't want you to saddle a horse just for me."

"It's already done," Trey said. "Come on."

A few minutes later she was seated on another Arabian, this

one also sired by Daddy's favorite horse. They rode at a brisk pace as they covered the distance between the barn and the edge of the property. There was no need for conversation. The comfortable silence that stretched between them fit the day and the moment.

"Sessa?"

Startled, she found him watching her. "What?"

"Thank you," he said.

"For what?"

He shrugged. "All of this."

She shook her head. "I don't know what you mean."

"Never mind." He nodded toward the barn off in the distance. "How do you feel about seeing what these ponies can do?"

She grinned. "Aren't we too old for that?"

"Trust me," he said with a wink. "I'm a doctor." And then off he went.

"Hey, wait for me!" she called. He beat her to the barn but not by much, and they were still laughing as they dismounted.

After brushing the horses, they ambled back toward the house. "I haven't had that much fun in years," she said. "Thank you for bringing me out here today."

"I can't think of anyone I'd rather have shared this with." He stopped short. "I didn't know about your dad's horse, Sessa, but I'm glad I can bring those Arabians back to the barn."

"He would have liked that."

"You two," Annette called. "Come on in here and see what we've got simmering on the stove. Your Pansie's expecting to stay for supper, and I'd like it if you'd join her."

"Join her?" Sessa said with a laugh. "That depends on our chauffeur."

"Your chauffeur would be happy to stay for supper."

Not only did they stay for supper, but they also gathered sticks and built a bonfire just big enough to roast marshmallows and chase fireflies. By the time Trey dropped them off at home and Sessa tucked Pansie into bed, she was sticky and exhausted, too exhausted to awaken the sleeping girl to give her a bath.

That would wait for tomorrow.

And so would her attempt to sort out the feelings that spending an afternoon with Trey Brown had caused.

CHAPTER THIRTEEN

A week later, Trey sat at his desk in the medical building downtown, but he still hadn't managed to get the image of Sessa and those horses out of his mind. If he'd thought her beautiful before, that moment, now hopelessly locked into his mind, elevated her to something even beyond.

Then there was Sessa helping Pansie to roast marshmallows, Sessa's laughter as Pansie tried in vain to capture fireflies in the Mason jar Annette offered her, and finally Sessa carrying the sleeping child into the house.

The progression of images played on an endless reel in his mind. Each following the other until they blended into one image of a woman who he knew had changed something inside him. Before prison, he'd had a single-minded focus on his career. Even his relationship with Vikki had been more about what they could do for each other than romance or love.

But somehow knowing Sessa had not only changed his direction, it had also brought laughter and even a lovely little girl into his life. And a whole town of strangers who were quickly becoming friends.

Trey shifted and tried to focus on the stack of medical records spread across the desk in front of him. The surgery he'd promised to scrub in on with Santini was Friday, and as of this morning, he still hadn't decided whether he'd go through with it.

The only medicine he'd practiced since he left prison was delivering the Chance's baby in Sugar Pine. At least he'd managed to successfully slice his bagel this morning.

A knock distracted his thoughts. "Come in."

Charlie Dorne stuck his head in the door. "Thought I'd come

by and see if you were really here. I was beginning to think Brown sightings were as rare as catching a chupacabra or filming Big Foot in the wild."

Trey laughed as he gestured to the chair across from him. "Get in here quick, or they'll know I'm here."

Charlie complied, his expression turning thoughtful as he seated himself. "Seriously man, how are you?"

"I'm good." Trey leaned back in his chair. "Better than I've been in a long time, actually."

"I can see that." Charlie looked him over. "Where've you been?"

"East Texas. Roofing a barn. Oh, and I bought a pair of Arabians."

If Charlie was surprised, he didn't show it. "Whatever works to get you back to medicine, man."

"I delivered a baby," he added. "So I have done a little doctoring, although that's only because the midwife had car trouble and the baby was breach."

"Anything else?"

He shrugged. "I did successfully cut my bagel this morning without throwing up, so I'm making progress."

It was instantly obvious that Charlie wasn't amused. "You're making light of something that has me worried, Doc."

Trey sobered. "You heard I'm scrubbing in with Santini?"

"On Friday, yes," he said. "It's Wednesday afternoon, Trey. You've got less than forty-eight hours to get your act together and operate on a man. Are you ready?"

Trey's shock must have showed because he added, "Didn't you read the records?"

"Of course I did," he snapped. "But since when do we care about names around here?"

Therein was the issue. At some point, the patients had become numbers, not names. Diagnoses and surgical plans, not people.

Trey knew his friend only asked because he cared, but he didn't have an answer, especially now that he knew he'd be operating on Mr. Rossi. Or not.

"I guess we'll find out when I walk into the OR on Friday."

"I see." Charlie paused. "Guess you heard Santini and Victoria Rossi are an item."

Trey shook his head. "I didn't figure you for one who kept up with the social life of his colleagues, Charlie." At his friend's hurt look, he hurried to make amends. "Look, I'm sorry. Yeah, I heard. Santini told me. Better him than me, you know?"

Charlie nodded. "They've been an item for awhile. Well before you were released." Trey's surprise must have showed because Charlie leaned back and let out a long breath. "Yeah, didn't think you knew that."

"Hey, it's fine," Trey insisted. "It's just that she was coming on to me pretty strong on my first day back at work."

"I noticed."

"She said she'd made dinner reservations for us." He paused. "I didn't go."

Charlie shifted positions. "Look, I'm just going to lay it all out for you. I think it's possible that the two of them are plotting something."

Trey waved off the statement. "To what purpose? Vikki, I can see as devious, but Santini? No way."

"A man in love does what he's told, pal." Charlie let that sink in. "And an ambitious woman who wants her man to succeed will do what she can to see that happens, don't you think?"

"So...what?"

"My guess is Santini is banking on you getting into the OR and either screwing up the operation or just flat being unable to operate. He will then step in and earn Milo Rossi's undying gratitude—and probably his daughter and a shot at chief-of-staff—by saving him."

"He can have both of those things, but if I don't operate soon, I risk losing my spot at the hospital."

"A spot you'd rather trade for a roofing job, apparently."

The truth. And yet he wasn't completely sure he could walk away from what he'd worked so many years to achieve. "What do I do, Charlie?"

"That's something you need to ask the Lord, pal," he said. "But if it were up to me, I'd bow out and let Santini have his moment. Just step aside, even if you have to admit you aren't ready to return to surgical work." He paused. "So how did you end up roofing a barn?"

"It needed it. And I needed something to do. It's the craziest thing, but there's more. See, this barn belongs to a woman I can't stop thinking about."

"Oh?"

"You sound skeptical."

"I am," Charlie admitted. "A little, anyway. Don't you think this happened too fast?"

"Probably. Maybe. I don't know." He shook his head. "But I can't get her off my mind. She's funny and smart, and she rides a horse like nobody's business, Charlie. She's a wood carver and a painter. Oh, and she's raising her granddaughter. Can you feature it?"

"Maybe I'm being selfish, but I thought you'd come back to what you left. Seems like that's what you'd want."

"It was." Trey could still remember that pivotal moment in the therapist's office when Tom had called him on what he really felt holding a scalpel. "But now I want something else."

"Do you really?"

Trey thought about delivering Jared's baby, remembered that small feeling of triumph. He nodded. "I do. Really."

"All right, then. What's the problem?"

"The woman is Sessa Lee Chambers."

"Ross Chambers's mother?"

He nodded. "And the town I'd be hanging my shingle in is Sugar Pine, Texas. The only place in this whole state where I've always been known as that doctor who killed Ross Chambers. Now do you see the problem?"

Charlie seemed thoughtful. "Well," he finally said. "We do serve a creative God. My suggestion is you fix your heart and ask the Lord to fix the rest."

"That's what Sessa said."

"Well then, I think I'm going to like this gal. When do I get to meet her?"

"That, my friend, is a good question." He paused. "I'll let you know when I have a good answer. In the meantime, I've got an idea about how I might fix this problem with Santini, but I'm going to need your help."

"Am I going to regret it if I say yes?"

"Not as much as if you say no." He chuckled. "Seriously, I just need help finding out where Milo Rossi will be in the next twenty-four hours."

"Easiest place to find him will be where he's been every Thursday night since before you went to trial."

"The Fish Camp?" Trey shook his head. "You're kidding."

"Nope. He and the missus still go every Thursday."

He exhaled. "Well, that does make this a whole lot easier." Trey embraced Charlie in a bear hug. "Thank you, man. You're the best."

~*~

Five minutes after the last Greyhound of the day arrived, Sessa eased her car into a place just down the road from the bus station and waited. She'd had no more contact with Skye since her last cryptic text, and although she'd been sorely tempted, Sessa hadn't initiated any further texts to clarify the situation.

Better to let the girl forget all about her plan to see Pansie. Or, if she hadn't forgotten, at least not encourage it.

The bus drove away in a cloud of smoke and dust, leaving an empty parking lot. The sun still rode high on the western horizon, a sign of the long slide into summer.

Sessa released the breath she hadn't realized she'd been holding and shifted the car into drive. Even though the day was not yet over, one more day without the threat of introducing Skye to her daughter had passed.

Her phone rang, and Sessa snatched it up. Coco. She pressed the button to allow the call to come through the speakers on her car radio and then said hello.

"Just checking in," Coco said. "Guessing she wasn't on that bus, or you would've called me already."

"It was late, but yeah, you would have been the first one I called."

"Well, of course. So now that we've all dodged that bullet for another day, tell me about your doctor. Any news on that front?"

"My doctor?" Sessa slowed to a stop at the red light in front of the Blue Plate Lunchateria.

"Honey, he's been your doctor since the first day he answered that ad in the paper." She paused. "Well, actually he didn't answer that ad, did he? That was just what you two told folks. See, you were in collusion from the beginning. If that's not the start of a beautiful relationship, then I don't know what is."

Sessa spied a familiar truck at the Blue Plate. "Coco, I'll call you back."

She did a U-turn right in the middle of Main Street and slid her car into the spot next to Trey's. To her surprise, he was sitting in the cab of his truck holding his cell phone.

They both rolled down their windows.

"I was about to call you," he called through the portal. "But I figured you were waiting for the bus."

"How did you know?"

He glanced around at the crowded parking lot and then crooked a finger at her. "Get in and I'll tell you."

As she got out, she waved to Vonnette and Jim Bob as they drove past in Jim Bob's cab. When she had settled onto the seat beside him. Trey turned toward her.

"Your friend Coco told me."

Her eyes narrowed. "Told you what?"

He shook his head. "Don't get mad at her. She didn't mean to let it slip, but I saw her over at the hardware store, and we struck up a conversation."

"More like she struck up a conversation."

He laughed. "Come to think of it, yeah, that's true. Anyway, while we were talking, she mentioned that you'd probably be coming down the street pretty soon, since the last bus of the day was due in at six, and either way you'd be needing some company."

Sessa pursed her lips. Coco and her matchmaking...

But the truth was, she was worn slick. She did want to talk to someone.

"So," he said slowly, "do you need some company? Maybe dinner?"

She grinned as her stomach growled. "Sure."

"Then buckle up."

"Why not eat here?"

Trey shifted into reverse and pulled out of the parking space. "Because I've got a better idea." He passed at the edge of the parking lot. "Coco also told me that Pansie was spending the night with your mother. Is that true?"

"It is," she said warily. "I've got a mid-morning video meeting with my contact at the Smithsonian and Mama insisted I needed a break. I've been working on those Smithsonian horses day and night."

"Makes sense." He paused. "Okay, then. I've got a place I'd like to take you, but it's a little ways out of town. Hope that's all right."

"Sure," she said. "Why not?"

He set off in the opposite direction from Firefly Lane, and soon, the truck was pointed toward Houston. "If you want music, just press that button there."

She did, and the sound of George Strait singing about crossing his heart filled the truck cab. Sessa hummed along and then, as the song shifted to one about getting to Amarillo before the morning, she sang along.

"That's my favorite," he said when the song ended. "Reminds me of my rodeo days."

Sessa smiled. "I suspected you were a cowboy. Now let's see if I can guess what event you competed in." She looked him over as if assessing him. "Team roping?"

He shook his head.

"All right, then. Steer wrestling?"

"No." He changed lanes to pass a slow-moving log truck. "Guess again."

"You're too smart to be a bull rider." When he laughed, she paused. "Really? You rode bulls?"

"I did, although my best event was saddle bronc riding. I made the College National Finals. Oldest rider to place, at least at the time."

"How about that?" Something in his statement sparked the film vapor of a memory, just out of reach and slightly beyond recollection. "I took Ross to the College National Finals when he was five or six." That she did recall. "We had such a fun. He was such a sweet little boy."

Trey caught her gaze across the width of the cab. "I bet he was, Sessa."

They fell into a companionable silence as George sang about firemen, love without end, and falling to pieces together. Eventually, Sessa's curiosity got the better of her. "Where are you taking me?"

Though the shadows were gathering, she saw the doctor's grin. "Patience, Sessa Chambers. We're almost there. I will tell you it's owned by a friend of mine, and it's like nothing you'll ever see anywhere else."

She settled back against the seat and watched the miles pass. Deepest purple smeared over a pink and gold horizon, and the shadow of a pale moon could barely be seen. Finally, Trey put on his blinker and slowed the truck to turn onto what looked like a narrow farm-to-market road. With only the headlights to guide them, the truck glided along the pavement and then, after a few minutes, bumped onto a dirt road.

Here the shadows were thick, the road suspiciously narrow.

"I promise this will be worth the drive." He slowed to ease the truck over a rough patch of road.

She kept her silence for another few minutes, and then she spied what appeared to be the glow of lights through the thicket of trees. Trey silenced the radio and pressed the button to roll down the windows as he slowed the truck even more.

Instantly the night sounds filled the cab, sounds of crickets and lapping water. Along with the sounds came the rich scent of earth, the smell of rain on fresh green grass.

"Listen to that, Sessa," he said reverently. "That's better than listening to old George, and for me, that's saying something."

Trey made a sharp right turn, and suddenly they were in a dimly lit parking lot. At the far edge, just beyond the glare of the truck lights, a double-decker boat tied to a dock sparkled with strings of lights as it bobbed under the stars. Laughter and the sound of conversation floated toward them on the warm breeze.

"What is this place?"

"I told you it was like nothing you'd ever seen."

"Yes," she said slowly. "I do believe it is."

Trey pulled the truck into a parking spot between two vehicles that looked like they belonged at a country club instead of here in the middle of nowhere and then rolled up the windows. "Used to be a fishing camp. Until a buddy of mine lost a bet." He climbed out of the truck and jogged around to open the door for her. "Now it's a restaurant. Well sort of. It's more of a private club. Members only. Come on."

They wound their way through a parking lot filled with Porsches, Mercedes, and other expensive vehicles and then stepped onto a wooden sidewalk that led to the dock and a vessel of dubious construction.

"I thought you said it was a fishing camp."

He grasped her elbow and led her on. "It was, but then the camp floated away after Hurricane Ike. That's the bad news. The good news is someone's tugboat landed where the camp used to be. Bill—that's my buddy—figured he'd make the best of it, so he called a bunch of us to come out and make a bonfire of the thing so he could clear the land."

"What does that have to do with losing a bet and ending up with this?"

"Once we all got out here, Charlie Dorne—he studied engineering before he decided to become a surgeon—got the bright idea of floating the tug instead of burning it. Bill, he bet Charlie the tug would sink and figured firewood was the best way to go."

Sessa laughed. "I see."

Trey shared her laughter and then returned to his story. "There was much debate on this, as you can imagine. Charlie said give floating it a try, and if it didn't hold water, he'd pay to have the boat removed from the fish camp. If it floated, Bill Smith had to turn it into the most expensive restaurant in three counties."

"Why a restaurant?"

"Bill's cooking can't be beat. We always thought it was a real waste that he was operating instead of cooking. That's why we loved coming out to the fishing camp. It was the food, not the fish, that got us here."

"I see."

Trey nodded toward the bobbing vessel. "It floated just fine. The rest is history."

"What's it called?"

"Fish Camp, of course."

"Of course," she said dryly.

Trey led her across the gangplank that bridged the gap between land and vessel. "Hey." He waved to someone inside before glancing back down at Sessa. "Ready for an adventure?"

"Too late to ask that," she quipped. "It's been an adventure ever since you first walked up my driveway, Trey Brown."

More than just an adventure. If she were truthful, she had to admit she felt a connection with him that went deeper than mere friendship, and that scared her to death.

The idea occurred to her that she and Trey were on what felt very much like a first date. A good first date. And that scared her even more.

But she also liked it very much.

Again his smile dazzled her. "I feel the same, Sessa Chambers." He nudged her shoulder with his. "Oh, I probably should have warned you."

Sessa stopped short and peered up at him. "About what?"

"It's catfish night."

CHAPTER FOURTEEN

Oh, but she was beautiful. Those eyes looking up at him. That smile that said she was up for whatever fun the evening would bring.

"This is Texas. Lots of places have catfish nights, Trey. What's there to be warned about?"

He chuckled. "No spoilers. Surprise is half the fun."

She gave him a wary look. "I'm not sure I want to know what the other half is."

He pressed his hand to the small of her back and led her toward the open door. "That would be spending the evening with me."

He'd thought to bring Sessa Chambers to the Fish Camp as a distraction from his nerves as he faced Milo Rossi. Showing up alone would never convince Rossi that they'd met by coincidence. He owed the man an in-person thanks, and he was determined to deliver it.

He hadn't expected to be so caught up in Sessa that he could almost forget his reason for coming. She was so *vibrant.*

But Rossi was late. According to Charlie, Rossi still had the same table, and he always arrived right at seven. It was ten after, and there was no Rossi in sight as Trey guided Sessa through the maze of mismatched tables and chairs to a small two-seater in the corner. A cardboard square with *Brown* scribbled in Sharpie was propped against the saltshaker.

She gazed around, taking in the atmosphere, a small smile playing about her lips.

"There are no menus," she said when she caught him watching her.

"There are never menus on catfish night."

There were never menus, ever. Fish Camp didn't work that way. You ate what was put in front of you, and what was put in front of you was always amazing.

The waiter set a fisherman's tackle box in the middle of the table between them.

"What's this?" she asked.

"Miniature catfish pate eggrolls, or as the chef calls them, Bait a la Bill." He opened the tackle box with a flourish to reveal the first course. "Enjoy your appetizer. Oh, and save room for dessert. We've got catfish truffles tonight."

"You're kidding, right?"

"Not even close."

Sessa laughed and reached for an egg roll. "These look amazing." She popped one in her mouth.

And so do you, he wanted to say.

"Oh..." She savored a second eggroll. "Your friend is an incredible chef. Tell Bill I'm glad the boat floated."

"You can tell him yourself." He cast a glance at the empty table. Sure enough, Rossi's table was set for two and still empty at half past.

There was still hope his plan would succeed. Trey returned his attention to Sessa. Even if he couldn't talk to Rossi, he would still have spent the evening with Sessa Chambers.

And that was a whole other kind of success.

She dabbed at the corner of her mouth with a napkin. "What do you think they'll bring next?"

If the food he'd spied on the tables they'd passed was any indication, the next dish was some sort of catfish tacos served in a brown paper bag emblazoned with a picture of Fish Camp's infamous tugboat. At least they looked like tacos, though with Bill, who knew?

Trey opened his mouth to tell her that when a commotion outside the door stalled the words. He spied the waiter who'd served the egg rolls weaving his way through the tables in their direction.

"The boss needs you, sir. Says it's an emergency." He looked at Sessa, then back at Trey. "You'll need to come alone."

Emergency? It had to be medical if Bill was calling for him.

Adrenaline surged. His pulse thundered in his head.

"Go on," Sessa said. "I'll be fine."

Would he be? He smiled wanly. "I won't be long."

Trey rose to follow the waiter through the door. Bill met him just outside. Trey hadn't seen his friend since before the indictment, and his breath froze in his chest.

And then Bill took one look at him and wrapped him in his beefy arms. "You look good, Brown, but we're going to have to catch up later." He stepped back and clasped his hand on Trey's shoulder. "Come with me." He motioned toward the parking lot where there was some kind of commotion surrounding a limo on the far side. "I would've tried the Heimlich, but I don't know at his age... Besides I did pediatrics."

A wail rose from the back of the limo, and Trey broke into a sprint. He found a man face-down on the carpet between the seats and a woman leaning over him. "I told him those hard candies weren't good for him. We hit a bump, and he swallowed it whole, and now it's stuck!"

A younger man, presumably the driver, paced outside the door. "I didn't know! I drove as slow as I could even though they were fussing because traffic made us late. Oh man, oh man."

Pressing past the driver, Trey climbed in.

"Give him room," Bill called after him. "He's a doctor."

The woman scrambled to move out of the way, and allowed Trey to roll the man over. He froze.

"Mr. Rossi."

He looked at the woman. He hadn't recognized her in her hysteria. The woman who might have been his mother-in-law. Bill gestured for the driver to remove her from the limo.

"Brown." Trey jolted at the sound of Bill saying his name. He handed Trey a medical bag. "I gave up the license but kept the tools. Now save the patient."

Trey opened it to find a first aid kit that more resembled the doctor bag he used to carry when he was practicing general medicine. He did a quick assessment of Milo and determined his airway was blocked. Because of the older man's health, the Heimlich maneuver wasn't an option. There was only one way to dislodge the obstruction.

To cut.

He looked at Bill, hands suddenly shaking, his gut roiling. "What's the ETA on the ambulance?"

"Seven to nine minutes per security." He held the text up to show Trey. "Local guys coming first and Life Flight will meet them up by the highway."

Seven to nine minutes. An eternity when a man wasn't breathing.

Trey used an antiseptic wet wipe on his hands and reached for the scalpel. He nearly dropped it with his trembling hand. Deliberately returning the knife to its resting spot, he paused to lay his hands on Milo Rossi.

My hands can't do this, God, but Yours can.

His gut lurched. His hands shook.

But God said, *I can.*

Then He said, *I will.*

The old familiar adrenalin kicked in. His mind was set on his work, and his hands moved without a tremble. When the trach tube had been secured and the patient took a breath, Trey finally exhaled as well.

Only after the procedure was complete did he truly realize he'd done it. He'd operated. A basic procedure that a first year intern could do in his sleep, but an operation all the same.

"EMTs are here," Bill said as he clasped his hand on Trey's shoulder. "I had them lay off the siren and lights. No need to get the other diners upset."

Trey leaned against the wall and watched the EMTs load Milo on the stretcher and hook him up to the gear that would monitor him until he reached the hospital. His attention turned to Mrs. Rossi, who offered a trembling smile.

"I know you," she said. "You're the Brown boy. Victoria's doctor friend."

Not anymore.

He tried to match her smile but failed miserably as he climbed to his feet. "Yes, ma'am."

She pushed away the offer of assistance from the driver and moved toward him. "Thank you. You saved my husband."

"No, ma'am," he said. "Your husband saved me. Twice."

"Trey?"

He turned to follow the weak sound of his name and saw that

Vikki's father was extending a hand in his direction. Trey grasped that hand and found his grip still strong. Out of habit, he checked the older man's pulse. Also strong.

"You're going to be fine, sir."

"They've called in the chopper to get him to Turner Memorial," the EMT said. "He must be a VIP. Are you his doctor?"

"Not anymore," Trey said. "That would be Dr. Santini."

Milo Rossi shook his head. "You," came out on a rush of breath.

Trey gathered the older man's hand in his. "You'll be in good hands with Santini, sir." He paused. "And so will Vikki. And sir," he said slowly. "Meeting you here tonight was no coincidence. I hoped you'd be here, because I wanted to look you in the eye and thank you for what you did to get me out of jail. I didn't want to meet like this, though."

Rossi managed the beginnings of a smile and held tight to Trey's hand.

"Sir," the EMT said. "We need to get him loaded up."

"We'll let Dr. Santini know he's headed that way." The EMT paused to look over his shoulder. "That was some mighty fine work, Doc. You saved that man's life. You sure you don't want to ride in the chopper with him?"

Trey shook his head. "I'm sure."

A few minutes later, the medical helicopter took off with Milo Rossi on board. His wife drove off in the limo. Trey leaned back against the glass and watched. Bill, however, watched him.

"That was some nice cutting," he said. "Very nice cutting." Before Trey could protest, Bill continued. "Charlie told me. We've all been praying. Your hands were solid."

All Trey could do was let out a long breath. "Thank you."

"So if that's the only reason you're thinking of leaving medicine—"

"It's not."

He was surprised to find it was true. He'd thought everything would be settled once he could hold a scalpel again, but he didn't feel settled.

"Yeah, okay." Bill wrapped an arm around him. "You all right?"

"Not really," Trey admitted. "But I will be."

"Yeah," he said with a crooked grin. "I saw who you came in with. You're going to be just fine."

"She's just a friend."

"Whatever you say."

Rather than return directly to the table, he found his way to the men's room and stayed out of Sessa's line of sight. He stood over the sink and splashed cold water on his face, thankful he was alone.

Lifting his eyes to the mirror, he searched his face for signs that something was different. That he'd somehow become a doctor again. Instead, he found the same face that met him every morning.

The same man he always had been, and yet a new man altogether. A man whose hands were steady, not of his own will but of God's.

He reached for his phone and dialed Santini, half-expecting he would reach voice mail. Instead, the man answered. Trey could hear road noise in the background.

"Brown! I'm heading to Turner Memorial now. Sounds like tomorrow's surgery is off, but I'd rather make that decision after I've seen the patient. Are you in transit?" Santini asked.

"I'm not coming."

"I see." He paused. "You do understand what this means."

He knew quite well what the consequences would be, and he was fine with them. "Good-bye, Santini."

Trey squared his shoulders and walked away from the man in the mirror to join Sessa at the table. "You were gone a long time. I thought you'd left without me." She paused and seemed to be studying him. Thankfully, she didn't seem upset. "I'm kidding. Is everything all right?"

"Everything is perfect." He leaned across the table and kissed her on the cheek. Then he sat across from her. "Better than perfect."

"Trey," she said slowly, "what happened?"

He thought of several evasive responses and then decided to tell her the full story.

"...And so while I knew he would be here, I had no idea I would meet him that way. Or be called on to operate when I haven't been able to manage it since I left prison."

She looked pensive.

"What?" Then it hit him. "You think I used you as an excuse to be here so I could run into Mr. Rossi."

"You did," she said slowly.

He let out a long breath, his adrenaline slowly draining. "I almost came alone. But I wanted you with me. Not as a cover story but because I enjoy your company, Sessa. So yes, I had two purposes for being here tonight. I'm sorry I didn't tell you beforehand. Will you forgive me?"

Her expression softened. "Yes, but please be honest, Trey. That's important to me."

"And to me."

He ducked his head, and when he dared another look, she wore a wry smile. "You're forgiven for everything except one."

"What's that?" he said warily.

"Not warning me about catfish night."

"If I'd told you, you wouldn't have come."

"I might have."

He grinned at her, the last of the tension sliding off his shoulders. He nodded to the platter in the center of the table. "Pass the tacos, please. Oh, and prepare to meet Bill. Just keep one thing in mind."

"What's that?" She pressed her palm into the spot where he'd just kissed her.

"Don't believe a word he says about me." Trey upped his grin. "Unless it's a compliment. In that case, just assume he's understating the facts."

~*~

Trey pulled the truck to a stop next to her car in the parking lot of the diner. Sessa shifted to face him. "Thank you for an interesting evening."

His smile warmed places long cold. "You survived catfish night."

And a first date that was the opposite of a disaster.

"Happily," she said with a grin. "Bill's great. Now that I've met him, I can see why the restaurant is such a success. I'm still not so sure about his idea for artichoke night. I'm thinking I'll pass. Although I think he may be on to something with cookie night."

"I thought so, too," Trey said. "Until he started talking about shrimp gumbo cookies. I'm not sure I want to be the first to try those."

Sessa joined him in laughter and then grew silent. "Look, I may be wrong, but I feel like you've survived something more than catfish night." She reached across the seats to touch his sleeve.

His eyes were steady and filled with affection as he watched her. "Thanks for...being there. Supporting me."

"Hey, it earned me a kiss on the cheek."

Trey's expression went slack. "I did kiss you on the cheek, didn't I?"

She nodded. "Did you forget? I mean, I know I'm not the most memorable woman around, but hey..."

"You're wrong." His expression turned serious. "You are the most memorable woman I know. However..." He shook his head. "I kissed you. Right there in front of everyone." He ran his hand through his hair. "I guess I kind of got carried away. I wasn't thinking, and it just happened."

"Don't say it like you're sorry," she teased. "Let a girl have her pride."

"Oh." He swung his gaze to collide with hers. "I never said I was sorry. I only meant to say I'm sorry I didn't do it right."

"Okay, now I'm confused. What do you mean by that?"

"Sessa," he said softly. "You're not the kind of woman who deserves a quick kiss on the cheek over a plate of catfish tacos."

She wasn't? His words sent a thrill straight up her spine.

"Hey." She batted his arm playfully. "Do not besmirch the tacos. They were amazing."

"Yes, they were. But you..." He leaned toward her, and she smelled the subtle scent of soap and woodsy after shave. "You, Sessa Lee Chambers, are..."

Another few inches closer. Now she could almost feel him touching her, and her breath caught.

He cupped her cheek with his work-roughened palm. "Amazing," was a soft whisper against her ear.

Tap tap tap. "Sessa Lee Chambers, is that you parking in that truck with that boy? You keep that up, and your mama's going to find out."

Sessa jumped back, flustered. "Coco!"

She leaned against the seat and took a deep breath, then let it out slowly before pressing the button to lower the window. As the glass slid down, Coco's face came into focus. The grin she wore quickly turned to something between surprise and embarrassment as she must've registered Sessa's irritation.

"Oh," she said as her gaze flitted between Sessa and Trey. "I, um...oh."

Her bejeweled fingers went to her lips where she hid what was unmistakably a smile. "Well, I didn't expect you two really *were*—"

She shook her head and moved out of Trey's line of sight, then waved in front of her face as if she were in dire need of a cool breeze. "So I'm just going to get on out of here and leave you two to whatever you were doing...oh!" She ducked so Trey could see her again. "Hey, Doctor Brown. You still working on my friend's barn?"

"Yes ma'am," he said. "I've got to get that barn ready for the Arabians."

"I'm leasing the space to him for his horses," Sessa hurried to add. "And the pasture too."

"Well," she said just a little too sweetly. "I guess that means you two will be seeing a lot of each other."

Trey leaned forward, speaking directly to Coco. "That's my intention. I'd like to see a lot more of Sessa."

Oh.

Sessa's heart pounded. He wanted *more*. More than a first date.

And she wanted it too. Wanted to know him more. Wanted that connection, deeper than friendship from the very beginning. Wanted someone to stand beside her.

And she wanted it to be him.

Coco seemed to see the realization dawn on Sessa, because one of her perfectly plucked brows rose. "Well, good for you," she said to the doctor. "But I'm going to warn you that if you intend on seeing more of Sessa, then you're probably going to be seeing a lot more of Sugar Pine." She paused, her eyes narrowing. "We love Sessa, and we don't cotton to anyone who mistreats her."

"All right," Sessa said, mortified. "Good-bye, Coco." She pressed the button to raise the window. "Well, that was embarrassing."

She dared a sideways glance at Trey and found him looking straight ahead. His shoulders began to shake, and a moment later he began to laugh.

"Trey?"

He faced her. "I'm sorry, Sessa." He swiped at his eyes. "It's been a very long time since I got busted for parking with a girl."

"Well, guess what, buddy? This is a first for me. More than halfway to fifty, and someone is finally going to tattle to my mother that I was parking."

This made him laugh again, and she joined him. Finally she reached for her purse. "It's been fun...memorable, actually, but I really should go."

Trey got out and trotted around the front of the truck to open her door and help her climb down. Instead of backing up to let her pass, he remained standing between her and her empty car.

Moonlight slanted across his face, taking years off his age and causing her heart to do a flip-flop.

"You know," he said slowly, "I was just thinking. Your friend Coco, she's not going to keep her mouth shut about catching us doing what looked a lot like kissing."

"But wasn't," she amended.

"But wasn't." He leaned toward her. "So, since the whole town is going to think I kissed you right here in the parking lot of the Blue Plate Lunchateria..."

"Yes?"

"I might as well..." He was close now. Very close. Sessa's breath caught as her hands clamped in his shirt at his waist.

"Yes?"

He didn't finish the sentence. Instead, he wrapped his arm around her back and gently drew her to him.

And then he kissed her.

It had been a long time since she'd kissed a man, but Sessa was pretty sure kissing had never been like this before. After eons, or moments, Trey stepped back to hold her at arm's length.

She leaned against the truck—held on tight lest she topple— and did the one thing she could do. Smile.

"I meant it when I told your friend that I want to see more of you." He leaned against the door frame and rested his hand on her shoulder. "Are you scared of all this?"

Yes. "No," she managed.

His lips turned up in the beginnings of a grin. "Well that makes one of us. I'm scared to death."

She leaned forward and rested her cheek on his shoulder then wrapped her arms around him. Contentment filled her. "Good night," she told him. "I had a great time."

"Let me follow you home. Just to make sure you get inside all right and nothing happens."

Sessa shook her head and ducked under his arm to attempt her retreat. "This is Sugar Pine, Texas. Nothing ever happens here, so don't worry. I'll get home just fine."

"I care that you're safe, Sessa, so would you at least call me when you're home?"

"I will." She pondered the idea of actually having someone in her life who cared that she was safe. Someone besides Mama or her friends, that was.

Trey followed her around the front of the truck and waited while she climbed into her car. She rolled down the window. "Trey, I've got a confession to make."

He leaned down to rest his elbows on the car door. "What's that?"

"I'm terrified, too."

Trey once again cradled her cheek with his palm, although he made no move to kiss her. Probably just as well, since the eyes of Sugar Pine were on them out here in the open.

"Then we'll be terrified together. I've got meetings tomorrow and plans for Saturday, but I want to see you as soon as I can."

"Oh?" Somehow she was right back to junior high. Right back to those days when the mere attention of a cute boy would cause her to be a tongue-tied and blushing mess.

He lifted his hand to press a tendril of hair behind her ear. "How about you and me and Pansie have a cookout on Sunday afternoon?"

She smiled. "Yes, I would like that."

"So would I." He warmed to the topic. "I saw you've got a decent grill out there in the shed. I'll bring what I need to get it working again."

"Daddy would like that," she said. "What do you want me to cook?"

"Oh, Sessa." He caressed her name. "I am going to do the cooking, so don't you worry about anything." He shrugged. "Unless you want to make a pie. I understand you're in that book club where everyone makes pies, so you've probably got a favorite recipe, don't you?"

"Pie," came out as an embarrassing squeak. "Sure. Yes. Pie."

Shut up, Sessa. You're embarrassing yourself.

"All right." He leaned in and gave her a kiss on the cheek that matched the one he had given her at the Fish Camp. "Good night, Sessa Lee Chambers."

She thought about his kisses all the way home to Firefly Lane. In between ignoring texts from Coco. However, when the headlights reflected a person sitting on her front porch, all other thoughts fled. She would know that auburn hair and upturned nose anywhere.

Skye.

CHAPTER FIFTEEN

Sessa gathered up her purse and stepped out of the car, moving deliberately toward Skye. Though her heart beat a furious rhythm, she refused to show it.

"Skye," she said when she reached the porch. "I didn't expect you'd be here." Not once the bus had departed that afternoon. How long had the girl sat out here?

Pansie's mother looked older by more than just the two years that had passed since Sessa last saw her. Her hair was still long, still swept up in that style the kids called a messy bun, but while it had been a garish color before, she looked much more natural chestnut brown now.

Even in the moonlight she could see that Pansie's mother bore a healthy glow that she hadn't had when she left Sugar Pine. Still thin, at least the girl appeared to be eating better. Or perhaps just more regularly.

"I know I asked you to pick me up at the bus station, but I caught a ride from Houston, so I didn't ride the bus. At least not that last part of the trip."

She rose and nodded to a green military-issue backpack. The sides and front had been decorated with what appeared to be multi-colored paint pens, and several key chains of differing types were affixed to every zipper.

"I hope you don't mind, but I don't really have anywhere to crash tonight."

"Where did you crash the last time you were here?" she snapped before thinking better of it. Her emotions were so close to the surface that her politeness filter was malfunctioning. "Never mind." She brushed past Skye to open the door. "Come on in."

Skye followed her inside timidly, her big brown eyes darting around the room until they came to rest again on Sessa. Looking for Pansie? Her pulse pounded in her ears.

"Pansie's not here tonight," she said.

"Oh." Skye shrugged. "I hoped she would be."

"She's with..." Sessa paused. No, she wouldn't tell this stranger where to find Pansie. Selfish or not. "So, are you hungry?"

"I could eat." Skye remained by the door clutching her backpack. "But really, don't worry. I've got some Twinkies in my bag, and some beef jerky too. Protein is important."

"Yes, it is." Sessa nodded toward the kitchen. "Just leave your bag right there and come with me. I think I've still got enough ham to make a sandwich. There might be pie left, too."

Skye followed to sit at the table in the spot Sessa indicated. She watched the girl while she made the sandwich.

What did she want? Sessa's mind whirled. There was only one good answer. Pansie.

But the girl that Sessa saw—only nineteen or twenty— appeared ethereal, as if she might be an apparition. As if she might disappear if Sessa blinked long enough.

It took Sessa, Mama, and a whole legion of friends to give Pansie the care she needed. What did Skye think she could do for Pansie if she took her away?

Sessa shut down that thought before she could get a good upset boiling. She didn't know for sure that Skye wanted to take Pansie.

She needed to handle this whole situation carefully.

"Sweet tea?" She set the plate in front of Skye.

"Sure. If it's not too much trouble."

Sessa poured two glasses and brought them to the table, then sat across from Skye.

The girl bit into the sandwich as if she hadn't had a decent meal in far too long.

"What brings you to Sugar Pine?"

Skye paused to take a sip of sweet tea and then met Sessa's gaze. "My daughter, of course."

To visit her or take her? she wanted to say. "About that," Sessa said instead. "This is the only home Pansie has ever known. I can't imagine it would be good for her to be removed from what's familiar." She paused, allowing the words to come. "So I thought maybe you and I could arrange some sort of formal agreement. Something legal and binding. For Pansie's peace of mind, of course."

"Mrs. Chambers." Skye set her tea glass down. "I know I've got a lot to learn. But I seriously doubt a two-year-old is worried about peace of mind. Maybe you're the one concerned about that. Am I wrong?"

"No," she said slowly. "You aren't."

Skye nodded. "Look, I love that you love my Pansie-girl. You've taken good care of her. Much better than I could have. But I'm her mama."

The statement swept through Sessa with the power of a cyclone, shaking her down to her foundations, but Skye seemed not to notice. She stuffed her mouth, humming with appreciation.

Then she looked up again. "A child needs her mama, don't you think?"

Sessa struggled for words, struggled to breathe. There was a part of her that couldn't deny Skye's simple statement. But...

"I think that depends on the mama," Sessa said.

Skye's plate clanked as her hand knocked against the table. There was no mistaking the hurt in her eyes or the tremble of her lips. And that didn't make Sessa feel quite right either.

"And the child," she added. "Pansie is a very strong-willed little girl. She likes her routines. Change isn't easy for her."

Skye shrugged, now looking back down at the plate.

The girl yawned, and Sessa's maternal instincts kicked in. Along with her desire to end this conversation. What passed for healthy in the moonlight now looked more like exhaustion. "Where have you been all these years, Skye?"

"Around," she said. "You know, getting my head straight and stuff."

What exactly did that mean? "So is it straight now? Your head, I mean."

"Sure."

"So you've got a plan? You know where you're going and how you'll take care of Pansie?"

"Well, kind of." Another yawn. "See, I know she's got to love the same things I do, so I thought maybe the beach."

"So you'd go live in Galveston?"

Not too far. This is doable. She kept her attention on Skye even as she thought of what was good. What was right. What was best for that precious little girl.

She shook her head. "I was thinking Florida. Maybe back to California."

Not with my Pansie, she longed to scream. "Well, not tonight," she said instead. "It's getting late. Why don't I get you settled in the guest room, and we can talk more about this tomorrow?" She paused. "After Pansie gets home."

Skye rose. "Good idea. I could use some sleep in a real bed. That bus isn't the best for sleeping. Too loud and bumpy."

Sessa showed her into the guest room and then closed the door behind her. Resting her head on the door, she lifted the only prayer she could manage at the moment: *Lord, help Pansie and me. But help Skye, too.*

Sleep proved impossible, so Sessa slipped out the back door. Her nervous energy could be applied to getting some work done in the workshop. She would have to run the ad for help again, too. This time she'd branch out and look for help in other cities, Houston maybe. Surely somewhere there was a decent woodworker looking for a new job.

Though the evening had been warm, the night air felt less so, and the stars twinkled beneath a slender fingernail of crescent moon that called her to sit beneath it. Bypassing the workshop, she followed the path around the side of the building to where a pair of rockers used to sit beneath the pecan tree when Daddy was alive. The winter after he died, she'd put the rockers in the shed and never brought them out again.

Life wasn't the same. It never would be. And yet avoiding the issues—her lingering grief—hadn't solved anything with Ross. And avoiding Skye wasn't going to make her go away.

She'd spent so long avoiding, she didn't know if she had the guts to start facing things again. But maybe it was time to try.

Sessa found the flashlight just inside the garage door and used it to follow the path out to the shed. A few minutes and two trips later, she had the pair of rocking chairs back where they belonged. She sat down.

Leaning back against wood that could use a coat of fresh paint, Sessa closed her eyes and inhaled the earthy night air until she felt her taut nerves begin to relax. The structure was dark and quiet now, but she couldn't wait for Trey's Arabians to take up residence in her barn.

Trey.

Her eyes flew open at the reminder of the doctor. Of the kiss. She'd forgotten to call him, but she'd have to make it up to him tomorrow.

A flicker of light over near the edge of the house caught her attention. And then another. And another.

Fireflies. Sessa smiled.

Lightning in a jar.

As if drawn by those same flickers of light, Skye stepped out of the back door with something in her hand. Ross's jar.

Her white nightgown whipped around pale coltish legs as a warm breeze kicked up. She picked her way down the path barefoot, her hair hanging down below her shoulders in soft chestnut waves.

If she were not the mother of Sessa's granddaughter, she might have thought Skye to be a sleepwalker. Or a teenager slipping away from her parents for a night of fun.

She spied Sessa and waved. Sessa returned the wave, albeit weakly. The last thing she needed was to have her peace shattered by this girl.

Whatever is true, whatever is noble...

For the first time, it occurred to Sessa that it might not just be *her* peace that had been shattered. Perhaps Skye's had been as well.

She patted the rocker next to her. "Come and sit with me," she said, not because she wanted to share this time with Skye, but because she had a deep sense of knowing—a feeling beyond logical understanding—that Skye was supposed to spend this time with her.

The girl sat down and tucked a tendril of hair behind her ear revealing her profile. A profile Pansie shared. *Oh.* How could a child look so much like one parent and yet from another angle look exactly like the other?

The object of her thoughts turned toward Sessa, her arms cradling the jar. "I saw the fireflies from the window, and I remembered how Ross used to tell me that he had this jar on the shelf in his room to catch them in. He called it—"

"Lightning in a jar," Sessa supplied.

"Yes, that's it." She looked down at the jar. "That was a good memory for him. He loved that about you, that you would help him catch those fireflies."

"Oh, that's not completely true." Her soft chuckle rumbled across the field. "Ross did all the catching. I just cheered him on."

Skye grinned. "That makes sense. I couldn't imagine him letting someone else do anything for him."

The statement gave her pause. "You know my son well." She shook her head. "You *knew* him well." It was still hard to fathom she would never see him again.

Skye's fingers, with their neon chipped nail polish, traced the top of the jar. "It's still hard to believe he's gone, isn't it?"

"Very," Sessa said. "Sometimes I think I should call him, or that he should call me. And then I remember."

"I see the scar," she said softly. "Every day I see it, and then I remember."

Sessa reached over to touch Skye's arm. "What scar, sweetheart?"

She set the jar on the ground beside her, swiveled in her chair to face Sessa, and then unceremoniously unbuttoned her nightgown to show her stomach. "There." She pointed to a thin sliver of a scar extending downward from just below her navel.

"You had a c-section."

Skye nodded. "They told me when I woke up that the doctor had to do it this way because it was an emergency, and he had to think of saving a life and not whether I could still wear my bikinis."

"I'm sure you're thankful that the doctor was able to save Pansie's life."

She looked at Sessa with eyes that matched her daughter's. "No, Mrs. C. Not Pansie's. Mine."

Oh.

"The doctor told me I shouldn't try and have her, because I might not live to see her born. I told that doctor what to do with his advice." She gave Sessa a sideways look. "Can you imagine the world without my Pansie-girl in it?"

"No," she said softly.

"Me, either."

Sessa waited to see if Skye would offer more, but she did not. Instead, the girl buttoned her nightgown and retrieved the jar. Without a word or a backward glance, Skye made her way to where the fireflies were still dancing among the shrubs.

Her first attempt at catching the flickering creatures was pitiful. "Honey, you need a net," she called. "Just wait there, and I'll get you one."

She rose and took the flashlight, then went around the house and into the garage to climb the ladder into the storage space over the rafters. There, next to Ross's fishing poles and tackle, was his net. She grabbed it and returned to the yard.

"All right." She handed the net over to Skye. "Now try."

Skye proved to be a quick study. Before long, she was easily catching the bugs and depositing them into Ross's old jar. Sessa made her way back to her rocking chair, where she offered encouragement as the girl laughed and swiped at the dancing critters with the net.

Finally Skye tired of the project and set the net aside. As she walked back toward the rockers, Ross's jar glowed golden in the moonlight and illuminated her far off smile.

She settled back on the rocker. In that moment, she was a child, not Pansie's mother. A barely-grown young woman with her whole life ahead of her.

Or at least that's what Sessa saw.

But looks were so very deceiving.

For this young woman had already given birth. Had chosen to save her daughter's life at the risk of losing her own. Had given her baby to someone who could offer what she could not.

Had sacrificed.

"We were going to do that together someday, Ross and me," she said softly. "He was going to teach Pansie how to catch lightning in a jar. It was important to him that she know."

She shouldn't be surprised that her son had known he would be father and did not share that news with her. Somehow, however, she was. "And she will," Sessa said. "When she's older."

That seemed to satisfy Skye, for a moment later she stood. "There's something else I have to do. But I want you to do it with

155

me."

"All right." Sessa rose, their quiet conversation steadying her somehow. She felt a camaraderie with Skye that she hadn't earlier. "What's that?"

"Come with me."

Skye turned away from the house to walk toward the barn. When she reached the fence at the paddock, she handed the jar to Sessa and then hitched up her nightgown, climbed over, and retrieved the jar.

The girl walked to the barn door and stood in the glow of the security light. "What are you doing?" Sessa called, but Skye ignored her to disappear inside. A moment later, the light went off and the paddock was plunged into darkness.

"Skye?"

She returned to the paddock, though all Sessa could see was the glowing jar and a glimpse of night gown and pale arms and legs. Then Skye began to turn in slow circles. With each turn, the jar appeared, then disappeared. And Sessa realized Skye was singing.

"Twinkle, twinkle little star. How I wonder where you are. Up above the sky..."

The twirling stopped. Then, in a rush of airborne gold, the fireflies flew from the jar.

"Good-bye, Ross Chambers." Skye's whisper barely carried to Sessa's ears. "I loved you."

How long they stood there—Sessa leaning against the fence and Skye standing with the empty jar in her arms—it was hard to say. Time seemed to slow to a stop, and even the stars overhead ceased to exist. There was nothing but one woman, one girl, and an empty jar.

And a fragile peace that Sessa hadn't felt in over two years.

Finally Skye found her way back to Sessa and handed her the jar. They returned to the chairs again, but Skye seemed uninterested in sitting. Instead, she watched the fireflies and held both palms against her belly.

"Sweetheart," Sessa said. "Don't you have people you need to contact? Family?" At the shake of Skye's head, she continued. "Surely there's someone. A parent? A grandparent?"

Again she shook her head.

"But there has to be someone," Sessa gently insisted.

Their eyes met across the distance between them, a distance that had more to do with life than space. "Just you," she said. "And Pansie."

"Oh." Before tonight, this admission might have felt like a burden to Sessa. But now it felt like a gift.

She shrugged and turned her attention to the stars dotting the wide Texas sky. "It's okay. I mean, I've decided it is."

"But surely there is someone who—"

"No," she said. "There isn't."

"Okay." Sessa paused to let the sound of the night birds fall between them. "What's your last name, Skye?"

"Chambers. Or at least that's what I tell people. But are you asking what it was before I met Ross?"

"Yes."

She began to worry with a button on her nightgown as a lock of dark hair fell forward, obscuring her face. "I don't know. Not really. I mean I was given a name but..."

Silence. Then a shuddering sob. Enough of this line of questioning, Sessa decided. The topic could be revisited another time.

"Skye," she said softly, resisting the urge to gather the woman-child into her arms. "Do you know about Jesus?"

She nodded. "He and I are friends. I wish I'd met Him sooner though, instead of when I was in that place waiting to have Pansie." She paused. "They were nice there. It was a home for girls like me. It was where I belonged then."

"Where do you belong now?"

Enough time passed that Sessa figured she wouldn't get an answer. Then Skye turned to face her. "That's what I need to figure out. For Pansie and for Ross."

"Honey." Sessa wrapped the girl in an embrace. "Figure it out for you. Everything else will fall in line once you do that."

"For someday."

"What do you mean?"

She smiled. "You can't figure something out on your own time, right? I mean, it would be great if there were instant answers. But there usually aren't. Sometimes, yeah. But mostly you have to live for the somedays."

157

"Live for the somedays." She gave Skye a squeeze. Such wisdom from one so young. "I like that. And I think I'm going to try and figure out how to live for the somedays, too."

Skye nodded against Sessa's shoulder and then pulled away. "Thank you," she said. "For everything. But mostly for loving Ross. And loving Pansie."

She turned toward the house and disappeared inside before Sessa realized that once again, the girl's concern had been for others and not herself. For the ones she loved.

Indeed, she might learn a thing or two from this young woman.

This time when she tried to sleep, Sessa found she had no trouble. It seemed as if she blinked, and she was dreaming about fireflies. The next moment the sun was shining through the curtains. She rose and gathered her robe around her.

Pancakes would be good. Bacon, too.

Skye needed to put some weight on. Needed a healthy breakfast. Then together they would go and get Pansie. How she would explain who this woman-child was to the two-year-old was a thought for later. For now, she would see that Skye knew there was someone else who cared about her, too.

She padded down the hall to find Skye's door still shut. She knocked and when Skye didn't answer, decided to start breakfast. Perhaps the smell of bacon cooking would awaken her. It always worked with Ross.

However, once the bacon was made and the pancakes were cooked and warming in the oven, there still was no sign of Skye. Worried, Sessa grabbed a slice of bacon and chewed on it as she headed back down the hall.

"Wake up, honey." She tapped the door twice and then opened it slowly. "Come have some breakfast and then we will go and fetch..."

The bed was made and all traces of Skye were gone. Even her backpack was nowhere to be seen.

Sessa scrambled out the door and down the hall. No sign of her in the paddock or barn. She snatched up the flashlight and net from the spot where they'd been left overnight and deposited them in the garage, then went back inside, leaving the jar beside the rockers.

Where could she have gone?

Sessa went back down the hall to get dressed. If Skye'd gone into town, she might have deduced that Pansie was with Mama. The idea that her mother might have a stranger on her doorstep looking for Pansie caused Sessa to find her phone and dial Mama's number.

"You're up early," her mother said.

"Not so early," Sessa countered as calmly as she could manage. "How's our Pansie-girl?"

The use of Skye's pet name for the child wasn't deliberate, but it made her all the more worried about where the girl had gone.

"She's being a sleepyhead this morning. I haven't heard a peep out of her."

Oh no.

"Mama," Sessa managed, "please go in and check on her."

"Oh, I don't think that's necessary. She's just—"

"Please," she snapped. She forced herself to sound reasonable. "It's necessary."

"All right."

Sessa gripped the phone and forced herself to breathe. Skye couldn't have taken her. She wouldn't have.

And yet she had every right to.

"Oh, look at you, you sweet little princess. Are you playing with your toys and being quiet?"

At the sweet sound of Pansie's reply, Sessa sank to the floor and allowed the tears to fall. *Thank You, Jesus.*

"Are you satisfied? She's fine."

"Yes," she said. "Thank you."

"Sessa, what's going on?"

She closed her eyes and swiped at her damp cheeks with the sleeve of her robe. "Nothing. I just had this awful feeling that..." That what? She'd not cause worry when it didn't need to be. "Never mind. I'll be over to get her soon as I can."

"Don't hurry, sweetheart. Vonnette wanted me to bring her out to play with her grandson. He's not in town much, and you know how Pansie likes to play with Seth."

"Yes, all right. Just let me know when you're done, and I'll come get her."

"I'll bring her home. You go on and get some work done

while you've got the free time." Mama paused. "Unless you've got plans to go out again with that cowboy."

So she'd heard. Irritation swelled, but there was also a part of Sessa that secretly thrilled that she had something *good* in her life to be gossiped about.

"Don't bother to try and explain why you didn't tell me you were having a fling with that man. I know how you hate to admit it when your mama is right."

A fling? "Really, Mama, it's not what you think."

"It is exactly what I think," she said. "Sugar Pine is a small town, Sessa Lee Chambers, and if you don't want your business being discussed, then do not conduct your business—or in this case, your kissing—in a public place like the parking lot of the Blue Plate."

"Bye, Mama."

"We will talk about this later," was Mama's parting shot before she hung up.

Sessa sent several texts to Skye that went unanswered, then tossed her phone on the bed and went back into the room where Skye had slept to see if she'd left any clue. Finding nothing, Sessa dressed and retrieved her phone to stick it in her back pocket.

Pansie had been down to her last pair of clean shorts when Sessa packed her up for the trip to Mama's. She needed to throw a load of Pansie's clothes into the washer before she logged on for the meeting with the Smithsonian curator. Two steps into the little girl's room, she spied the folded note on Pansie's pillow.

For Mama's Pansie-girl.

As with the note that had been tucked into Pansie's diaper bag, the "I" in the girl's name had a heart drawn over it. Just beneath the words was a child-like drawing of a jar with tiny yellow lightning bugs escaping.

Below the jar was something more: *For someday.*

Sessa thought to open the note, then decided against it.

No doubt Skye would be back someday. Maybe sooner than Sessa was ready for. But her interactions with the young woman over the last twenty-four hours had settled something inside Sessa.

Skye was so much more than she'd expected.

With a soft sigh, she reached up to slip the piece of paper under the old red cowboy hat. It wasn't someday yet.

CHAPTER SIXTEEN

The first week of June in Texas meant heat coming up in waves off the concrete and blowing in warm blasts across the field. Today, however, the late afternoon clouds hung low and looked as if they were about to spit rain.

If Trey thought they'd be grilling, he probably ought to think again.

The sound of a car door jolted Sessa from her job sweeping off the back porch. When Trey ambled around the corner with a bag of charcoal slung over one shoulder, she hurried out to meet him.

"Hey beautiful." Trey wrapped his free arm around her and then paused to give her a hug.

"Hey yourself." She hugged him back. "Can I help?"

He shook his head. "I've got this under control. You just go do what you usually do on Sunday afternoon."

"That could be anything from nap to read a book to clean house." She shrugged. "I'd rather see what you're up to out here."

"Suit yourself. But don't blame me if I put you to work."

The next thing she knew, Trey had her handing him the things he needed for scrubbing the grill and then sent her inside to chop onions for the meal that he refused to disclose. Of course, she had to go and check her makeup after completing her task, such was the strength of the onions he chose.

"Gwammy's been crying," Pansie said when Sessa went in to fetch her after her nap.

Sessa hugged her close. Although she felt slightly more settled after Skye's brief appearance in their lives, today she couldn't resist holding her granddaughter for just a moment too long.

"Not crying, sweetheart," she said. "Grammy's been helping Dr. Brown make dinner. Would you like to help, too?"

She ran to the kitchen as fast as her chubby legs could carry her and headed straight for the lower cabinet where Pansie's own cooking tools were kept. She found her favorite wooden spoon and a child-sized pot. "Okay, Gwammy. Let's cook."

Sessa ushered Pansie out onto the porch where she could see the clouds were gathering tighter, closer, darker. "Let's go see what Dr. Brown is doing."

She hurried into the back yard with Pansie beating a rhythm with her spoon and pot. By the time they reached the shed, their arrival had been well announced.

Trey's smile gleamed, but the rest of him was covered in soot. "Who do we have here?"

"You need a bath, mister," Pansie said.

"Yes, I do. But maybe I'll just dance around in the rain until the dirt falls off."

Pansie gave Sessa a *can-he-do-that* look.

"And why don't you call me Uncle Trey?"

"We came to help," Sessa said. "Put us to work."

"I'm glad you're here. What do you think of putting the grill over there under the covered porch? I think we're far enough from the house to cook safely." When Sessa nodded, he maneuvered the now-gleaming grill into place.

"Now what?" Sessa said.

"Well, I guess if you've got the pie ready, then there's really nothing else to do but sit there and look pretty while I work."

She laughed at his joke and tried not to let her horror show. In all the drama with Skye and then her call with the Smithsonian, she had forgotten the pie.

Now what? She could tell him the truth, but... she wanted to impress him.

"Pansie, sweetheart. Why don't you come inside with Grammy while I check on the pie?"

"Gwammy, you don't make pie."

She picked up Pansie, heat rising in her cheeks, and then turned her attention to Trey. "Silly girl. She's always teasing. Come on, Pansie."

Hurrying inside, Sessa set her granddaughter down and

hurried to the kitchen to see if she had anything she could defrost that might be passed off as homemade. Failing that, she picked up the phone and called Coco.

"Is Skye back?" was the first thing Coco said.

"What? No. I haven't heard anything from her. Actually, it's about Trey."

"Well of course it is. Before you tell me whatever it is you called to tell me, you could start by telling me what that man's intentions are."

"His intentions?" Sessa echoed. "Right now his intention is to grill something—who knows what—and then have pie that I baked."

Coco laughed. "But you don't bake pie, honey."

"I know! But he thinks I do, and I forgot to tell him I don't." She paused. "Okay, it's not that I forgot. I just, well, I let him think I can bake pies, okay. I figured I'd have time to either learn or buy one from the diner, but then when the thing happened with Skye—"

"Still no word?"

Coco was the only person she'd told about her overnight visitor. And even then, she'd kept the entirety of the tale to herself, only mentioning how they had a nice visit and then she woke up to find Pansie's mama gone.

"Right," Sessa said. "Not a word."

"Well, we can thank the Lord for that, I suppose." She paused. "Now about this pie. What are you going to do?"

"I think it's a little late to admit I can't bake pies, don't you?"

"No, honey. I think now's the perfect time to admit it."

"But he's going to a lot of trouble to make dinner for Pansie and me. What do I serve for dessert?"

"You got Blue Bell?"

Sessa went into the pantry and opened the freezer. "Several cartons. Why?"

"There's your solution," Coco said. "Just toss a couple of them into a container and throw them into the freezer. Your fellow won't know the difference between Blue Bell and homemade."

"I cannot pass off Blue Bell Ice Cream as my own. This is Texas. It's just not done."

Coco laughed. "And yet you were planning on passing off

someone else's pie as yours? Really, Sessa. You need to get your priorities straight."

She turned to lean against the cabinet. "Oh, Coco, I am hopeless."

"No, you're not." She paused. "You're infatuated."

Coco went on, but Sessa's ears must've stopped working, because all she could hear was the echo of Coco's word. *Infatuated.*

Was she?

Who wouldn't be? Trey was handsome and kind, but beneath the surface, he was so much more. He understood her conflicting feelings about Skye. They both grieved Ross.

Before, the realization of the depth of her feelings might've scared her, but with him here, feeling the same depth of emotion, somehow she felt...hope. Anticipation to see where this thing could take them.

Coco was still talking in her ear. "...here's what we're going to do. Carly is always making those fancy pies. I'm going to call her and see if she's started her baking for book club next week."

"She's always on top of it when it's at her house."

"If she's got something made and in the freezer, I'll see if I can't convince her to let you have it." Again she paused. "You know I'll have to tell her why."

"Gwammy," Pansie called. "I want a juice box."

"After what Trey did for her and Jared, I don't think she'll mind feeding him."

"Probably not," Coco agreed, "although she won't be getting the credit, will she?"

Sessa put the phone on speaker as she reached into the fridge for a juice box for Pansie. "I should tell him."

"Only if he asks. Now get on out there and make nice while I do my magic. I'll stop by and leave the pie in the mailbox then I'll text you and let you know it's there."

"You're a genius. I owe you, big time."

Sessa put on her most innocent face and went back outside, once again with Pansie trailing a step behind. "Okay, all set for dessert. What can I do out here?"

"First you can tell me what kind of pie we're having." He paused to smile. "I do like homemade pie."

"Well," she said slowly, as she wrestled her conscience.

"We're having box pie," Pansie said with a grin.

Trey knelt down to be eye level with the little girl. "And how do you know that?"

"Auntie Coco does magic and leaves pies in the box." Pansie tugged at her hand. "She said so, didn't she, Gwammy?"

~*~

There had to be some truth in the little girl's statement or Sessa wouldn't look so red-faced. However, Trey had learned a long time ago not to ponder too hard on anything a woman said, whether she was 3 or 30.

Besides, Sessa's embarrassment was adorable. And she managed to look gorgeous even with that flush of crimson coloring her cheeks.

Instead of asking, he put both females to work, and just about the time the rain started in earnest, it was time to eat. They gathered mismatched chairs around a battered farm table under the porch's tin roof and spread out their feast. The softly falling rain creating its own symphony against the roof.

The steaks were a hit with Sessa, but little Pansie was more interested in trying to eat the corn on the cob. She wore more of the butter and corn than she consumed, but it was great fun watching her make the attempt.

Finally he pushed back from the table and surveyed the damage. While he'd managed to finish off two rib-eyes, Sessa had taken the smallest one and shared it with Pansie. Now the little girl was happily drawing on a piece of blue construction paper and Sessa looked plain nervous.

"I've been so busy talking about the Smithsonian horses that I haven't even asked about you, Trey." She paused and seemed to be assessing him. "Is there an update on your job at the hospital?"

"I'm going to turn it down." There was much more to it than that, but ultimately the end result was he would walk away from his career in Houston without caring to look back. And he'd never felt better about a decision.

"Oh?"

He could tell she didn't know what to say, so he decided to help her. "I'm going into private practice. At this point in my life,

I would rather be spending my time helping people on a more personal basis. When I did surgery, I rarely got to know my patients."

"So you're thinking of slowing down?"

He shrugged. "As slow as a doctor's pace can be, but yes. I would like that very much."

They shared a smile.

"Well," he said slowly, "I guess it's time for pie."

"Pie." Her eyes went wide then, quick as that, she shed her expression and put on a smile. "Yes, let me just go get that pie."

"Out of the box," Pansie said. "From Coco."

Trey watched the exchange between his two hostesses with amusement. Something was going on here, and it appeared Pansie knew more than Sessa wanted her to.

Sessa allowed her gaze to linger on the little girl and then shook her head. "Would you mind keeping an eye on her, Trey?"

He nodded. "Absolutely. I'm just going to let her tell me some stories while you're getting that pie."

Sessa stepped away, moving toward the back door, though he didn't miss the look she sent over her shoulder or the lip she held between her teeth.

"Say, Pansie." He leaned down toward the tot. "Can you tell Uncle Trey about how you and Grammy made pie today?"

He could tell she wasn't going to answer. The set of her jaw and the way her attention was clearly on her work told Trey he could say anything but the little girl would hear none of it.

"I bet you like making pie, don't you?"

Still nothing from Pansie, but out of the corner of his eye, he watched Sessa linger in the doorway. She might be surveying some dust on the doorframe, but he knew good and well that she was feeling guilty about something and hoping that little girl didn't tell on her.

Finally, Sessa disappeared inside.

He caught Pansie studying him and grinned. Maybe she had been listening.

"What do you figure she's doing in there?" he asked her.

"Going to the mailbox," the girl said matter-of-factly.

Oh, this was going to be good. "Why's that?"

She shrugged. "'Cause Coco said to."

"How about we go see what Coco left in the mailbox?" This was going to be fun even if Sessa wouldn't appreciate it. Trey rose and motioned for Pansie to follow, pressing his index finger to his lips.

Pansie grinned and copied his gesture and then tiptoed off the porch to follow him around the side of the house. As they passed the kitchen window, Trey ducked so that Sessa, who seemed to be pulling plates out of the cabinet, wouldn't see them. Again Pansie mimicked him although at her size there was no way she could be seen from the window.

Getting from the side of the house to the mailbox without being spotted was going to take some doing. He paused to lean down and whisper to Pansie. "You and I are going on an adventure to the mailbox. Follow right behind me and be really quiet, okay?"

"Okay Uncle Trey! Let's go!" she said loud enough that Sessa surely heard.

"Shhh...." He crouched down and then took off briskly walking, stopping only when he knew he was hidden behind his truck. True to her word, Pansie kept right behind him. Another sprint to find cover behind an overgrown azalea bush and then they were at the mailbox.

"Okay, Pansie," he said to his co-conspirator. "Let's see what Coco left in the mailbox."

"I want to open it!" she demanded.

He loved little kids, though he rarely spent time with them. Pansie's honesty and her wide smile melted his heart. "All right. You can open it, but Uncle Trey's going to have to lift you up so you can reach."

After hefting the tiny thing up to the mailbox, he watched her fumble with the latch and then open it. "What's in there?"

"Coco's pie," she said as she wriggled out of his arms. "Told you."

He looked inside and sure enough, there was a pie. And judging from the temperature inside the mailbox, it was still warm.

"Well, how about that." He looked down at Pansie. "Now it's time for the next adventure. Are you ready?"

"Yeah," she said with an enthusiasm that melted his heart. This little girl was wiggling her way into his affections almost as quickly as her grandmother. "Where we going now, Uncle Trey?"

"Oh, well, this is going to be extra hard." He knelt in front of her. "See you and I, we're going to take Coco's pie and we're going to surprise Grammy by bringing it to the table for her. What do you think about that?"

"Yeah," she said again. "Can I carry it?"

"Well honey, I think Uncle Trey ought to carry it." When she stuck her lower lip out as if to protest, he had to think fast. "See, carrying the pie, that's not the important job. The important job is being the leader. Now, I could be the leader if you wanted to carry this pie, but then you'd miss all the fun."

"I want the fun," she demanded.

"Okay then. Here's what we're going to do. I want you to run fast as you can to that spot behind the azalea bush where we were hiding a minute ago. Can you do that?" When she nodded, he continued. "When you get there, you motion for me to follow you." He showed her how to wave him forward. "Then I'll come over there. Ready?"

Before he could say go, off she went. Thankfully, Sessa was nowhere near the window, because there was no precision or planning to their return to the table. With him trying not to drop the pie and Pansie just running as fast as she could, they would have been pitifully easy to spot.

Just as they rounded the corner of the house, Trey heard the front door open and close. "Hurry." He cradled the pie with one hand and herded the little girl toward the porch with the other.

"Okay now, Pansie," he said as he settled back onto the chair where he'd been sitting during the meal. "Now we're going to play pretend. You color a picture of this pie, and I'm going to hide it."

"Why are we doing that?"

He grinned. "It's part of the surprise."

"We're surprising Gwammy!" Her brown eyes widened. "Yay!"

"Okay, you start drawing that pie." Once the girl was too involved in her work to notice, he slid the pie toward him and hid it on the seat of the chair to his right. A few minutes later, Sessa walked out looking particularly worried.

"Welcome back," Trey said. "We missed you, didn't we Pansie?"

She ignored him and continued to draw. He shrugged in

Sessa's direction and motioned for her to sit.

"No, I can't," she said. "I'm still..." A phone rang inside. "Still working on the pie. Will you excuse me a minute?"

She hurried inside, and Trey had to contain his laughter as snatches of Sessa's frantic conversation drifted toward him. "No, I checked. Gone. Yes, I'm sure."

He switched his attention to Pansie. The dark-haired darling was oblivious to her grandmother's distress as she put the finishing touches on an interesting looking piece of art. He could see that the circle was probably the pie, but the rest of the design—from the dashes of yellow to what looked like a jar and a red hat—baffled him.

"So, change of plans," Sessa said as she came through the door with a container of Blue Bell Homemade Vanilla ice cream, a bowl of strawberries, and a smile that was pretty but probably not sincere.

"Oh," he said innocently. "Trouble with the pie?"

"About that pie." She set the ice cream and strawberries on the table and turned to head for the door again. "It's a funny story, actually. But let me go get the bowls and spoons and then I'll tell you all about it."

"Can't wait to hear it," Trey called as she disappeared inside. "How's that drawing coming, Pansie?" She held it up for him. "Oh, that's nice. Now fold it in half so Grammy can open it like a present when she comes back out."

Pansie complied then aimed a broad grin in his direction. "I like adventures, Uncle Trey."

"Me too." Life with these two would be a constant adventure, one he happily considered. He heard Sessa's footsteps approach. "Now remember. Don't show her the drawing until I tell you to, okay? That's part of the adventure."

She nodded.

Sessa stepped out onto the porch and deposited three bowls and three spoons on the table. "Who wants strawberries and ice cream?"

"I want pie," Pansie demanded. "But ice cream too. And strawberries."

Trey shrugged. "She wants pie. Too bad that didn't work out." He let out a long breath. "What was that funny story about the pie you were going to tell us?"

Her smile wavered, and he wondered if he'd done the right thing in playing this joke on her. "Well, see—"

"Sorry to interrupt so early into your story," Trey said. "But what kind of pie was it exactly?"

"Kind of pie?" she echoed as if buying time. "Well, it was...you know, a pie."

"Not very descriptive, but go on."

She nodded. "Yes, well, see I have been a member of the Pies, Books & Jesus Book Club for years. Whoever hosts that month makes four pies."

"Yes, Jared told me about it. He was rattling on about it the night their baby was born."

"Well, anyway, I have a confession to make." She paused to look at Pansie. "See, I'm a good cook. Just ask anyone. I can make just about anything. But..."

"You can't make pies?"

Her face fell. "How did you know?"

"I didn't." He nodded to Pansie. "Give Grammy your present." Trey returned his attention to Sessa. "You can't make pies but your granddaughter can."

The little girl leaned forward to watch Sessa unfold the paper. "See Gwammy, it's pie with lightning bugs."

"Why, yes it is," she said with a genuine smile. "And what's this?"

"That's Daddy's hat." Pansie turned to Trey. "It's on the high shelf in my room, so I can't touch it 'cause I'm not big enough yet. It's for somedays."

Sessa's eyes softened, and Trey knew the little girl had said something that touched her deeply. "Waiting for somedays is important," Sessa said. "But don't ever give up on someday coming, sweetheart."

Oblivious to her grandmother's change in mood, Pansie giggled as a few weak rays of sunshine peeked through the clouds. "Uncle Trey, your turn."

"Your turn for what?" Sessa asked him.

"For the surprise," Pansie said. "We went on an adventure, didn't we, Uncle Trey?"

"We sure did."

"We had jobs, and I was the leader," she said, nodding. "That's important."

"Yes it is." Sessa shifted her attention to Trey, her eyes narrowing. "And what was your job?"

He couldn't contain his grin as he reached under the table. As much fun as he was having, it was time to give poor Sessa a break. And he really wanted to taste that pie.

"Trey?" she said.

"He carried the pie!" Pansie exclaimed and then clasped her hands over her mouth. "Oops, that was the surprise."

Trey slid the pie out from its hiding place and set it on the table in front of her. "Look what Pansie and I found in the mailbox."

Sessa turned the prettiest shade of pink and then laughed. Trey joined her, as did Pansie, although he doubted whether the little girl had any idea what was so funny.

"So, Sessa," he said. "What kind of pie is it?"

She swatted his arm with her napkin and reached for the knife. "I have no idea. I told Coco I'd take whatever Carly had."

"Pansie." He looked past Sessa to the little girl now busy coloring on another page of blue paper. "Time for another adventure." She sat up at attention, her grin firmly in place.

"What're we doing now, Uncle Trey?"

"We're having pie." A few fat splatters of raindrops indicated the next round of showers had arrived. "And then maybe we'll go have that dance in the rain. What do you think?"

"Yay!"

As it turned out, the pie was some variation of blueberry, possibly with goat cheese and rosemary, according to Sessa's description. It was hard to tell, and yet the flavors blended to fill the flakiest crust he'd eaten in a long time.

While Sessa dabbed daintily at the corner of her lips—lips he intended to kiss again very soon, if she'd let him—Pansie seemed to be wearing a good portion of her slice of pie on her face. A trail of blue splotches decorated the front of her pink dress and covered her hands.

"Oh goodness, Pansie," Sessa said. "You've made a mess of yourself. Sit right there and I'll go get a wet washcloth."

As soon as Sessa disappeared inside, he felt the void of her absence. Trey gestured to Pansie. "Come on," he told her. "Let's have another adventure."

She climbed down from her seat, leaving a smear of blueberry on the edge of the table and down the back of the chair. "Where are we going?"

He took her hand and felt a blueberry mush smash against his palm. Oh well. It was worth it to hold onto the little girl who held Sessa's heart.

"We are going out in the rain. It's time to dance, Pansie Chambers."

~*~

Sessa returned to find a grown man and a little girl carrying on like fools in the rain. Not just dancing, but twisting, turning and jumping. Pansie's blueberry-stained dress stuck to her, and Trey's pearl snap shirt was drenched to his skin.

She backed into the shadows, and her heart melted. If she hadn't already been falling for the man, this moment would have sealed the deal.

The frolicking stopped when Trey motioned for Pansie to move closer and put her feet on top of his boots. "Just hold on to my hands and don't let go while we dance." She complied, and they began a slow twirl, something between a waltz and a Texas two-step.

"Good job," Trey told her. "See, that's how princesses dance in the rain with cowboys."

This. This was what she'd missed in Ross's life. What she hadn't been able to reach out and capture for him.

She tossed the washcloth on the table and leaned against the doorframe, arms crossed, and watched the cowboy and the princess dance.

"This is like at school," she heard Pansie tell Trey. "We're making a joyful noise." Then Pansie spied her. "Gwammy, come dance!"

Trey aimed a grin at her, and her knees nearly buckled. "That's right," he said with an *I-dare-you* tone. "Come dance!"

She moved to the edge of the porch. "Oh, I don't know. It looks like the cowboy already has a princess to dance with."

Trey knelt down and whispered something in Pansie's ear. A moment later, the little girl came running toward her, damp curls flying, her grin broad.

"Come on, Gwammy." She tugged at Sessa's hand and urged her out into the rain.

Sessa felt the first few drops of rain slither down her neck, and she shivered despite the warmth of the evening. Pansie pulled her closer to Trey as the downpour dampened her hair.

"Hey, cowboy."

Pansie left her in front of Trey to chase the raindrops.

Trey grasped one of her hands and then took a step back to offer a courtly bow. "Hello, my queen." He then closed the distance between them to wrap his arm around her waist. "Shall we dance?"

Unlike the dance he'd shared with Pansie, this dance was slow, deliberate, a conversation without words. His eyes never left hers, and she didn't dare look away.

The warmth of his palm at the small of her back distracted her almost as much as the width of his chest and the breadth of his shoulders. Of the muscles she could feel as she held tight to his arm.

Don't let go.

She held on tighter, and he smiled. "Doing all right, your majesty?"

"Oh yes, cowboy."

"Then don't let go." He hauled her close, and the horizon slipped as he dipped her backward.

And then he kissed her.

She didn't realize her eyes had closed, but a sudden giggle surprised her into opening them. Pansie appeared in her line of sight. "Hey there, princess," Trey managed. "This cowboy's kind of busy right now."

"Blueberry kisses!" she shouted as she planted sloppy kiss on Sessa's cheek. Then, being the diplomat, she did the same for Trey.

"Blueberry kisses," he said as he swiped at his cheek and then stuck his finger in his mouth. "Tasty." He paused. "And unforgettable."

Then he kissed her again.

CHAPTER SEVENTEEN

June meeting of the Pies, Books & Jesus Book Club
Location: Carly Chance's home
Pies: one bubble gum, two caramel apple, and one bacon cheesecake
Book title: AT THE SOUND OF WATER by Jamie Livingston
Turner

"She didn't really kiss him in the parking lot of the Blue Plate, did she?"

"Of course she did," Sessa said as she walked into the living room, catching Vonnette and Mama with their heads together. "And why not? Everyone in Sugar Pine was going to hear about it anyway."

"Hear about what?" Mama said coyly. "Far as I know, there's nothing going on. At least nothing that you've told your mama about. Of course there's plenty going on, as the whole town knows."

"I do believe you've rendered her speechless," Vonnette said.

Sue Ellen shook her finger at Mama and Vonnette. "Oh, y'all leave her alone. If she's got some kind of flame kindled with that handsome doctor, I'm sure she'd tell us." She turned to face Sessa. "Wouldn't you?"

Carly looked up from nursing her baby and added her agreement, which led to the rest of the woman chiming in. All Sessa could do was stand there like a deer in headlights.

Coco stood and clapped her hands to get their attention. "All right, ladies. As Sessa's acknowledged best friend since as long as either of us can remember, I am going to settle this once and for all so we can get back to what we came here for."

"Pie?" Vonnette quipped. The others giggled.

"Well, yes of course," Coco said. "I know we've got several new types to try, thanks to Carly's love of all things *Epicurious*."

"I never did understand what *Epicurious* is," Mama said. "Sounds like something the preacher wouldn't approve of."

Carly shook her head. "No ma'am. *Epicurious* is a magazine for cooks who like gourmet food. I have lots of other places I like to find recipes, but I get some of my best ideas from there."

Sessa offered a smile of thanks that her best friend had steered these women onto another topic. *Bless her heart.*

Carly beamed. "Now I'm going to hand this little man off to his gran-gran so I can go get those pies cut."

As soon as Carly was out of earshot, Robin leaned forward. "Okay, y'all. That pink bubblegum pie is delicious. I was suspicious, but it really does taste like Double Bubble. She listened to good sense and made two plain old caramel apple pies, so you probably can't go wrong there. Or at least that's what she told me they were. I didn't actually see her make them. I've got to warn you, though. I'm just not sure what to make of that bacon cheesecake."

"Bacon cheesecake?" Vonnette shook her head. "What is this world coming to?"

"I know." Robin held her grandson against her shoulder and patted his back. "But you never know. Keep an open mind, that's what I say. Well, an open mind and an open bottle of Pepto-Bismol."

Carly returned with a tray filled with slices of pie. "All right, ladies. Those are the caramel apple. I'll be right back with the other two, although I understand the surprise might have been ruined just a little by my dear mother-in-law."

"Oh honey," Robin said. "You know I love your cooking. I was just bragging on you."

"Sessa," Carly said. "Would you come help me?"

"Sure." She rose to follow Carly into the kitchen. "What can I do?"

"Bragging indeed! That woman, for all I love about her, sometimes she just stomps all over my last nerve. Does she think I didn't hear the Pepto-Bismol comment?" Carly shook her head. "Oh, don't listen to me. I'm just exhausted. Much as I love my son, I would sure like him to learn the difference in night and day and spend more of the night asleep."

"Babies are a full-time job. Maybe he'll learn quickly."

"I sure hope so." She placed the slices of pie and cheesecake on another tray.

"Thank you for sending the pie over," Sessa said.

"I heard what happened." She giggled. "When Coco told me about Trey and Pansie finding the pie, well, I laughed until I cried."

"It *was* funny, after I got over my embarrassment." She paused. "Honestly, I don't know how I could have looked Trey in the eyes and claimed to have baked anything as amazing as what comes out of your kitchen. And speaking of, is that the bacon cheesecake? It looks delicious."

"It is." Carly grinned and reached into the microwave, where a generous slice had been cut and was waiting on a paper plate. She must have hidden it there before setting out the pies.

She grabbed two forks and handed one to Sessa. "A good chef always saves a piece for tasting. Here. Try a bite."

"Oh, Carly." She swallowed the interesting concoction. "I'm going to need that recipe."

"Yeah?"

Sessa nodded and snagged another bite. "Yeah."

Relief flooded the younger woman's face. "Oh, thank you. I'll email you the recipe. But first I think we need just one more bite."

"Just one more wouldn't hurt," she agreed. "Or two."

"What're y'all doing in there?" Vonnette called. "The caramel apple's almost gone."

"Go ahead and finish it off," Carly called. "We're bringing out the other in a minute." She returned her attention to Sessa. "Before I go back in there, I need to tell you something."

"All right."

She pushed the tray aside and reached for Sessa's hand. "I just want you to know that, no matter what happens with you and Dr. Brown, he saved my son's life. I know he did. He was breach, and we live out in the middle of nowhere, and there wasn't a midwife and poor Jared..."

Sessa patted her hand. "Honey, it's okay."

"Well, anyway, he barely knew Jared. So for him to come out

there and do that for me... For us. Well, it speaks of what kind of man he is. So if anyone thinks to slight him because of what happened with Ross, they're going to have to go through me and Jared to get to him."

Sessa breathed in deeply, letting the mention of Ross and the pang of grief it carried slip away. And then Carly's words really penetrated, bringing a rush of warmth and gratitude toward the younger woman. "Thank you for telling me that."

And of course, at that very moment, Mama's voice intruded.

"Go ahead and eat the rest of the pie, ladies. I bet they're talking about Sessa's cowboy. I told her that was the man God sent her, but *no*, would she listen to her mama? Might as well call my great granddaughter and say good-night. At least she listens to me."

Sessa shook her head. "That woman. Much as I love her, she can truly be a pain. I cannot wait until she finally says yes to Dr. Easley and goes on a date. You can be certain I'll be giving her every bit as much trouble as she's giving me."

Carly grinned. "You mean you didn't know?"

She gave her friend a sideways look. "Talk to me, girl."

"Well, " Carly said, "guess who has not only joined the choir but also the Quilt Guild?"

"No."

Carly nodded. "Not only that, but I understand he and your mama have spent more than the last four Tuesday afternoons planning quilts over lunch at the Red Lobster in Sively and then going to the fabric store to pick out material."

"No!"

"Or at least that's the story I heard at the diner from one of Vonnette's customers, and she heard it while she was getting her hair done."

"Surely not."

She paused as if trying to decide whether to say more. "I saw them holding hands in that same parking lot where you and that cute doctor were locking lips."

Sessa chuckled. "Well, how about that? Thank you, Carly." She moved toward the door. "Mama!"

"Hush. Do you really want to bust her right now?"

"In front of God and everybody she cares about? You bet I

do. She surely doesn't mind doing it to me."

Carly shook her head. "Don't waste it, girl. If your mama's going to that much trouble to hide it from you, I say save it for when it counts."

"Carly, I swear you and Sessa are going to have to arm wrestle Bonnie Sue over the last piece of caramel apple pie," Vonnette called. "If something's that interesting, come and tell all of us."

"We all know she's talking about that cowboy. What did I tell you?"

"Should I use it now?" Sessa said as she lifted her brows.

Carly shook her head. "Nope. Save it." She grinned. "That caramel apple pie she's so fond of?" A giggle. "There are no apples in it. Or caramel. Go in there and insist she get the recipe. I'll handle the rest. Trust me."

"You are devious, Carly Chance."

She laughed. "And exhausted. Let's get that book club meeting started. Bedtime can't come soon enough for me."

"Well, look who has decided to join us," Mama exclaimed when they returned to the room. "I just called the babysitter to check on Pansie, and guess what your granddaughter told me."

Sessa cleared a space on the table for the tray Carly was holding. "What's that, Mama?"

"That she and Uncle Trey danced in the rain after they stole pie from the mailbox."

Sessa froze, glad her back was to the room. "You must have misunderstood."

"We all heard her," Vonnette said. "Bonnie Sue had her on speaker phone."

She turned around slowly and found every eye in the room on her. "Oh?"

Coco grimaced. "There's more."

She focused on her best friend. "I'm sure she was just making things up."

"Like blueberry kisses?" Mama said. "I believe she said something about the princess and the cowboy."

"We all figured you were the princess," Vonnette said. "And it was obvious who the cowboy was. As to the blueberry kisses..."

Sessa sat across from her mother and let out a long breath. "Well, you're half right. The princess, however, is Pansie. And yes, she *did* dance in the rain with Dr. Brown. And the blueberry kisses were because she was covered in blueberries after eating Carly's pie." She paused, still thrilled by the memories. "Well, anyway, you kind of had to be there."

Mama's perfectly plucked brows rose, and those lips that matched her pink ensemble pursed as she lifted her glass of tea. "I suppose so, Sessa, but none of us were invited."

"It was just a cookout. And while we are on the subject of not being invited, I'm wondering why all of a sudden you've stopped trying to get me to go to Quilt Guild meetings with you."

Her mother almost sloshed sweet tea all over her. "I'm sorry. What?"

Sessa gave her an *I-know-all-about-it* look. "Just thinking I might want to start going to the meetings. What say I pick you up for the next one? We could have some lunch at the Red Lobster over in Sively, and then maybe after we could head over to the fabric store to look at material."

Carly grinned from her perch on the rocker behind Mama. Mama, however, wore a decidedly less mirthful expression.

"You know, honey. I've always felt bad that I put so much pressure on you to go to those meetings. Don't feel like you have to." Her hand shook as she set the tea glass down in front of her, completely missing the coaster.

"Oh, no pressure at all. In fact, I would *love* to, Mama. I know how lonely you get when you have to do things by yourself. Speaking of doing things, got anything you'd like to share with the group? Maybe I could make a call on speaker phone to a certain Doc Eas—"

"Well, I don't know about the rest of you, but now that I've had my pie, I'm ready to talk about this month's book." Vonnette leaned over and placed the coaster under the glass. "Am I the only one who couldn't figure out what water was supposed to smell like?"

Sessa continued to stare at her mother, refusing to be the one who looked away first. It was childish, but she didn't care.

Finally her mother turned her attention elsewhere. Sessa called that a victory.

One thing she'd learned recently was to savor the victories. And the memories.

And someday she would learn not to live for the somedays.

"I heard someone bought the old Landrum house." Carly sidled up to her. "Wonder who that was."

"I don't know," Sessa said quietly, letting the other ladies continue their discussion of the book. "It's been vacant for years. I'm surprised anyone would want it."

"It is next door to the Blue Plate." Coco joined them. "Prime location for a business. Maybe Sugar Pine is finally going to get a cute little boutique or maybe a spa. Oh, wouldn't a spa just be the best thing ever?"

"I've seen pictures. That old place used to be a real showplace," Carly said. "I remember when it was the prettiest house in town. Whatever goes in there will be nice, I guarantee you that."

"Are you girls talking about Sessa and that man again?" Vonnette called. "Because we're here to talk books, not men."

She smiled. "Actually, we were talking about the Landrum house. Anyone know who bought it?"

The general consensus was that the purchaser was a mystery. Sessa smiled. *Not for long.*

Nothing in Sugar Pine remained hidden very long. She gave Mama a look. Nothing at all.

CHAPTER EIGHTEEN

Two days after dancing in the rain with Sessa, Trey walked out of the Chief of Staff's office with a weight lifted from his shoulders. Of course, the chief thought he'd lost his mind. Trey knew he'd only just begun to find it.

Charlie Dorne fell in beside him as he headed toward the elevator. "Just heard the news," he said. "Good for you, cowboy."

"That didn't take long." He shook Charlie's hand.

"Apparently the chief's secretary and Santini's OR nurse are thick as thieves. I left Santini to close and came to find you."

Trey punched the button for the elevator. "I'm glad you did. I was going to call you." He paused as the elevator dinged. "When I got settled, that is."

"Where will you go?"

He stepped into the empty elevator and grinned. "I've got some plans, but there's a certain person in Sugar Pine, Texas, I need to run them by first."

Charlie clasped his hand on Trey's shoulder. "Glad to hear it. I guess your visit to the therapist really paid off."

"Speaking of paying, I need to stop by his office and handle something." Trey walked out into the ground floor atrium and then shook his friend's hand once more. "I'll see you soon, Charlie." He pulled his hand away to wrap his arm around the surgeon. "Thank you, man. For everything."

Charlie chuckled as they stepped apart. "Everything, huh? That's a pretty broad category."

"Okay, let me rephrase," Trey said. "Thank you for everything starting with buying that Bible and ending, I hope, with the Lord leading me to the future He meant me to find."

"Now that's more like it." Charlie's phone rang and he reached for it. "Stay in touch. I mean it, Trey."

He gave Charlie the thumbs up sign and then headed to his truck. Dialing the counselor's number, Trey waited until he got the recording that indicated there was no one in the office. "Hey, it's Trey Brown. I owe you a belated thanks. Your idea for me to go and make amends to Ross Chambers' family changed my life. One of these days, I want to tell you about it, but not on the phone. If you're ever in Sugar Pine, Texas, give me a call." He then left his number and hung up.

There was one more stop to make before he left Houston, and that was the one he was least anticipating. He pulled up in front of the familiar white columned mansion with the circular drive in the River Oaks area of town, and then sped right past. Slowing to a stop around the block, he took a deep breath and prayed, then turned around and went back.

He parked and walked up to the massive front door to ring the doorbell before he lost his courage. A maid let him in, led him to the parlor, then left him alone.

A few minutes later the door opened and Milo Rossi wheeled himself in with a uniformed caregiver following close behind. "Scoot," he told the woman, and she did exactly that, leaving them behind closed doors.

The décor had changed since the last time he'd been here. More African safari and less English manor, or at least that was his observation. Trey walked past two mounted antelope heads to shake Mr. Rossi's hand.

"Welcome," he said. "I understand you tendered your resignation at Turner Regional this morning."

"Word travels fast."

"In my world, information is power." He gestured to the sofa. "Sit, Trey. I'm interested in why you needed to see me. Do you need a job?"

"No, sir."

Mr. Rossi lifted one broad shoulder. "A pity. I'd give you one in a heartbeat. Anything for the man who saved my life."

"I did as I was trained to do, nothing more." He leaned forward. "I'm only here to thank you."

The older man waved away any further discussion. "I'm in

your debt, not the other way around."

"But without your intervention, I would still be in that jail cell. I owe you my life, sir."

He shook his head. "Oh, son, if you would only see the big picture. Do you think I wanted to have you out of that prison? No, I'll tell you. I did not. Any man who breaks my daughter's heart, well, suffice it to say prison is not even sufficient punishment for such an offense."

Trey's gaze sunk to his boots. He hadn't thought about Vikki and what ending their relationship might have done to the rest of the Rossi family. Back then, he'd rarely considered anything beyond himself.

"However," Mr. Rossi said with enough authority to recapture Trey's attention. "Much as I am the one who many people answer to, there is One to whom I answer." He shrugged. "What I did not want to do, I did for Him."

Trey shook his head. "I don't understand."

"Neither did I," he said. "Until that night at Fish Camp when you saved my life. Sometimes we don't know what disobedience could have cost us, but just imagine if I hadn't pushed Ross's accomplice to testify for you. Where would I be today if you were still locked up instead of at Fish Camp on Thursday? Come here."

Trey rose to move closer as the older man struggled to his feet. He reached to offer help, but Mr. Rossi shook his head.

"There," he said when he found his balance. "I am eye-to-eye with you, which is as it should be. See, this is not only between you and me, Trey Brown. Thank you. Because of your skill with a knife, I am still here."

He thought to say something to argue but couldn't quite decide what. Instead, he merely dipped his head and said, "You're welcome."

The older man remained standing as he pressed a button attached to the lanyard around his neck. An instant later, the uniformed attendant returned to help him into the chair.

"Now leave, Trey. And stay away from my daughter."

Not a problem. In fact, he only had one woman on his mind—one woman he'd fallen in love with—and it was not Victoria Rossi. "Yes sir."

Unfortunately, he returned to his truck to see Vikki sitting in the passenger seat. "So, did you and Daddy have a nice chat?"

He reluctantly climbed inside and stuck his keys into the ignition.

"Get out, Vikki. I just promised your father I would stay away from you. I no longer break promises."

"Well, isn't that noble of you." She sighed. "All right. I just wanted to know why you didn't scrub in on the surgery with—"

"Your boyfriend?" he snapped. "Ask him."

She chewed her index finger and watched him from across the seat. "I did. He won't tell me."

"I don't want to play your games." He turned to place both hands on the steering wheel. "Our conversation is done." *They* were done. Vikki might be able to forget everything that had happened before his exoneration, but he couldn't.

Trey climbed out and slammed the door. Vikki did the same and then followed him as he walked down the driveway toward River Oaks Drive. If he had to walk the whole way home, it would be a small price to pay compared to spending another minute with her.

"What kind of idiot are you to walk away from all of this?"

More to the question, what kind of idiot had he been to think of staying? Of marrying her?

The kind of idiot who needed a Bible and a lengthy period of solitude in which to read it, apparently.

"You're different, Trey," she said. "And I don't think it is prison that changed you."

Trey stopped short. "You're wrong, at least in part." He pressed past her, returned the truck, and pulled the Bible Charlie had given him from behind the seat. "If I hadn't been stuck in prison, I wouldn't have had time to read this. No, that's not true. I wouldn't have *taken* the time."

"So you're saying prison was a good thing?" Her expression conveyed a level of disbelief. "Really?"

"Prison was worse than you can even imagine. The only good thing about it was that I finally had nowhere to run." He sat the Bible back on the seat and climbed inside. This time he was quick to lock both doors, but he did open the driver's side window. "If you're looking for advice—"

"I'm not."

He ignored her words and gave it anyway. "I wish someone had told me just to be still and listen."

"I don't get it."

Trey started the truck and shifted into drive. "You will if you listen long enough."

He left Vikki standing in the driveway and pointed the truck toward Sugar Pine. With each mile that fell behind him, he listened a little more.

~*~

Sessa sprinkled flour over the wooden counter top and reached for the bowl. "I will get this pie crust right if it kills me."

"And it just might."

"Mama!" Sessa righted the bowl just before its contents would have spilled onto the kitchen floor. "You scared me to death. What are you doing here on a Tuesday? I thought you had Quilt Guild."

"And I thought you wanted to go with me."

Swiping the towel, she cleaned off her hands and turned to face her mother. "You and I both know what that was about."

Mama nodded and even had the decency to look contrite.

"Why didn't you just tell me?" Sessa demanded. "Especially after all that pushing to get me to open up about Trey."

"Because it's not easy being on the other end of...well..."

"Teasing? Pushiness? Oh, maybe control?"

Her mother waved away the questions. "No, none of that. I just didn't want to be in the spotlight. Walter and I, we are taking things slow. Or were."

"Were?"

Mama grinned. "Last night while we were eating supper, he popped the question."

"Oh Mama!" She crossed the room and gathered her mother into an embrace. Though she would always miss her daddy, Sessa was truly happy that Mama had found love again. "I'm so happy for you."

"Are you?" She seemed to be studying Sessa's face. "Because after your daddy died, well, I just didn't think I'd find another man like him." She held up her hands. "And honey, please understand

I haven't found someone like him, but I have found someone who I like. No one will take Daddy's place, but he never did want me to be alone. Does that make sense?"

"It makes perfect sense." She surreptitiously wiped away a tear. "So when's the wedding?"

She shook her head. "Oh, I haven't said yes yet."

"Why not?"

Mama put on her most stubborn face. "Honestly, Sessa. I am a catch. Don't you think I'm worth a proposal with a little more thought put into it?"

"I, well..." She covered her smile with her hand. "Yes, of course," she managed.

"Darn right I am. I told that old coot he'd better get down on one knee and make a show of it. And not at the Pancake Hut either. Goodness, how tacky would that be? And that floor, well he'd probably stick to it if he knelt down, what with all the syrup that's been spilled there."

Mama went on, but Sessa tuned her out and concentrated on her piecrust. To her surprise, she managed to roll out what appeared to be a perfect crust.

"Sweetheart," Mama said. "I don't think I'd have believed you made that if I hadn't seen you do it right there in front of me."

"Thank you, Mama." She crimped the edges and cut slits in the top then finished off the crust with egg wash and stuck it in the oven. "How about we sit down and have a cup of coffee while the pie bakes?"

"Shouldn't you be working on those horses? I thought you said you were up to your eyeballs in work?"

"I am," she said slowly, "but since I haven't found anyone to hire to help, I'm doing it all, and that gets overwhelming. Sometimes I just have to walk away and close the door for awhile."

"And bake pies instead?"

"Exactly." Sessa nodded toward the coffee pot. "Are you sure I can't convince you to have some coffee?"

Mama shook her head. "I can't. I'm missing lunch, but I did mention to a certain someone that I'd still be going to Quilt Guild. If he's got good sense, he'll figure out he needs to take me to supper in Sively and practice his knee bends and *please-marry-mes* before I lose interest."

"If he has good sense, he'll run," she said under her breath.

Mama looked back from the window, where she'd been studying something out in the pasture. "What's that, Sessa?"

"Nothing, Mama. Have a good time. Let me know if you elope."

"Oh child, you are just too funny." She kissed Sessa on the cheek and then snatched up her keys and purse. "This is Sugar Pine. No one elopes here."

After setting the timer on the oven, Sessa went to the window to see what Mama had been looking at. Sitting in a rocker beneath the pecan tree was Trey Brown, and he looked quite pleased with himself.

She brushed the flour from her clothes and joined him outside. "What are you doing out here?" She looked around, then turned back to him. "And more important, where's your truck? I didn't see it in the driveway."

She thought to brush a kiss across his cheek, but he slid his arm around her back and drew her down into his lap. Trey rained kisses on her forehead and then slanted his lips over hers. His kiss left her breathless and made her heart race.

"No, you wouldn't have seen the truck," he said when Sessa climbed to her feet. He patted the empty rocker. "Join me?"

She glanced at the clock on her phone. "Just for a few minutes. I've got a pie in the oven."

He smirked. "Don't you mean the mailbox?"

"For your information, cowboy, I have been practicing, and I do believe I've made the perfect peach pie." At his skeptical look, she added. "Even my mother agrees. Would you like me to call Bonnie Sue to come back here and have her confirm this?"

"No," he said quickly. "No need for that."

"Well, trust me, it's going to be good."

He gave her a sideways look. "Does that mean I'm invited for supper?"

"I hadn't thought about supper, but you're definitely invited for pie."

Trey dipped his head. "I would be honored to share pie with you and the princess."

"Oh, she's not here tonight. She's doing a girlie sleepover with

Aunt Coco."

"I thought you were keeping her close."

"I was," Sessa admitted.

"And now you're not." His eyes were too perceptive, but she managed to hold his gaze. "How're you holding up?"

It had been two long weeks since he'd been here for their Sunday date. She'd missed him more than she wanted to admit, but they'd talked on the phone for hours, like they were teenagers again.

She'd told him about Skye's appearance. He'd been a good listener, not trying to tell her how to solve things but supporting her when she'd told him about her conflicted feelings.

And now the clasp of his hand over hers was a comfort. "Surprisingly...okay."

He squeezed her hand. "Given that you and Pansie are the most important people in my life, I decided to do a little discreet checking. Since Jared said he'd do me a favor if I needed one..."

"Wait...we are?"

His eyebrows lifted. "Have I not made that clear?"

She grinned as warmth spread all through her. "You have now." She thought about his *checking*. Exhaled slowly. "I'm terrified if I think about her coming back and wanting to take Pansie with her. But... Let's just say my faith has grown with each day that it doesn't happen."

"I see."

"I just have to face the fact that Skye may come back someday, and she may want her daughter. Until then, I have to trust that Pansie is safe with me." She paused. "Besides, as you said, Sugar Pine is a small town. I can't imagine that Skye could slip out of here with Pansie and not be seen."

Even as she said the words, Sessa shuddered. That, of course, was her biggest fear.

"I've never had kids of my own," he said slowly, "so maybe I'm not the one to comment on this, but I can't imagine just walking away from my own flesh and blood and never coming back."

Sessa sighed and thought of what Skye gave up, of how she sacrificed so her daughter could have more than she could offer. "Me, either."

They were silent for moments that stretched long, comfortable. Then he leaned forward in the chair, his hands on his knees.

"Sessa," he said softly. "I'm falling in love with you. You got a problem with that?"

His admission caught her by surprise. Oh, but she wanted to say something witty, something that would make this memory one she could look back on with a smile. But suddenly her ability to speak had vanished quicker than a mud puddle on a hot Texas afternoon.

Instead, she finally managed a shaky, "I don't."

"All right then." He reached across the distance between them to grasp Sessa's hand.

"All right then," she echoed, still searching for those words that might charm him further and reassure him he hadn't chosen a woman with nothing but a head full of fluff.

"I do love you, Sessa Lee Chambers." He slid her a sideways look, his expression softening. He didn't seem to mind her fumbling for words. "You have no idea how much I love you."

"Ditto." She cringed. What in the world was wrong with her? Couldn't she just tell him she loved him? Just say the words that refused to slip past her tongue?

She couldn't, but she would. This much Sessa determined as they sat and enjoyed the quiet. Until the sound of the smoke detector shattered the silence.

CHAPTER NINETEEN

"I do not care if you believe me or not, Trey Brown. That pie was going to be perfect. Even my mother said so."

Trey opened the door of the Blue Plate Lunchateria and laughed as Sessa slipped inside. A glance around told him Jared had not yet arrived.

Ditto.

It wasn't the most passionate response he could've hoped for. But it was more than nothing. More than he deserved.

Gratitude and anticipation buzzed in his veins, and he found it so very easy to tease her. "There is no shame in admitting that you're just not able to make pies."

"I can make pies just fine." She lifted her chin a bit and waved at the woman behind the cash register. "Hey Sue Ellen. Just two tonight."

Every eye in the room turned their way. Great. He'd been so busy enjoying spending time with Sessa that he hadn't given much thought to what the citizens of Sugar Pine would think about having a killer in their midst.

"Oh honey," Sue Ellen said as they approached. "I finally get to meet the famous Dr. Brown!" The woman's broad smile seemed genuine enough, and her easy manner was definitely welcoming. Trey relaxed slightly.

Sessa made the introductions and then grinned at Sue Ellen. "You should have seen the peach pie I made. Mama said it was perfect."

"But the smoke detector said it was burned to a crisp," Trey added.

"Oh no." Sue Ellen leaned toward Trey. "Too bad about the

191

pie, but tonight's special just happens to be peach pie! Oh, and we have fried chicken."

She looked at him as if he ought to know the significance of that statement. "Good," seemed to be the appropriate answer.

"It's better than good," she said sweetly. "It's not often we offer our fried chicken anymore, because the only one who knows the recipe is Melba, and she's been retired for longer than I've been alive. Or rather she's been trying to retire since then."

Sessa exchanged looks with him. And he added, "I guess I'm having the fried chicken, then."

"Oh honey, don't decide that until you sit down and look at the menu." She looked at Sessa. "Is he always in such a hurry?"

"I really couldn't say," Sessa managed, smiling at Trey's discomfort.

Sue Ellen picked up two menus. "Y'all come on and sit down. Now that I'm thinking about it, I need to go check on Melba. She gets a little forgetful. If she's gone home, then you might as well forget about having the chicken tonight."

An image of an ancient confused woman leaning precariously over a boiling pot of oil while chicken bubbled beneath her gnarled hands arose in his mind. He shook it away to follow Sessa and Sue Ellen to a booth in the center of the room.

Of course.

Trey caught a pair of camouflage-clad men and their dates openly staring and offered a nod of greeting. The men returned the gesture, and one of the women smiled. The other didn't offer any response.

Well, all right then.

"So," Sessa said as she opened the menu. "You didn't tell me where your truck was."

"No, I didn't." He tried to give the appearance of reading the list of items offered at dinnertime. When he glanced up, he caught her staring.

"Well?"

"Well what?" He closed his menu.

"What's the mystery about your truck?"

He shrugged. "No mystery. So, is the chicken as good as your friend says, or should I go for the meatloaf? I liked it before."

"It's not that I minded driving you here," she said demurely, "but I'm just curious. Is it in the shop?"

"No," he said, enjoying this immensely. "And thank you for driving. Next time I'll do the honors."

"So you're buying a new car?"

"No need." He opened the menu again. "Why buy new when what you've got works just fine?"

"If it works just fine," Sessa said, "then why not drive it?"

"Because you gave me a ride."

Sessa glared in his general direction but said nothing. Oh but this was fun.

Finally. He waved at Carly Chance and her husband Jared as they stepped inside the door. While the ladies behind the counter *ooh-ed* and *ah-ed* over the Chance baby, Jared made his way to their table and tossed Trey the keys to his truck.

"Thanks buddy," Trey said as he shook hands with the former Marine.

"Any time." He winked in Sessa's direction. "Be nice to this guy." He left to join Carly and their son in a booth near the cash register.

Sessa gave him a pointed look. "What was that about?"

Trey dangled the keys in front of her and then stuffed them in his pocket. "Got my truck back."

"I would ask from where but I assume you won't answer."

Trey shrugged. "I'd say the answer is obvious. I got it back from Jared. Now, about the chicken. What are the odds Melba hasn't wandered off?"

"Oh, she's here," Sue Ellen hurried to a stop at their booth.

"Then chicken for me," Trey said. "And sweet tea."

"Me too," Sessa echoed.

Sue Ellen wrote down their orders and then seemed reluctant to leave. Finally, she looked down at Sessa and grinned. "Oh," she said before she hurried back to the kitchen.

Well of course. It had obviously been too much to hope that Sessa's friends would be able to keep their mouths shut for thirty minutes.

"What in the world?" Sessa said.

She knows. Trey groaned. "Maybe Mabel wandered off."

Sessa shook her head. "Whatever it is, I'm sure I'll hear about it before bedtime. Sugar Pine's a small town with big mouths."

"Apparently." He watched Sue Ellen return from the kitchen to confer with Carly. Carly handed the baby to Jared and set off with Sue Ellen for the table with the camo-clad men and their women.

"So," Sessa said. "I'm getting a little worried."

So am I. "About what?" He spied Carly and one of the camo-dates conferring. Apparently his secret was out. He gave Jared a pointed look, and the man shrugged. Surely his new friend hadn't given away the secret that Trey had been plotting for weeks.

"You know about the work I'm doing for the Smithsonian, right?" At his nod, she continued. "Well, I knew the scope of it, and yet now that I am actually in the middle of it, I'm a little overwhelmed."

"Hence the pie baking today?"

"Yes." She held up her hand to stop him from responding. "And before you say it, you are a good hand at the work you've done, but you belong in a doctor's office and not carving in my workshop."

He reached across the table to grasp her hand. "I have a feeling you're going to find a solution, Sessa."

She seemed to be considering the statement. "I guess I could run the ad again."

"Yes, you could. And I'll see what I can do to be more helpful." He paused to chuckle at her expression. "But you're right. I do belong in a doctor's office, so any help I'd offer would have to be part time."

She contemplated his words with a tilt of her head. "So you're going back to the hospital?"

"I didn't say that."

"Then I don't understand. If you're going back to practice, then wouldn't it be at the hospital where you—"

Thankfully Sue Ellen returned to set plates in front of them and then stood back and beamed. She patted Sessa on the shoulder and then leaned down to hug Trey.

Yes, she definitely knows.

Trey glanced around the room. Again, every eye was on him. He gestured for Sue Ellen to lean close. "Does everyone know?"

Her eyes darted to Sessa and then returned to him. "I doubt she does."

He groaned. "But everyone else?"

Sue Ellen offered a guilty look. "Only the ones who've come in to the diner tonight. Or the ones they've called and told."

Trey nodded toward the front of the diner and then looked at Sessa. "Will you excuse us a minute?" He stood, linked arms with Sue Ellen, and escorted her back to the cash register.

"Look," he said none too gently. "I went to a lot of trouble to plan this for Sessa, and if you are her friend, then you will not ruin the secret. Do you understand?"

Sue Ellen looked surprised. "Oh. You're so right! Oh, no. I need to fix this."

"No." Trey saw that all eyes in the room were still on him. "I guess I do."

He cleared his throat and clapped his hands until all sounds in the diner ceased. "Can I have your attention?"

Sessa turned at the sound of his voice. "Trey, for goodness sakes, what are you doing?"

"Trying to salvage a plan."

He heard her soft echo. "*Plan?*"

He ignored it. "Now, as to the rest of you, how many of you have heard what I'm planning?"

Almost every hand in the room went up. Again, he groaned

"All right. How many of you want to ruin this for Sessa?"

This time all hands dropped back down.

"That's what I figured." His heart pounded, and his throat threatened to constrict. He felt as nervous as a teenager on his first date, and yet he somehow managed to continue. "Now, as long as I am at it, I might as well come right out and ask how many of you are bothered by the fact that a man with my background is sitting here in your town tonight and keeping company with the prettiest girl in Sugar Pine?"

One hand went up. Jared.

"What the heck, Jared? You never told me you had a problem with me dating Sessa. Not that I'm going to stop. I love her."

"Why not tell the world?" she said as her cheeks turned the prettiest shade of pink.

"Give me time, and I will, darlin'."

A few of the diners chuckled.

Jared pointed at Trey. "The only problem I've got is with you wasting a nice evening in here when you could have gotten your chicken to go."

Trey grinned. "Sue Ellen?"

"On it." She hurried to their table to retrieve the plates.

Sessa rose to join Trey. "What are you doing?" she whispered.

"What I should have done the minute Jared walked in." He gathered her into his arms and kissed her soundly. "Sue Ellen," he called. "Hurry up with that chicken."

She ran back from the kitchen with a bag and two sweet teas in to-go cups. Handing the food to Trey, she looked at Sessa and giggled.

"What is going on?"

Trey ushered her out of the diner and into the parking lot.

They walked past his truck, and she must have noted the heavy crusting of mud it wore. "Looks like you were stuck in the mud. When did you...?" Her words trailed off.

He had been stuck. Instead of telling her that, he shrugged and kept her moving forward. When she attempted to turn toward her car, he eased her back into the direction of the sidewalk.

"Where are we going?"

He stopped on the sidewalk in front of the old Landrum house. "Here. The soon-to-be Sugar Pine Medical Clinic."

"You?" she said in a rush of breath.

"I bought it, yes." He set the bag of chicken on the porch rail and reached for his key. "There's still a lot to be done, but come in. I'd love to show you around."

~*~

Sessa walked up the steps of the old mansion, and what she saw caught her breath. How nice of Trey to use some of the money he made as a Houston surgeon to help revitalize downtown Sugar Pine. Was that what all the quiet whispers had been about in the diner? Her date had certainly seemed to be the talk of the town.

The porch had been painstakingly returned to its former glory. Even the ceiling of robin's egg blue had been repainted and now shimmered a pale color above the freshly painted porch. She'd noticed the new paint when they drove in but hadn't thought about it until now. He must've been busy over the last two weeks, but how had the entire town kept it from her?

"Come in," he told her. "Remember, there's still a lot of work to do."

He opened the door and moved aside. She stepped in. "Oh," she whispered. "Trey, this is absolutely beautiful."

The walls on either side of the old entry hall had been removed to create one large open space with windows that gave a one-hundred and eighty degree view of Sugar Pine's main street. With the sun setting to the west, its orange close hidden behind the Blue Plate, the room was cast in a golden glow.

Straight ahead was a double staircase that split in the middle and then descended on either side of an antique partners desk. Above the desk was a light fixture that had to have been original to the house.

"My receptionist will sit here." He gestured to the desk. "Soon as Carly's finished with her maternity leave, that is."

Oh. *His.* The meaning of his words penetrated the fog in her brain and settled there.

"Carly?" Sessa shook her head. "Wait. Do you mean all of this is yours?"

Trey set the chicken on the desk. "Yes. After I met you, I couldn't stay in Houston. There's just nothing for me there anymore."

"Oh." Her thoughts raced, but she couldn't manage to get anything else out of her mouth.

"So, putting down roots in Sugar Pine just makes sense." He glanced around him and then returned his attention to Sessa. "Doc Easley told me there's been no doctor in this town since he retired."

"You talked to Doc Easley?"

Trey nodded. "I wanted to get his opinion. He was the doctor here before me."

"But he didn't tell a soul."

Trey grinned. "Apparently a rare trait in this town."

Sessa waved away the statement with a smile and then headed up the stairs. "What's up here?"

"Nothing yet." He followed her. "I'm still trying to decide what I'll do with all of these rooms. One will definitely be set aside for Carly's son, should she decide to keep him with her at work." He paused to look around and then shrugged. "As to the rest...those answers will come later."

He grasped her hand and nodded toward the stairs at the end of the hall. "Did you know there's a third floor to this place?"

She followed him up the narrow set of stairs to what she figured was the attic. Instead, she found every wall had been removed and every window opened to the slowly setting sun. Where the downstairs glowed with highly polished woodwork and leaded windows, the space up here was pristine. Even the rafters had been painted a brilliant white. Spanning the length of the old home, the room would easily hold several hundred people.

She couldn't believe he'd done all this and managed to keep it a secret!

She twirled in a circle to take it in. "What will you do with this?" She settled under a massive chandelier that hung in the center of the room.

"The possibilities are endless. Or at least that's what your friend Cozette says. Her idea is to turn this into an event center. Parties, reunions, weddings. Things like that. I think it's a great idea. What about you?"

"Coco knew about this?"

He shrugged. "Don't be mad at her. I asked her not to say anything. I wanted this to be a surprise."

"Well." She admired the chandelier, the walls, the view from the windows, and then turned her attention back to Trey. "It's definitely a surprise. And I think it's a great idea."

Trey looked relieved. "I hoped you would say that. Now come back downstairs and take the rest of the tour. I'd especially like your input on my office."

Sessa allowed Trey to escort her through the remaining rooms on the ground floor, pointing out changes and answering his questions about decorating along the way. Finally they ended up in a room that most certainly had to be his office.

Oh. If Trey were putting down roots, if he intended to begin practicing medicine here, what else did he intend? Sessa cast a sideways glance at the cowboy doctor she'd fallen hopelessly in love with and allowed herself to hope, just for a moment, that his earlier declaration meant she might fit into his plans.

New furniture had already been delivered, and shelves spanning one wall sported a decent array of books and framed photographs. A massive desk held court in the center of the room, and a leather chair that looked quite impressive sat behind it. Two more chairs of a similar style gathered between the desk and the fireplace.

She ran her hand over the carved wood. "This is beautiful."

"It was my father's."

Sessa turned her attention to the line of leather books, most of them medical in nature, and ran her finger over their spines. A photograph of Trey with an older couple caught her attention.

"Your parents?"

"At my medical school graduation."

She smiled and returned the photograph to the shelf and then reached to the shelf above it. There she found two photographs mounted side-by-side in one frame, both obviously from his rodeo days. The picture on the left was of a much younger Trey sitting astride what appeared to be a bronc awaiting its turn to flee the chute. The one on the left, also of Trey, featured the cowboy kneeling down to speak to a little boy.

Something in the black-and-white picture seemed familiar. The dark-haired child's face wasn't visible, but from the way the cowboy smiled, their exchange must have been memorable to both of them. Trey seemed quite interested in whatever the boy was holding in his hands. Was it a hat? Maybe a program. Hard to tell.

"What did you find?" He closed the distance between them.

"Rodeo," she said as she held the photograph up for his inspection.

"That was a long time ago. Those were the days, though. My mom loved those two pictures. I believe they came from the local newspaper, or maybe one of those sports magazines. I really can't remember. Anyway, she had them framed and kept them where everyone who came to the house could see them."

"Sounds like your mother was proud of you."

He wrapped his arm around Sessa. "She was. My dad, too. I miss them."

Rather than ask what happened, she leaned her head on his shoulder and looked up at the picture of the little boy. What was it that seemed so familiar?

"So," Trey said as he broke off the embrace. "You approve?"

"Oh, yes," she said. "I definitely approve."

He nodded toward the door. "Then I've got one more surprise for you."

She gave him an incredulous look. "You don't think this is enough surprise for one day?"

"Trust me." He ushered her out of the front door and then locked it behind him.

"Wait." Sessa pointed inside. "We forgot the chicken."

Trey laughed and went in to retrieve it. When he returned, he placed a hand on the small of her back and urged her toward his truck. "Come on, woman. Time for a picnic."

"What'd you have in mind ?"

He helped her inside and then handed her the bag of food. "Just wait."

Trey climbed into the truck and started the engine. A few minutes later they were headed toward Firefly Lane. Just when Sessa figured Trey was taking her home, he made a sharp left turn and headed down a dirt road that ran parallel to her street. They bounced around under an almost purple sky until he slowed to a stop in front of a familiar gate.

"This is the Landrum ranch," she said.

He grinned. "I know. I negotiated both properties as a package deal."

"But this place—"

"Backs up to yours?" he supplied. At her nod, he upped his grin. "I know. Now come see what I've been doing here."

Once they got inside the gate, Trey drove the truck to the old farmhouse and stopped. Apparently he'd spent much of the past two weeks here, too. The exterior lights lit the grounds so well that it could have been midday. Had she been so busy with the Smithsonian horses that she had missed commotion this close to home?

"I haven't touched the house yet except to make it comfortable enough to sleep. It'll need a complete redo if I decide to keep it."

"Why wouldn't you keep it?" She surveyed the grand old farmhouse from her spot in front of the truck. "It's just about the prettiest thing I've ever seen."

"No, Sessa." He stood beside her. "That would be you."

She thought he would kiss her then, but he didn't. Instead, he took her hand and led her down the path toward the barn. Here, too, there was plenty of light, thanks to the spotlights positioned in the tops of trees and on poles all around the perimeter.

She wandered into the barn. "What are you going to do here?" The room was hidden in shadows, no lights to show off any of his handiwork.

"Stand right there." A moment later, the room filled with light, revealing a glorious barn with stables for two dozen horses and a tack room that would be the envy of any horseman.

"Oh, Trey," she whispered. "Wow."

"My feelings exactly." He turned her to face him. "Wow." And then he kissed her.

A moment later, she stepped out of his embrace, her mind reeling. Trey must have sensed it, because he slid his arm around her waist. Together they walked the length of the building's first floor.

"Those doors open onto the paddock. Beyond the paddock is a pasture." He paused. "And on the other side of the pasture—"

"Is my pasture."

He nodded.

"And the Arabians?"

"I guess we'll share custody." He laughed, and she joined him. "Long as the gate is open between our properties, they won't know the difference."

"Considering what this place looks like in comparison to mine, I think they'll know."

Trey shook his head. "Horses go where the feed is. And the love." He traced the length of her jaw with his knuckle. "I'd say your place is as good as mine if that's the measure." He nudged her toward the door. "Now come on. I've got one more thing to show you."

She followed him out of the barn and back to the truck. The cab smelled like chicken, and her stomach growled. In all the excitement, she had not yet had a bite of Mabel's specialty.

The truck roared to life again, and Trey slid her a sideways glance across the seat. "I have to warn you about something." He gunned the engine and headed out across open pastureland.

She grabbed the door handle to keep from being jostled out of her seatbelt.

"Last time I drove down here, I got stuck."

Great. She looked around. "Seems like it's okay to drive on now, right?"

"Probably," he called over the sound of the engine.

"When did you get stuck?"

He flashed her a wicked grin. "This afternoon. Jared pulled it out with his tractor."

"And that's why he had your keys?"

"Yep." He gestured to a spot just ahead. "We're here."

He helped her from the truck and then grabbed the chicken. "Follow me, but watch your step."

She did as he asked, inching her way behind him through the thicket until they reached a clearing. There she spied a gazebo lit with tiny white lights that twinkled and shimmered on the lake beyond.

"It's beautiful."

"Come and sit, Sessa. I want you to see this."

He led her forward, now holding her hand until they were inside the gazebo. There she spied a jar on the table.

Full of fireflies.

"Oh, Trey," she whispered.

He held her hand and then reached over to plunge the gazebo into darkness. "Look, Sessa."

She did, and gasped.

Not only did the jar take on the ethereal glow of the lightning bugs, but the combination of the water and the thicket surrounding it brought out thousands more of the creatures. Trey continued to grip her hand as he dropped down on one knee.

"Sessa Lee Chambers," he said gently. "I love you like crazy. Will you do me the honor of becoming my wife? And will you share all of your somedays with me?"

"I love you too." Sessa paused to savor the words she'd finally managed to say. "I love you," she said again. And again. Finally she came to her senses. Goodness. The man had asked her to marry him!

"Say something." He looked up at her with those eyes she

loved. With that smile she couldn't forget. "Say yes."

Sessa looked around, took in all of it. Then she grasped for a ragged breath before returning her attention to Trey. "It's all so beautiful, and as much as I want to say yes, what about Pansie? She's part of my life, and I have to consider her in any decision..."

"Say yes, Gwammy," a sweet little voice called from somewhere on the other side of the thicket.

"Pansie?" Sessa called.

"Come on, Auntie Coco. Let's have an adventure."

The sound of footsteps hurrying toward them made Sessa smile. Pansie wore her favorite princess costume along with half of Coco's many bracelets glittering on her arm. A rope of pearls and glow-in-the-dark scepter completed the ensemble.

Atop her head was...oh.

The little girl touched the brim with her scepter. "Auntie Coco said I could wear the red hat, because it's someday now."

The red hat. The one Ross had worn.

"It's beautiful." The image of Ross's daughter shimmered through her tears. "Absolutely beautiful."

The little girl stood by Trey. "Did you ask her yet?"

"I did," he told her. "But she hasn't answered yet."

Pansie climbed up into Sessa's lap and gathered Sessa's face into her tiny hands. Then she moved in so close that the rim of Ross's cowboy hat covered them both.

"Gwammy," she said in a stage whisper. "We love him."

"Yes, sweetheart," she managed through the tears that were threatening. "We do."

"Then say yes. Tell him we love him."

Sessa looked around her granddaughter to the man still kneeling before her. "Yes," she said. "We love you."

Coco let out a whistle that her sons' coaches would have been proud of. "Looks like we're going to put that third floor event room to good use, Dr. Brown."

"Long as she doesn't elope."

"Mama?" Sessa watched her mother and Doctor Easley step out of the thicket.

"Hi," Pansie called to her great-grandmother. "I'm having an adventure."

"So am I," Mama called. "You're not eloping, Sessa Lee

Chambers. Do you understand? I've got a mother-of-the-bride dress I've been hoping to wear and—"

"Hush woman," Doc Eisley said. "If that girl wants to elope, let her. In fact..." He clambered down on one knee. "Bonnie Sue, you're the woman for me. Now marry me, and let's spend whatever time we've got left together? What do you say?"

Mama actually giggled. "Oh now, you're teasing me."

He held up a ring. "Does this look like I'm joking? Now, go tell your daughter good-bye and let her get properly engaged without us old folks here."

To Sessa's surprise, her mother did exactly as the old doctor said.

"Carry on, kids," Doc Easley said. "Bonnie Sue and I are heading for the state line, and I'm not bringing her home until I've made an honest woman out of her."

They both laughed that time, and Sessa joined them.

"Well now," Trey said. "Where were we?"

"We were planning that wedding at your new event center," Coco said. "We really need to name that room, Trey. You need to get on that."

"Let's not get ahead of ourselves. Right now I'm going to get this evening back on track, and there will be no talk of wedding facilities, and nobody else is getting engaged but Sessa and me." Trey reached for the jar and set it in Pansie's lap. "Pansie, remember how we practiced it?"

She wriggled free and carried the jar out of the gazebo and down a few steps toward the lake. "Right here?"

"Yes, there," he said.

While Sessa watched, Pansie began to twirl, her floral dress catching the light as she turned, just like her mama had.

How had Trey known?

After a moment, she stopped and then set the jar on the ground. She opened the lid and allowed the fireflies to escape in a shower of light.

As the last lightning bug left the jar, Pansie reached inside.

"Bring it to me, please," Trey said, and she did, slipping something that sparkled into Trey's palm.

"Now look under the table, Pansie," he said. "Uncle Trey has a surprise for you."

She climbed under the table and came out with a child-sized net affixed with tiny blue lights around the rim. "Auntie Coco, do you think you could help her fill that jar again?"

Coco took Pansie by the hand, leaving with a wink in Sessa's direction. "Let's go see what we can catch while Uncle Trey finishes what he started."

When they had disappeared toward the lake, Trey reached for Sessa's hand and placed something in her palm—a ring of sparkling white diamonds centering a yellow diamond the color of fireflies in the summer.

He took the ring from her hand and placed it on the third finger of her left hand. "Sessa Lee Chambers." He rose and urged her to stand. "I want as many adventures with you as there are days left between us. We can live on either side of the pasture, downtown, or anywhere on earth just as long as we're together, all three of us. Will you do me the honor of becoming *my* Sessa. My wife?"

The fireflies danced around them to the melody of Sessa's answer. "Oh yes. Yes, I will."

"I'll be your Pansie, too, Uncle Trey," came the tiny voice from the edge of the lake. "And I know where we're gonna live."

"Where is that, Pansie-girl?" Trey called.

"We're gonna live happy ever after." She adjusted her red hat and reached for more summer fireflies. "That's where."

And they did.

ABOUT THE AUTHOR

"I write because I can't remember a time when I wasn't making up stories in my head. I love the creative process of actually seeing those stories into print, and I especially love hearing from readers whose hearts have been touched by something I have written."

Bestselling author Kathleen Y'Barbo is a multiple Carol Award and RITA nominee of more than fifty novels with almost two million copies of her books in print in the US and abroad. A tenth-generation Texan and certified paralegal, she has been nominated for a Career Achievement Award as well a Reader's Choice Award and several Top Picks by *Romantic Times* magazine. Kathleen is a proud military wife and an expatriate Texan cheering on her beloved Texas Aggies from north of the Red River. Find out more about Kathleen or connect with her through social media at www.kathleenybarbo.com.

LOVE'S A STAGE
RENE GUTTERIDGE & CHERYL MCKAY

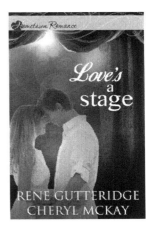

Grad student and future marriage counselor Aly Brewster had a perfect childhood with perfect parents. Now she's heading into her own perfect life: Finish her Master's. Build a successful practice. Husband at twenty-six. But when her parents blindside her with the news they're getting divorced, her perfect world shatters.

Actor Nick Armstrong has been in love with Aly since they met during freshman year. He's happy to accept his assigned place in her Friend Zone because it lets him be close to her. But it's been over five years—time to move on. Then the usually-unflappable Aly comes to him begging for help to save her parents' marriage. Nick has the perfect plan: fake an engagement to each other to inspire her parents to fight to save their marriage. And who knows? It might trigger Aly's feelings for him. But when Aly takes the ruse to the next level—planning a *wedding* in her parents' backyard and hiring additional actors to play his family—enough is enough!

As the lines between acting and reality grow decidedly blurred, these two improvised fiancés must decide: are they going to finish the play...or exit stage right. Alone.

KISS THE COWBOY
JULIE JARNAGIN

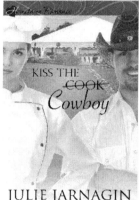

If you can't stand the heat...

All Lucy Pickett needs to become executive chef in one of Dallas' finest restaurants is to pull off the high-profile wedding she's catering. Unfortunately, she's forced to share duties with a modern-day chuck wagon cook, and she's determined not to let Dylan Lawson's rugged looks and cowboy charm knock her off her game. When she learns the restaurateur is considering Dylan for the position instead of her, the wedding shapes up to be a winner-take-all event.

Dylan Lawson longs to prove he can do something more than just being a ranch hand and this investor can give Dylan the opportunity he needs. The only thing standing in Dylan's way is the fiery chef who's fighting for the same position. Will the dicey competition scorch any chance they have for love?

Made in the USA
Middletown, DE
21 August 2015